In Two Weeks

NY State Trooper Series

Jen Talty

Jupiter Press

In Two Weeks: New York State Troopers Series, Book One

Publishing History: previously published by Triskelion Publishing, 2007 First Champagne Rose Edition,
Published in the United States of America
Previously Published by The Wild Rose Press 2009
Previously Published by Cool Gus Publishing 2010

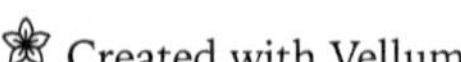
Created with Vellum

In Two Weeks

New York State Trooper Series Book One

USA Today Bestselling Author

JEN TALTY

Sign up for Jen's Newsletter (https://dl.bookfunnel.com/82gm8b9k4y) *where Jen often give away free books before publication.*

Praise for Jen Talty

"I positively loved *In Two Weeks,* and highly recommend it. The writing is wonderful, the story is fantastic, and the characters will keep you coming back for more. I can't wait to get my hands on future installments of the NYS Troopers series." *Long and Short Reviews*

"*In Two Weeks* hooks the reader from page one. This is a fast paced story where the development of the romance grabs you emotionally and the suspense keeps you sitting on the edge of your chair. Great characters, great writing, and a believable plot that can be a warning to all of us." *Desiree Holt, USA Today Bestseller*

"*Deadly Secrets* is the best of romance and suspense in one hot read!" *NYT Bestselling Author Jennifer Probst*

"A charming setting and a steamy couple heat up the pages in a suspenseful story I couldn't put down!" *NY Times and USA today Bestselling Author Donna Grant*

"Jen Talty's books will grab your attention and pull you into a world of relatable characters, strong personalities, humor, and believable storylines. You'll laugh, you'll cry, and you'll rush to get the next book she releases!" Natalie Ann USA Today Bestselling Author

"*Dark Water* delivers an engaging portrait of wounded hearts as the memorable characters take you on a healing journey of love. A mysterious death brings danger and intrigue into the drama, while sultry passions brew into a believable plot that melts the reader's heart. Jen Talty pens an entertaining romance that grips the heart as the colorful and dangerous story unfolds into a chilling ending." *Night Owl Reviews*

"This is not the typical love story, nor is it the typical mystery. The characters are well rounded and interesting." *You Gotta Read Reviews*

"*Murder in Paradise Bay* is a fast-paced romantic thriller with plenty of twists and turns to keep you guessing until the end. You won't want to miss this one..." *USA Today bestselling author Janice Maynard*

From the Author

This is the first book I wrote and the first book to be published. Ryan and Jared are near and dear to my heart. The story is set on Cleverdale in Lake George, New York, where I spent many summers during my childhood. Jared's house is modeled after my best friend's house at the time. The carriage where Ryan lives, though modified in the book to make it 'bigger,' was in my friend's backyard and our playground. Behind her house is a bar called Sans Souci. In the book, it has been renamed the Mason Jug.

This is the first book in a series of seven (and two novellas), all set in Lake George. I loved writing this series and hope you enjoy my world as much as I do!

Chapter One

Ryan O'Connor shut her cell phone, dropping it in her purse. She smoothed down the front of her new denim miniskirt in a lame attempt to calm her nerves. She hated hang-ups and this was the third one today.

She adjusted her overpriced, lace-trimmed camisole. The expensive cotton caressed her skin as if it were silk. She glanced in the mirror one more time, then pointed a finger at herself. "I hope you know what you're doing, sister." She grabbed her purse, flicked off the lights, and headed out the door.

A sudden burst of cool Lake George air smacked against her skin and goosebumps trickled down her arms. In this part of New York, spring temperatures ranged from freezing to bathing suit weather, but she'd always enjoyed the diversity.

The moon shone high in the dark cloudless sky,

casting an eerie glow. A small fishing boat hummed along the shoreline while she walked the half mile from her rented carriage house to her brother's restaurant, the Mason Jug.

The sound of rubber spinning wildly on the pavement caught her attention. Headlights flashed on, almost blinding her as a car whizzed by, sending pebbles in the air, pelting her legs. The wind swirled as the car sped past.

She jumped to the side. "Jerk," she muttered, combing her fingers through her hair. Hopefully she'd gotten all the strands back in the proper place. She wanted to look perfect. Sexy. She glanced over her shoulder and listened to the tires screech as the car rounded the corner and out of sight. Idiot didn't even honk his horn.

She gave up on the hair and slowed her steps to a snail's pace. Propositioning Jared Blake last night hadn't been her most brilliant idea. He barely even viewed her as a grown-up, much less a bed partner. Not that it mattered. The hunky state trooper had accepted a job transfer and would be moving in two weeks.

Broken gravel crunched under her shoes as she made her way up the path toward the main door of the converted old barn. Her brother had done a bang-up job of remodeling. He had spent a small fortune on making the building look like a cozy log cabin. He'd even put in fresh perennials around the entire building. The bright neon sign hanging above the doorway was the only indication that this structure was indeed a bar and not a home. Well, that and this stupid gravel parking lot. She'd begged her brother to pave it, but he thought it added to the *rustic* feel of the place.

The smell of baby back ribs sizzling on the grill assaulted her nose. There wasn't anything better than a barbecue on a cool spring night.

She clasped her hand on the doorknob, knowing her best friend Penny had been up to something. She turned her wrist and pushed back the door.

"Surprise! Happy birthday!"

She gasped, covered her mouth, and did her best to look shocked. Penny leaped at her, hurtling her into the door. "Geez, let me breathe, would ya?" Ryan laughed as she glanced at all the balloons dancing against the rugged beams. The inside of the Mason Jug still looked more like a barn, but that was part of the charm.

Her friends pulled at her like the rope in a game of tug-of-war. Although not a surprise, the party did give her a chance to relax. She'd never planned a one-night stand before. Heck, she'd never had one. But what scared her most was that Jared hadn't run for the hills when she suggested they take a walk on the wild side.

Although he hadn't agreed to participate in anything. Actually, he'd chuckled, kissed her temple, and left her leaning against her door, breathless. He'd probably thought she'd been joking since he had ignored the proposition.

"Wow, Pen. Great job." Ryan checked out the decorations. Fresh red and white flowers filled the center of every table and booth, matching the checkered tablecloths. Leave it to Penny to make sure nothing clashed. A big 'happy birthday' sign dangled above the bar. "I can't believe you did this."

"Yeah, well." Penny shrugged. "Come on, let's mingle."

Ryan spent the next hour alternating between laughing and looking over her shoulder for Jared. Just once, she would have liked him to put something before his job. She winced. Sex with her probably wasn't high on his to-do list.

She licked her fingers after stuffing her mouth with the best chocolate cake in town. "This is from the baker we use at the hotel." She poked Penny in the arm. "Who'd you get to help you with all this?"

"Not telling. Did I surprise you?"

"Not really." The front door opened, and her stomach jumped into her throat. She held her breath for a long moment, but it wasn't Jared who had stepped into the restaurant. Closing her eyes, she exhaled. What had she been thinking offering herself up like a desperate schoolgirl? And to Jared of all people. She blinked open her eyes only to find Penny looking at her as if she were some pathetic spinster or something. "Don't look at me like that."

"Like what?"

"Like you feel sorry for me or something."

"Well, I did hear that Jared took a transfer to some

unit in Rochester, New York. And he's selling the house. You okay?" Penny offered a hug.

"Why wouldn't I be okay?" Ryan pulled away.

Penny tilted her head. "Please, it's me you're talking to. I know you've got the hots for him."

Ryan used to think he'd never be able to see her as anything other than his best friend's dorky kid sister. "And I'm going to have him tonight. Who's the stud?" She pointed to some guy who had "Penny's latest" written all over him.

With a sparkling, pearly white smile, Penny responded, "Chuck. I told you about him..." Her jaw dropped and her big brown eyes looked like they were going to pop right out of her head. "What did you say?"

Ryan tried not to laugh. "I talked Jared into spending some 'quality time' alone with me."

"He agreed to do the dirty with you?"

"Not exactly." Ryan quickly glanced around the room. "I can't believe you just said that."

"Hey, you brought it up." Penny rested both hands on Ryan's shoulders. "Did you ask him to sleep with you?"

Ryan tugged at Penny's arm, pulling her to a table. "Not in so many words, but I think he understood my drift." Ryan narrowed her eyes. "I just took your advice."

Penny sat down and stared at her. "What, that romance is overrated, and sex is not, and that you should give it a try sometime?"

"Yep, that would be what you said." Ryan shook her head. "You told me to stop going after the boring tax accountant type."

"That didn't really include Mr. Loner." Penny leaned into the table with a scowl. "Your brother's right."

"About what?"

"Get Jared off 'God' status, because he's just a man, a man who isn't interested, and there are a dozen men out there who are."

"Wait one minute. You told me to put my cards on the table." Ryan folded her arms. "You've always said I should ask for what I want."

Penny sighed. "That's the problem, hon. You don't want sex with him. You want him for the long haul."

"Long haul and Jared don't mix." Ryan took a deep breath and put on her best smile. "He's moving in two weeks. Besides, I know exactly what I'm doing. Now tell me about this Chuck guy."

Penny pursed her lips. "Fine, but don't come running to me when he breaks your heart." Her eyes shifted past Ryan. "Chuck is hot."

"You like him a lot?"

Penny's eyes twinkled. "That's the difference between you and me. I never go into something thinking he's the one." She winked. "But someday I'll find my frog when I least expect it." She stood and stared down at Ryan. "Now get drunk and forget about Jared."

Sashaying away, Penny ran her hands through her

thick, shoulder-length, sandy-blond hair and did a quick sassy toss for good measure. She might not have been tall and sexy, but she had all the assets that men required. Large round breasts, a tight ass, and a personality to die for.

Ryan's purse vibrated. She dug into it and pulled out her cell phone and muttered a curse. She wouldn't answer a blocked call again. Whoever this was knew they had the wrong number, so why did they keep trying? "Buzz off." She tossed the phone back in her purse.

"Who?" Her brother sat down at the table with a concerned look on his face. Considering everything she and Pat had gone through, she knew that he meant well. But his overprotective ways were almost as annoying as Jared's.

"No one." She grabbed a handful of popcorn from the basket. "You hear from Jared?"

Pat's face scrunched even more. "Why?"

"Because he said he'd be here." Mindlessly, she raised a single buttered kernel to her lips. Over the past few months, Jared had been sending her mixed signals. She'd finally had the courage last night to call him on it.

"Then he'll be here. Did he put the house on the market yet?"

She shrugged. Finding a new place to live did concern her. Jared charged her next to nothing for rent and she loved the area, even though it took forever to get to work in the snow. "He didn't say."

Pat leaned closer. "I know Jared's move has upset you. But it's about time you got him off that pedestal you've had him on for the last few years."

"I don't have him on a pedestal." She grabbed a napkin, wiped the grease from her fingers, and tried to ignore her brother.

"Come on. I see how you look at him." He tried to bat her nose with his finger, but she swatted it away.

"Oh, shut up, will you? I'm not twelve, if you hadn't noticed." She gave him the evil eye.

"Could've fooled me," he grumbled, crossing his arms. "You can't possibly have real feelings for the man. He's my age."

She tossed the napkin on the table. "Of course I have feelings for him. He's been a dear friend to both of us, or do I need to remind you of everything he's done?"

"That's not what I'm talking about. You have to let him go."

"Get off it. I'm just worried about moving. I've lived in that carriage house since I was seventeen." She waved to a couple of girls she had gone to high school with.

"Didn't Jared say the real-estate agent was listing the property with a moneymaking tenant?"

"Jared has no control over what the new owners

would charge, or do with me. I'm better off renting an apartment near the hotel in Bolton, anyway."

Pat took both her hands in his. "You could always come live with Marci and me."

"Not." At twenty-three, Ryan had been living on her own since her brother had married five years ago.

Pat leaned back in his chair and scanned the room. "So, how'd your date go last night?"

"How did you know I went on a date?" She glared at her brother. It seemed she couldn't do anything without dear old brother and Jared knowing about it. Or having a say in it.

"Jared told me."

"Figures. He was hanging out on the back patio when Tom brought me home. I have to say the date wasn't anything to write home about, but thanks to Jared, well, let's just say I won't be going on a second one with that guy, ever." Jared had made telling Tom to take a hike a little easier, but it drove her nuts that he acted more like an older brother than a friend. He had this horrible habit of scaring off her dates before they even began.

"Jared said the guy looked like a moron."

"He thinks everyone I date is a moron." She rolled her eyes. "Where is he? He should've been here by now."

"I'm sure he offered to stay late or something," Pat suggested.

He better not have. She glanced at her watch.

"This week will be hard on him," Pat said. A sudden sadness washed over his face. "I told him. Too much change around this time of year wouldn't be good for him, but he'll never listen."

"He listens to you, and he's getting better every year," she said softly.

Pat rested his hand on her shoulder. "Now that I'm about to be a father, I can have a little empathy for what he must go through."

"It's not his fault his son died," she whispered.

"That's not what he believes." Pat rose and pushed the chair in. "Look, I've got to get back to the kitchen." He nodded toward the door. "Jared's here."

Ryan rose and stood next to her brother as Jared approached. His broad frame stood well over six feet, and his emerald-colored eyes sparkled with mischief. She took in a deep breath, trying to simply smile without letting her eyes roam over his perfect body.

An electric pulse shot up her spine when Jared touched the small of her back. Staring into his jewel-like eyes, she swallowed. His full lips brushed her temple the same way they always did when he said hello. It was just his way, but it always sent her ability to speak on a temporary vacation.

He chuckled as if he knew the effect he had on her, then ran his hand across his freshly buzzed head. "Sorry I missed the big surprise."

"She wasn't surprised, but she faked it nice," Pat said. "I'm short-handed tonight, so I've got to get going. Don't you go running off to the western part of this state without letting me get you good and drunk for old times' sake."

"You're on." Jared smiled wide. "Come on, Ryan, I've got a surprise for you."

She swallowed, then chomped down on her tongue, making sure she didn't sound like a schoolgirl when she spoke. "Jared, you didn't need to get me anything."

"Don't spoil my fun," he drawled, slipping his arm around her waist.

The noise around her seemed to disappear. The only thing she could concentrate on was his firm, muscular body and his bad boy good looks. She tried to breathe normally, but his aftershave, mixed with his own unique scent, was just too good to pass up.

Her heart beat frantically. The only thing he truly loved was his job, and that was okay. Tonight would be a onetime thing. She'd been afraid he hadn't heard her last night. But the way his thumb rubbed her hip and slid under her shirt to touch her bare skin told her he finally saw her as a woman.

"Ryan, wait," Penny yelled, waving something in her hand. "I found this on the table over there." She pushed her way through the crowd, panting. "Hey there, hot stuff."

"Hi, Penny." Jared chuckled.

"It looks like we missed a gift somehow." Penny handed her a long box.

"Someone has a secret admirer," Jared said. "Looks like a flower box."

Ryan examined the gift. The tag had her name on it, but nothing else. She glanced around the room. The people she would expect to give her a gift had already done so, except for Jared. Her heart fluttered. He'd never given her anything like flowers before.

"Open it." Penny poked her in the arm.

Ryan pulled back the bow and lifted the box open. She shoved the tissue aside, then gasped, staring down at a single dead rose with a note that read: "I'll get you, you bitch."

Jared grabbed the box. "Where did you get this?"

"I found it on that table." Penny pointed across the room with a trembling hand. "Who would do such a thing?"

Shaken, Ryan stumbled backward.

"What's going on?" She heard her brother's voice behind her.

"Someone just threatened your sister. I'll get the locals down here. For now, make sure no one leaves this bar." Still clutching the box with the single dead rose in his hand, he started bellowing orders at everyone at the party.

"Penny?" Ryan whispered.

"Right here, girlfriend." Penny guided Ryan to a chair. "Some idiot is just playing a stupid joke."

"My stepfather said those exact words to me the day he tried…he almost…"

"Your stepfather's in jail. He can't hurt you anymore."

Ryan wasn't so sure about that. George McIntosh might be in jail for murder, but he wasn't dead. And that meant he could someday get out.

About an hour passed while Jared and a local sheriff questioned everyone in the bar. No one knew where or how the box had shown up. The bar had been open to the public, with only the back room closed off for Ryan's party. Anyone could've snuck in and left the box.

"Hey, babe. How are you holding up?" Jared asked after the majority of the guests were allowed to leave. He knelt down in front of her, holding both her hands in his.

She cleared her throat in an absent gesture to achieve calm. "Do you think George could've somehow sent that to me?"

"That's what I'm thinking." Jared pulled her to her feet. "Let's get you home." He placed his hand on the small of her back and pressed his lips to her cheek. "I didn't drive, did you?"

She shook her head. "He's never tried to contact me before. Why now?" Her hands clenched into tight fists as if ready to strike back at any moment. She took a deep cleansing breath in through her nose, then exhaled slowly. No way would she give that man any power.

"Let me worry about George." Jared opened the door for her, then looped his arm around her.

"He didn't try to rape you." She leaned in close to Jared as they made their way down the road. She glanced over her shoulder as a car slowed, then drove by.

He tugged at her, turning toward the driveway. "Nope, just put a bullet hole in my arm." He lifted the sleeve of his T-shirt. "Bullet went in there and came out over here."

"Sorry, I didn't mean to—"

He stopped her at the front door of the carriage house. A firm finger hushed her words. "I know, babe." His gaze dropped from her eyes to her lips. His mouth hovered over hers for a moment, but before she could find the courage to close her eyes and kiss him, he pulled away. "Where are your keys?"

She dug into her purse and handed them to him. The gentle splashing of the lake against the shoreline calmed her nerves. She looked out over the dark waters lit up by the moon and stars. Even in the dead of night, she could see the majestic structure of the main house, thanks to the fresh coat of white paint setting off the traditional black shutters.

The rattling of the door brought her attention back to her home. The carriage house may have been an eighth of the size, but the mini replica had the same sense of hominess.

"For now, I want to make sure all your windows are

locked, and this door is secure." Jared stepped into the kitchen, then flicked on the light. "I don't think you should take any chances."

"I can't imagine anyone else wanting to frighten me like this." She pulled out her cell. Only one missed call. The blocked call. And no message.

True to his cop form, he scoped out the room before letting her in. "What about the dipshit you went out with last night?"

"Tom? Why would he do something like that?"

"I have no idea. But he wasn't too thrilled when you agreed to talk to me instead of having him in for a nightcap." He ducked into her bedroom, then the bathroom, checking the windows. "Besides, I don't trust him."

"You don't even know the guy." She planted her hands on her hips. "You don't trust anyone."

"Not true." He lifted a brow. "Besides, that dipshit last night didn't want to take no for an answer, if you remember correctly."

"I remember all right, and I was handling Tom just fine all by my little self." She brushed her hair from her face. Tom was persistent, but that was all. "Stop acting like a crazed older brother or something. Drives me nuts."

"I'm not your brother." He pursed his lips and let out a whistle. "And in that outfit…" His eyes roamed over her body in a very unbrotherly fashion. "You'd attract a monk."

"You don't like my outfit?" She smiled and leaned against the sink.

Running his hand across his head, he took in a breath. "I like it. A lot. You're a beautiful woman, but you're too nice. Naïve."

"I am not."

"Yeah, actually you are, and some guys might try to take advantage of that."

"Right. But since I'm not naïve, as you put it, there is no way I can be taken advantage of. I'm not a child, if you hadn't noticed." She flashed him her best sarcastic grin.

"Oh, hell. I've noticed," he said. "Why can't you just be that dorky kid with pigtails and freckles?"

"I still have freckles." She laughed. "On my ass."

"I didn't need to know that." His eyes darted around the small kitchen. "Listen, about tonight."

"What about it?" Her pulse increased, sending intense messages to other parts of her body.

He stepped toward her. "Sorry I was late for your birthday."

Her breath caught. She raised her hand to her throat and tried to swallow. Her gaze locked with his in a magical moment. The beating of her heart pounded wildly against her chest.

He approached her, putting his hands on the counter by her waist. He dipped his head, smiled, and said, "I'm going to install a new lock on that door tonight."

"That's not necessary." She barely managed.

"Yes. It is." He stood tall and reached in his pocket. "And so is this." He held a small package in his hands. "Happy birthday, Ryan."

Her eyes glanced between the small box and Jared. "You didn't have to do this," she whispered.

"Open it."

With shaky hands, she took the present and fumbled with the wrapper. Sometimes there was no arguing with him. But this gift just didn't seem like Jared. In the past he'd given her practical things: a cell phone, a laptop during her college years, and a membership to Triple A after she'd landed the job at the Lakeside Hotel.

She blinked and then lifted the top of the box. A sparkling emerald attached to a silver chain graced her teary eyes. "Oh, my. It's beautiful."

"It's your birthstone."

She lifted her gaze to meet his. He smiled like a big kid who'd just done something amazing, then scowled. "You're crying?"

"You shouldn't have done this." She placed her trembling hand on his chest. "It's too much."

"Don't you like it?" He shoved his hands in his pockets and retreated as if wounded.

"I love it, but…" She saw the disappointment in his eyes. Jared never did anything unless he wanted to, this she knew for certain. "Thank you." She pulled the necklace out of the box. "Would you help me put it on?"

His smile returned. "I know it's not my usual, but everything is different now."

She turned and closed her eyes as she lifted her hair. Water welled in her eyes. *Different.* He was right. Things were different and everything was about to change.

"There." He patted her shoulder, then backed away.

She turned and did her best to smile as if all was perfect. He stared at her for a long moment. It wasn't a sexual glance, or even a friendly gaze. He just stared. It was as if he was meeting her for the first time.

"Well, I'd better fix this door. I've got to get back to the station and do some paperwork."

"Tonight?" Her stupid tears must have frightened him away. She really needed to learn how to behave like a grown woman, or she'd never get the kind of goodbye she really wanted.

"I want to make sure that this dead rose thing doesn't fall through the cracks." He raised his thumb to her chin. "Sometimes threats like this get put on the bottom of the pile." He pressed his mouth against hers, but pulled away before the kiss even began. "I'll stop by in the morning and we can talk then." He turned and headed toward the door. "I've got one of those latches hotels use in the shed. I'll go get it and my tools."

She swallowed her frustration. She knew him well enough to know tonight wouldn't be the night. "I think you're overreacting. If it's George, he can't do anything from behind bars."

"Did the dead rose scare you? Be honest."

"Of course it scared me."

"Then I'm not overreacting. But I'm more concerned that some sicko has decided to stalk you."

Her heart skipped a beat. Jared had that "I'm a cop, so you'd better listen" look on his face. The one where he didn't blink, he just stared at you with raised brow and tilted chin.

"You'll find out who sent that rose, right?" Fear prickled up and down her spine. Even if George was behind it, someone else had done it and that alone gave her the heebie-jeebies.

"That would be the plan." He ran a hand across his head. "Hopefully before I move." He turned and closed the door behind him.

She reached for the refrigerator, then a beer. After twisting the top off, she chugged half of it. Jared could be overbearing. Honestly, he was downright controlling, especially when it came to his job. Under the circumstances, that could only be seen as a good thing. She'd seen enough stories in the paper about how stalker cases were often swept under the rug. She wiped the beer that dribbled down her chin. The only problem was that Jared would most likely demand to be at her side all the time. He'd tell her what to do, how to do it, even when to do it. She smiled. His being so close all the time would give her the opportunity to seduce him.

Her smile faded knowing someone planned on "getting her." She shivered as she remembered her stepfather's dirty hands on her body. "Bastard," she whispered. It had to be George. Who else would want to do such a thing to her?

Chapter Two

Jared slammed the phone into the cradle. The neatly stacked files he'd set on his desk crashed to the floor. Papers scattered at his feet. "Shit." He bent to collect them, aimlessly shoving them in a folder. He didn't need an open case on his desk, especially one involving Ryan. She'd been like family. So why did he all of a sudden have the hots for her?

"What are you doing in at this hour?" Sergeant Harmon asked. The rookie stood at attention just one step into Jared's office.

"Would you relax?" Jared said, rolling his own shoulders as if that would relieve the newly formed tension.

"Sorry, sir."

Jared blinked. This kid was going to drive him nuts.

"Do me a favor and run a background check on Thomas C. Grady."

"Am I looking for something specific?"

"Just a general check." Jared snagged a sheet from the top of the crumpled papers. The Warren County Sheriff's Department had filed their report, but nothing would come of it unless Ryan was somehow injured. A thought that sent his heartburn into overdrive.

His friend in Auburn, New York, had spoken with George, but George claimed he didn't know anything. The warden assured Jared that they'd keep a close eye on George. So the question remained: who sent the rose? And could Jared find the culprit before he left for Rochester?

"I'll get right on it," Harmon said. "Will you be sticking around?"

Jared stood. Normally he preferred the comfort of his bland office to the big empty house on the lake. "Just call my cell if you find anything."

Two weeks and he'd be on his way to a more challenging and demanding post. He slipped his arms into his coat when a vision popped into his mind of Ryan lounging in some silky black number, waiting for him with a glass of wine. He shook his head, then slammed the station house door and headed toward his pickup. He tried to remember when Ryan had turned into a woman.

Not many cars were out this Saturday morning.

Jared weaved his way through the twisted roads in record time.

He pulled into his driveway and parked in his spot, right next to Ryan's shiny white SUV. He stared at it for a moment before stepping from his truck. She'd always been such an independent kid. What choice did she have? Her childhood had sucked, but somehow she'd managed to make the best of it.

She'd always been strong and stubborn, and deep down he'd known she would make it. Determination should've been her middle name. A trait that scared the crap out of him. When she wanted something, she went for it, both barrels loaded.

He pounded on her door, then turned his back and waited. But no one answered. "Ryan?" He banged one last time before taking out his key. It was early for a Saturday morning, but he'd never known her to sleep past eight.

The key didn't slip in easily, but when he turned it, the lock clicked. He pushed back the door, but something stopped it. He chuckled. At least she'd used the chain. "Ryan," he said into the small crack. "It's me, Jared."

"Damn you." She scurried from the hallway in her robe, with a towel on her head. "You scared me."

She almost shut the door in his face when she released the chain, then pulled back the door. "I had started dialing 9-1-1 when I heard your voice."

"Sorry, but I wanted to let you know what George had to say."

She tightened the red terrycloth that covered her damp, creamy flesh. When her eyes locked with his, blood rushed throughout his body.

"And?" She lifted the towel from her head, releasing her hair. She ran her hands through the wet light-brown strands, letting it fall past her shoulders before she tossed the towel on a kitchen chair. "Are you going to stand there and stare at me or tell me what George had to say?"

"Sorry," he said, forcing his gaze to her face. "George claims he didn't even know it was your birthday."

"Yeah, right. You want some coffee?" she offered with a forced smile. The slight tremble in her voice hadn't gone unnoticed.

For months after George had attacked her, she'd been withdrawn, and Jared feared she'd be forever tainted. "I'd love some." He pulled a chair out, spun it around, and straddled it. "He can't hurt you anymore."

She rested her hand on his shoulder. "I know." Briefly, her eyes caught his. "I won't let him get to me."

"That's the spirit."

"You hungry?" Her sparkling blue eyes couldn't hide the internal scars her stepfather had left behind. She might have the drive and determination of a pit bull, but he knew her better than anyone, and she still hurt. He understood that pain, more than he cared to admit. He also understood how important it was for her to be seen as a strong, independent woman. Well, no denying the woman part anymore.

"Nope." She'd turned her back to him, and his eyes automatically darted to her toned legs. "Damn," he whispered.

"Damn, what?"

"Damn legs," he admitted, unable to look at anything else.

"Excuse me?" She twisted and turned, looking down at her legs. The robe barely reached the middle of her thighs and when she moved, so did the robe.

"You realize you're serving me coffee practically naked." He tried to line his voice with a hint of sarcasm, but it didn't work.

"You realize you're an ass." She adjusted the robe high around her neck before lifting two mugs, setting one down in front of him.

"Just trying to make you laugh." He sipped the strong black liquid.

"Thanks." She graced him with a broad grin, then laughed.

"When do you want to go to the cemetery?" Visiting her mother's grave every year had become a ritual. One he would miss after he moved.

"I need about half an hour. Does that work for you?"

"Sure." He glanced at her, annoyed that he couldn't keep his mind from wondering what she looked like under that damn robe. "You do have nice legs." He scowled. This certainly wasn't the time or place.

"Thanks." She eyed him suspiciously.

"Just thought you should know." Forgetting the world around him, he rose and strode over to her. "I think you're beautiful."

"I'm fine, really." She leaned back, tilted her head, and looked at him with a puzzled expression. "You don't have to keep trying to distract me."

Only *he* was the one who was distracted. He lifted her hand and kissed the hollow of her palm, then placed it on his shoulder. "You sure opened an interesting can of worms the other night." She smelled like a combination of soap and exotic fruit. The room spun and he couldn't see past her.

"I did?" she questioned with wide eyes. Her breath sounded raspy, and he felt her wild pulse beat against his chest. Her pink tongue peeked out and smoothed over her full lips. He moistened his own, while her radiant sky-blue eyes rolled closed in anticipation. Then the phone rang, and she jumped, knocking him in the nose with her forehead.

He stumbled backward, his eyes watering. "Damn. That hurt."

"Sorry." She winced and reached for the phone. "Hello?"

He stepped away, rubbing his nose and giving himself a mental lecture. Since when didn't he know how to charm the pants off a woman? Since when did he want to with this woman?

"Hello?" she repeated loudly. "Who is this?"

He glanced up from her sexy, bare legs and frowned. "What's the matter?"

She stared at the phone and shook her head. "I hate hang-ups. This is about the tenth one this week. Even if you dial the wrong number, you should apologize before you hang up." She slapped the phone on the wall cradle, and it rattled. "People can be so rude."

"Don't you have caller ID?"

"Blocked number." Once again, she adjusted her robe, and then she inched toward him.

The closer she got, the stronger the smell of peaches affected his already tense body.

"Sorry about your nose."

"Sorry I scared you," he said.

"You don't scare me."

"Don't tease a man when you're wearing nothing but a robe," he whispered. The cold countertop pressed into his back.

She lifted herself up on tiptoes, leaning into him. "You started it, and who says I'm teasing?"

His gaze dipped below her luscious mouth, to the red material puckering open across her chest. She didn't have cleavage, just a sexy space between two perfectly rounded breasts. "You're playing with fire, babe." He toyed with the belt holding her robe closed, easing her closer, their mouths a half-inch apart.

Her feminine curves pressed against his body in all the right places. A single spark ignited the moment his lips brushed against hers, shocking him in an erotic dance he couldn't resist. He darted his tongue into her mouth and let the purest form of passion take over.

She tasted of coffee and sugar, and she smelled like heaven. He ached to find out how her skin felt beneath his fingers. When he cupped her face, her hair tangled in his hand. Releasing a few strands, he glided his fingers down her neck and rested his palm above her breast. Abruptly, he pushed her back. "We shouldn't do this."

"Do what?" She narrowed her eyes. "Thought you said I was beautiful?"

"Your beauty has nothing to do with it. You're much younger than I."

She glared at him with hurt in her eyes. "I'm not a kid. If you don't want me, that's fine. But don't play games with me. I hate that." She stepped from his clutches.

"I think you're the one playing games." He stumbled toward the door, raking a hand across his head. "I'll meet you by my truck in a half hour." With a hand on the door handle, he said, "And I want to know if you get any more hang-ups. Could be the same guy who sent you that rose."

Once safely outside, he marched toward the lake. He stood at the end of his dock and focused on the waves crashing against the shoreline across the bay.

The swirling wind did nothing to cool him off. There was no mistaking how much he wanted her, but having her would be insane. Stupid. He felt responsible for her because he was the one who'd arrested her stepfather. He knew exactly what George had intended to do to her. Jared shook out his hands.

He'd taken on the role of protector. Always making sure she had everything she needed, and then some. Even when her brother came back to take care of her, Jared couldn't back away. She'd been just a kid and didn't deserve what had happened.

She sure as hell didn't deserve to be used and dumped. And that's what would happen if he got involved with her. No matter what she said she wanted. A goodbye thing? What the hell was that? Nope, the only thing he planned to do was pack up and get the hell out of town before Ryan unglued him completely. But not before he figured out who'd sent that damn dead rose.

The following evening, Ryan perched herself at a table in the back corner of the Mason Jug. She fiddled with her cell phone and waited for Penny, who was late. Nothing new there. Penny would be late for her own funeral.

Ryan looked around the bar. All the regulars and a few new faces filled the room. A couple of guys she knew from high school waved, then continued with their pool game. The music wasn't too loud, but it drowned out the voices around her.

She'd worked her butt off to graduate from high school early. Then she crammed a four-year degree in business management into three intense years. She took a full load each semester and every summer, spending what little free time she had waiting tables.

She noticed her brother behind the bar. He gave her a glancing nod, then smiled as a waitress yapped in his ear. Against all odds, she and her brother had come out on top. She was finally in charge of her own life.

"Hi."

She sloshed her water before she looked up, trying not to cringe. "Tom, you scared me." Going on a date with him the other night proved to be a huge mistake. One she didn't plan on repeating. He had been irritable toward her all day at work, no matter how nice she'd been.

"Sorry. Mind?" He tipped his head toward the empty chair.

Oh, she minded all right, but she had to work with the numbskull. "Actually…" Looking around the room, she smiled when Jared stepped through the main door.

He strode across the floor in that cocky, arrogant cop stroll, like he owned the place. She wished she could take her eyes off him. But all she could do was stare at the sexy thing moving effortlessly toward her.

"Hey, babe." He squeezed her shoulder. "Tom, right?" He extended his hand to Tom.

Must have been quite the handshake considering how Tom's face scrunched as if he were in pain. She tried not to smile, but gave up as Jared sat down. Normally she hated it when he came to the rescue. Any other day she'd make it perfectly clear it annoyed her. However, considering what she had planned and the short time she had to achieve her goal, she'd put up with his interfering ways.

"I'll see you at work." Tom had the nerve to pat her shoulder.

She gave him a slight smile, reminding herself that being nice was always the best way to deal with people like him. "See you later." Slowly she turned to face Jared, knowing he'd have a huge scowl on his face.

"Something's off with that guy." Jared arched a brow. The lines on his face were set and hard.

She gave Jared a knowing nod but couldn't respond because his damn greenish eyes caught her attention and now she couldn't look elsewhere.

"Glad you agree. Now you need to stop being so sweet to guys like that."

"Being mean is only going to make working with him harder."

"Dating him is what made working with him a bitch."

"You're impossible. Can we stop talking about it, please?"

"Fine. Want a drink?"

"No, thanks. I'm waiting for Penny." The wild beat of her pulse pounded in her ears. Even when he made her mad, he had this strange ability to make her swoon.

Jared chuckled.

"What's so funny?"

"I think Penny's getting it on with some guy in the parking lot. Actually, I think I know the guy."

"Great." Ryan snatched up the menu and hid her blushing face behind it. Damn crazy fantasies of a naked Jared just wouldn't go away.

Jared gently took the menu from her hands, then touched the emerald necklace he'd given her for her birthday. The green rock fell down toward her breasts. He hesitated for a moment before touching her skin. "Looks real nice on you." He dropped his hand to his lap, leaving behind a hot pulse trickling to her midriff.

"What are you doing here?" she asked.

"Looking for you." His eyes sparkled, and a slow grin appeared on his face. "I want to apologize for my rudeness the other day."

"No need." She shrugged, but deep down she wanted to jump and shout. Jared apologized to no one.

"Don't you think this thing with us is weird?"

Weird? No weirder than the rest of her love life. Or lack thereof. She picked either guys who suffocated her or guys who dumped her right after they'd gotten into her pants. She smiled. At least with Jared the dumping would be mutual. "Because we've been friends forever?"

"That, and I've known you since you were, like, two." He scrunched his face as if he'd just eaten something sour.

"Okay, so that is weird, but so what." Tentatively, she rested her hand high on his thigh. "You're a few years older. Not a big deal."

"Try close to ten."

She rolled her eyes. "You're the one who started flirting and telling me how hot you think I am."

"You're the one who propositioned me." His gaze dropped to her hand. He lifted it in his and clasped his fingers through hers. "Why don't we try and go out on a date? A real date. Flowers and everything."

Holding her breath, she lifted her free hand and traced a path with her index finger across his jawline. "If you think that will help with whatever problem you're having."

He grabbed her hand and then pressed his lips to her palm. "I don't have a problem."

"Then what's the big deal?"

"Contrary to popular belief, I don't just jump into bed with anyone, or even on a whim."

That wasn't quite what she'd heard about his shenanigans over the years. Not to mention the women that came and went every so often from his house. "I'm not just anyone."

"Then humor me. Let me take you to a nice restaurant for dinner and maybe some dancing. A goodbye thing."

She forced a smile. "I'd like that." And she meant it, but not that he actually called it "a goodbye thing."

He glanced toward the door and laughed. "Penny's here."

Ryan watched Penny give her new boyfriend a wet, passionate kiss. "Oh, now that's just gross."

"Really?" Jared leaned in. "Close your eyes," he whispered.

Ryan sucked in a breath, then let her eyelids drop, but didn't take her sight off his luscious lips.

He grinned before pressing his mouth against hers. His hot tongue darted inside her mouth and ignited a fire deep in her belly. A rumble rolled from his lips to hers. Instinctively, she ran her hands up his thighs, hips, and fisted in his shirt.

He cupped her cheeks, staring at her for a brief moment before pulling away. "Not so gross," he whispered, then stood and walked toward the door, not looking back.

Ryan stared across the room. She blinked a few times but couldn't focus. The man had kissed her blind.

"Earth to Ryan." Penny waved her hand in Ryan's face.

"Yeah, yeah. I'm here."

"You looked dazed and confused." Penny sat down with her own look of discomfort as she fiddled with her pinky ring. "Sometimes I'm such a fool."

"Why?" Ryan said, still breathless. She touched her lips.

"Like an idiot, I told Chuck I loved him."

Ryan gasped, covering her mouth.

"Don't look so shocked. It was in the midst of multiple orgasms, so he probably didn't think much of it." Penny flapped her arms in her normal dramatic way. She shrugged her shoulders, but Ryan didn't miss the single tear rolling down Penny's cheek.

"Oh, my. You really do love him." Ryan giggled. She never thought she'd see the day Penny gave her heart wholly to a man.

"Yeah. I think I do. But I don't think he loves me." Penny sighed as she glanced around the room. "Oh, my God. It's like a freaking high school reunion in here. Doesn't anybody have anything better to do than hang out in the same old same old?"

Ryan laughed. "Come on." She pushed back her chair, feeling like a new woman. "This calls for an old-fashioned girls' night out. I'll get my brother to make us some wings to go with the tequila I got for my birthday."

"Oh, that *so* works for me." Penny stood, adjusting her hair behind her ears. "But now you have to explain the major sucking face with Jared." Her eyes twinkled.

"Not." Ryan covered Penny's mouth with her hand. "Don't say a word. I know what I'm doing."

Penny looped her arm over Ryan's shoulder. "No, you don't."

A few hours later, Ryan and Penny had sprawled out in the lounge chairs on Jared's front lawn down by the lake. He had never minded her using the yard. She couldn't help but wonder if the new owners would allow whoever rented the carriage house full use of the lawn. Somehow she doubted that.

Large shrub hedges lined the lush one-acre spread down both sides of the property for privacy. A few boats hummed by, their wake rolling onto the shoreline.

"Are you going to tell Chuck?" Ryan hiccupped, feeling the effects of the alcohol. "That you meant what you said. That you love him."

"Nope." Penny shook her head vigorously. "I don't think I can drive home. Mind if I crash here?"

"Not at all." As Ryan pushed herself to her feet, her legs wobbled. "Why do I do this to myself when I have to get up for work?" Pressing her shoulder blades together, she tried to keep herself from stumbling. Drinking had never been one of her strong suits.

"Because I'm such a bad influence." Penny's arm crash-landed on Ryan's shoulder and they nearly fell over.

"Yes, you are," Ryan said, doing her best to guide them to the carriage house. She gasped when she reached the gaping hole that used to be her front door. "Oh, my, God!" She froze. "What the hell?"

"Holy crap," Penny mumbled. "I know we didn't leave the door open."

"Maybe I should take a look around."

"Are you nuts? We need to call the cops."

Ryan glanced over her shoulder and looked to see if Jared was home. Relief flowed through her body immediately. "Jared's pickup is here, so he's got to be around somewhere." Frantically, she looked toward the main house, but all the lights were off. "Where the heck is he?"

"Right in front of you, babe." His deep throaty voice comforted her.

"Thank God." Her pulse increased as panic set in. Jared stood in her doorway, in his uniform, with latex gloves on his hands. "What happened?"

"Someone broke in." He peeled off the gloves. "I've got backup on the way." He directed his gaze to Penny. "Can you drive?"

She shook her head, her jaw gaping open and her eyes wide.

"Can you call your boyfriend? Chuck, right?"

"Yeah," she whispered, then pulled out a cell phone with trembling fingers. "You want to come to my place?" Penny asked, pressing the phone to her ear.

But before Ryan could answer, Jared said, "Ryan will stay with me. Just sit tight for a little while." He led her to his pickup and opened the tailgate, hoisting her up onto the cold metal. "Don't either of you move."

Red lights flashed in the sky when a police car rolled down the street. Ryan watched as some local officer chatted with Jared. "Penny?"

Penny jumped up and took Ryan's hand. "Is he always this controlling?"

"This is nothing," Ryan said. When Jared took over, the world was given no choice but to listen.

"Thank goodness it was a nice night out. I shudder to think what might have happened if we were inside. But I'm surprised they didn't go for the main house."

"I can't believe someone broke into my house, period." Ryan swallowed, remembering all the hang-ups.

Jared continued to talk with the other officers, but Ryan couldn't hear them. Her body had gone numb. Then headlights swept down the road and slowed by the driveway.

"Here's Chuck," Penny said, still holding Ryan's hand.

"A BMW?" Ryan eyed Penny. "You've left out a few details about your new love."

"Penny. Are you okay?" Chuck flew from the driver's seat, leaving the engine running and the door open. He scooped Penny into his arms and planted kisses all over her face before putting her down. "Are you hurt?"

"Just a little scared," Penny said as Jared approached.

"Jared, right?" Chuck stuck his hand out, but held Penny tight with his other arm. "I'm so glad you were here."

"You graduated with Randy, right?" Jared swiped a forearm across his head.

"Yeah, I think it was three years behind you. What happened?"

"Not exactly sure yet, but I didn't think Penny should be alone or drive."

"All right if I take her home?"

"That's fine. If I need her, I know how to reach her."

"Thanks. Please keep me posted." Chuck nudged Penny toward his car. "Are you okay, Ryan? Can I get you anything? Want to come with us?"

"I'll take care of Ryan," Jared said like it was his job or duty.

"Ryan can take care of herself," she said under her breath. But she quickly reminded herself that someone had broken into her home, and Jared was just doing his job. He was always just doing his job.

"I'll call you tomorrow." Penny waved as the BMW rolled down the road, red taillights fading out into the darkness.

"Ryan, this is Officer Jenkins," Jared said. "He needs you to go through the house with him and make sure nothing is missing."

She followed him into the house, tears welling in her eyes. A firm hand gripped her forearm as she made her way down the short hallway to her bedroom. "Oh, God." She stopped at the doorway and looked at her clothing strewn about the room. Her body trembled. "What were they looking for?" Her throat was too dry to cough.

"I need you to tell me what's missing." Jared

smoothed his strong hand down her back. The circular motion at the base of her spine comforted her. "But you can't touch anything yet."

She glanced around the room. "It's hard to tell, with most of my belongings on the floor. Seems like everything in my closet is out here." She inched toward her dresser, trying not to step on anything. The drawers had been pulled open and emptied. "I don't know." She continued to scan the room. Her clothes had been tossed to the ground as if they didn't matter. "The only thing I don't see is my...my...underwear and nighties."

"Doesn't look like there are any undergarments here," Officer Jenkins said.

She jumped, having forgotten the officer was in the room. "My underwear? Who would do such a thing?" Her stomach tightened. The taste of bile rose up to her throat.

"A pervert, ma'am," Officer Jenkins said.

"But who? And why me?"

"Could be an ex-boyfriend or a perfect stranger, but someone decided to fixate their issues on you, ma'am." The officer turned toward Jared. "I'll file a report, and our office will up our patrols. We'll need to get her prints so we can match them against the prints we've found here."

"State will take care of that and send them to you. What about a tap on the phone? She's been getting a lot of hang-ups lately."

The officer lifted his hat, then wiped his brow.

"Doubtful, but I'll check into it. You might have better luck than us."

"All right. Thanks for coming out."

"You can put your room back in order now, ma'am."

"Thanks." Ryan plopped on the edge of her bed and tried to make sense of what had happened while she and Penny had been having a quiet drink near the lake only five hundred feet away. If she didn't know better, she'd have thought her stepfather had returned. He used to go on rampages and trash the house, just because someone ticked him off. But George was behind bars.

She rolled onto her back and stared at the ceiling for what seemed like an eternity. Her eyelids sank heavily and her body demanded sleep. She inhaled deeply, then let out one slow breath. She couldn't believe this was happening to her.

Jared had already called his office for a list of every possible perp in the area, but nothing jumped out at him. The background check he'd done on Tom had turned up a few parking tickets, a speeding ticket, and a sealed file from juvie.

That sealed file could've been anything. Hell, Jared had been picked up twice as a teenager, once for lewd behavior and once for possession. Both times the cop had opted to warn him and send him home scared shitless. However, that didn't make him a criminal. Kids made stupid mistakes every day of their existence.

He ran his fingers across the splintered wood. Anyone could've kicked in the door. Jared grabbed a soda from the refrigerator before heading back to Ryan's bedroom. The thought that someone had her panties sickened him. There were a lot of heinous crimes out there, but sexual ones disturbed him more than most.

He paused at the base of her bed and sipped his soda. Ryan had curled up like a kitten and hugged her pillow. He hated the idea of waking her, but she couldn't stay here alone under the present circumstances.

He set the soda can down on the nightstand and hesitated for a moment. She looked almost peaceful. He slid his arms under her warm body.

"Jared?" Her eyes flew open.

"Relax, babe." But it was him who needed to relax. The muscles in his body ached like he'd been up for days.

"I have to work in the morning."

"What time do you need to get up?" He lifted her into his arms, and she nuzzled her face into his neck. Her hot breath tickled his skin.

"About six. I've got a big event tomorrow at the hotel."

"I'll set an alarm for you." Careful not to bump

anything, he made his way out of her room and through the carriage house.

"Are you taking me to your bed?"

"You can't stay here alone; the door doesn't lock anymore." That really didn't answer her question. He hadn't given much thought to where she'd sleep. Okay, so he had, but only in the name of protecting her. *Yeah, right.*

"Thanks." She cuddled close when he stepped outside. The cool breeze smacked him in the face like a cold bucket of water.

Her thumb glided across his neck and her warm breath heated his skin, reminding him of their kiss in the bar. He wanted to hold her. Make love to her in the moonlight. But not tonight. It wouldn't be right. He wasn't sure any time would be right with her. Not because he didn't want her, but because she deserved more than he could ever give anyone.

He settled her into his bed and took a step back. Deciding she couldn't possibly be comfortable in her jeans, he reached for her zipper. His fingers trembled. He fumbled with the stupid thing as if he'd never used one before.

"Need a little help?" she mumbled, pushing his hands aside. She slipped from her jeans with ease, then lifted her shirt over her head and tossed it to the side.

He blinked, then blinked again, but couldn't rip his eyes from her half-naked form. He kept telling himself to turn away, but instead he just stared at her matching pink bra and lace panties. “Damn.”

He yanked the comforter and tossed it over her. A soft, rosy scent filtered around him, sending his pulse into a frenzy. She shifted beneath the blanket, snuggled up with his pillow, and let out a sigh that sent him over the edge.

After ridding himself of all of his clothing except his boxers, he fluffed the spare pillow and climbed onto the bed, on top of the covers. With his ankles crossed and his hands tucked behind his head, he squeezed his eyes shut. But the rhythmic breathing of the beauty lying next to him couldn’t be ignored.

“Jared,” she mumbled. “Thanks for being there for me.” She shifted under the covers, inching closer but never touching him. Thank God for small favors.

“That’s what friends are for,” he whispered, resting his hand over hers.

She held it but didn’t move. She seemed to just drift off, and he knew she’d fallen asleep.

Her friendship meant a lot to him. He had started off as a protector, but somewhere it shifted to something more equal. He settled down and took a deep breath. But he remained restless. Friends shouldn’t share a bed with friends.

Chapter Three

Ryan took in a slow breath. A masculine scent filled her senses. But it didn't belong in her bedroom. Confused, she blinked open her eyes. Then she remembered her house had been broken into, and Jared had tucked her into a bed in the main house. "Oh, my." She recognized the room.

His room.

She stretched, enjoying the musky smell of Jared's aftershave. She had no idea a smell could be so alluring. Or so comforting.

She scanned the darkened room. She'd been in his house a million times, even his bedroom, but had never expected to wake up there. Only dreamed what it would be like to spend the night next to his strong body.

She wondered where he had slept as a warm glow peeked through the curtains. She adjusted the pillow behind her and scooted to a sitting position, letting the covers fall to her waist.

Lifting her arms high above her head, she released the sleep from her body. When she finished her cat stretch, she sighed and glanced across the room at the clock. She still had a few minutes before she had to get up, so she'd enjoy his bed, even if he wasn't in it.

She noticed a humming noise just before it stopped, then the bathroom door pushed open.

"You're awake," Jared said.

Unable to take her eyes off his sculptured body, she nodded. His chest hair glistened with water left over from his shower. A towel had been wrapped low around his waist. Too low. Steam drifted into the bedroom, carrying a soapy smell.

"You okay?" He adjusted his towel a bit higher.

"Huh?" She gasped and clutched at the covers as he sat on the edge of the bed, but the blanket didn't budge. "Fine," she whispered.

"Relax." He lifted the covers, but held them in his hand while his other hand smoothed back her hair. He traced a path across her cheek, down her neck, to the space between her breasts. His finger tickled up and down her skin, just above her bra.

Her choppy breath burned her lungs. Her heart pounded so fast she couldn't tell where one beat started and another one ended.

"You're so beautiful," he murmured. His eyes darted back to her face as he drew the covers across her chest. "I'll get you some clean towels for your shower."

She pulled the covers to her chin. "I need my clothes so I can go back to my place and get ready for work."

"Take a shower here. I'll get you some of my sweats, and then I'll walk you to your place so you can change."

"I'm sure I'll be fine getting ready in the carriage house." This was it, and she'd just blown it. She should've acted like a woman. Instead, she acted like a scared rabbit.

He stood, almost losing his towel. It didn't seem to bother him, because it took him forever to fix it. "You have to take these threats seriously."

"I do. But—"

"No buts." He waved his finger in front of her face. "I'd never be able to forgive myself if something happened to you." He opened a dresser drawer and handed her some clothes. Without another word, he ducked back into the bathroom, once again leaving her unable to catch a breath.

She slipped on the shirt, which hung to her knees, and opted not to put on the sweats. Her pounding headache demanded caffeine.

She slipped downstairs and started a pot of coffee. As she glanced out the window toward her carriage house, fear prickled at the back of her neck. Someone had broken into her house, touched her things, stolen her underwear, and she had no idea who or why. It didn't seem like something her stepfather would do. Besides, he was behind bars where he belonged. Although, she wouldn't put anything past that man. He was evil. Pure evil.

"Ryan?" Jared's footsteps clunked on the floor like a herd of elephants. "Damn it, don't run off like that." He stuffed his gray uniform shirt into his unbuckled pants, then zipped them.

That man was too sexy for his own good, even when he wasn't trying to be. "Just thought you might like some coffee." Licking her lips, she forced her stare to remain above his neck.

"Thanks." With capable hands, he pulled down two mugs. "Go shower, then I'll make sure you get off to work," he ordered.

She bit her tongue; fighting with him wouldn't be worth it. When he was on a mission, forget it. He'd win every time. "Thank you," she whispered. "Having you around last night made things a little easier."

"You're welcome." He bent over and pressed his lips against her temple. He'd kissed her like that many times before, but this time, there was something blatantly sexual about the way his mouth touched her skin. "Now scoot, I've got work to do."

"Should I call a door guy?" she asked with renewed hope. Maybe she hadn't blown it after all.

"I'm your door guy, babe." He snagged a dishtowel and swatted her bottom. "I'll fix it tonight, right after I cook you dinner."

"Well, now, I can't pass up an offer like that." She padded toward the stairs with a mixture of excitement and fear. She'd fantasized long enough. It was time to take action, consequences be damned.

Hours later, Ryan took a step back and glanced around the banquet hall with a satisfied smile. The sun sparkled through the clear windows, casting a beautiful shine across the grand room. She'd taken part in the design of all the hotel's renovations right down to the bold red carpet throughout the main dining room, and she couldn't be prouder. The manager had complimented her taste many times, saying she'd helped raise the hotel's status as one of the best resorts in the state. Maybe even the country. Her job had been the one thing she could count on. Well, besides Penny's friendship and Jared's overprotecting ways. She sighed. Too many things were changing.

She checked her watch. The ladies' club would be arriving any moment, and she couldn't have been more pleased with how everyone on her team had managed to save a near disaster.

"You outdid yourself," Rick Weston said.

Unable to contain her joy, she smiled wider. "Thanks. I'm happy with the way things turned out, considering the problems." Impressing Rick, the general manager, was important. Too many things had gone wrong leading up to this day, and it was up to Ryan to fix them. Hell, it was her responsibility to take the brunt of blame. If Ryan didn't know better, she might think someone was out to get her. Her smile faded. Someone might be. That thought chilled her to the bone.

"The ladies' club has been wonderful about the mix-up with the hors d'oeuvres. The chef has managed to pull a few strings, and we'll be all set with the correct entrees." Ryan ran her fingers across the deep-pink tablecloth. Mistakes had been made before, but this did seem over the top.

"Any idea what happened to the requests?"

Forcing her gaze to the centerpiece, a small bowl with a single gardenia floating in a sea of pink water, she swallowed. "I have a copy of everything in a folder on my desk. What I submitted and what Leo has are two completely different things."

"That doesn't make any sense."

She turned to her boss and kept her chin up. "Tom received the same papers that the kitchen did. I must have screwed up somewhere. I'm sorry." One thing Ryan had learned along the way was to always take full responsibility. The buck had to stop somewhere, and today it stopped with her. "I'll make sure it doesn't happen again."

Rick cast an appreciative look around the room. "You've always been very efficient. You've done a fabulous job here. I don't believe all this could've been your fault."

"Well, it is my job to make sure parties like this go off without a hitch."

"And you did." Rick smiled. "Don't forget about the changes in the golf tournament this weekend."

"I'll take care of everything personally." She pushed back the large double doors to the main lobby that glistened with sunlight. It had been her idea to add windows to bring in as much sunlight as possible. Also, the view of the lake against the backdrop of the tall mountains would only add to the ambiance, and she'd been right.

There was a freshness in the air, like walking into a flower shop. She made sure arrays of freshly cut flowers were strategically placed on every floor so the hotel always smelled like spring. A large chandelier hung proudly from the cathedral ceiling.

"I know you will."

She headed toward her office with a spring in her step. Not only did she do her job well, but also she knew without a doubt she was good at it. And she'd continue to make sure that no major screw-ups happened again. She would hand-deliver all her requests, and she'd confirm them and check on them herself. No way would she rely on anyone else and have to scramble like this again.

Dodging a few young patrons who ran down the hall, she tried to figure out how so many mishaps could happen on one project. The ladies' club had always held their banquets in the village, and she'd worked hard to land this account. She couldn't afford to have something like this happen again with any of the other major accounts she had convinced to change venues.

In the comfort of her small, cozy office, she adjusted the fresh daisies she'd received from her brother, then seated herself behind the oak desk. Penny had always accused her of being anal when it came to neatness. Ryan wanted to laugh out loud over how well Penny knew her as she ran her hands across the clutter-free desktop. She wouldn't describe herself as anal, but more of a go-getter of sorts. Maybe she was more like Jared than she cared to admit. The man did have a tendency to like things done his way and so did she.

Her to-do list caught her attention, reminding her she'd have to stop at the store on the way home. Hopefully Jared would forget to fix the door. Not that she didn't want him around, but she needed to feel as though she could take care of herself. Or maybe it had more to do with proving to him once and for all she was a full-fledged adult and didn't need him. Well, she wanted him in her bed, but wanted him more to see her as a woman. Her heart pounded in uneven bursts as she thought about the possibility of getting Jared alone for the night. This time she wouldn't screw it up. No way.

Inspecting the paperwork for the golf tournament, she opened her file drawer. "Oh, my God!" A bloody dead rat sprawled across her files, dripping red liquid across her hanging folders. Pounding her feet on the floor, she rolled her chair back and let out a piercing scream.

Fear gripped her heart as her pulse raged out of control. Her hands trembled when she reached for the phone, but she didn't know who to call first.

"Ryan!" A female voice rang out from the hallway. "What's going on?" Her assistant, Cheryl, bolted through the door.

Ryan ripped her eyes from the nasty thing dangling on the metal file holder. "A rat."

"A live rat?" Cheryl asked with wide eyes.

Ryan shook her head and swallowed the lump in her throat. "A very dead one." She lifted the receiver to her ear. "I'm calling 9-1-1. Get Rick."

A male voice answered.

"Jared?" She coughed, realizing she'd hit star nine instead of 9-1-1. Well, he was a cop, so this worked, too.

"Ryan? What's wrong?"

"I think someone decided to play another prank on me." Unable to look at the furry beast in her drawer, she stood and moved to the other side of her desk.

"What kind of joke?"

"There's a dead rat in my desk. I don't think he crawled in there and hung himself, either."

Cheryl let out a gasp as she peered over the desk. "That's disgusting."

"I'll call it in and I'll be there in…about ten." The line went dead just as Rick flew into her office.

"What's going on?" he asked with concern in his voice. He stopped and stared into the drawer. "What the hell?"

"I called Sergeant Blake. He'll be here shortly." Ryan fumbled her way into the hallway. "Why would someone do something so…so…" There were no words, and no reasonable explanation.

"Cheryl," Rick said as he paced in the hallway. "I'd like you to call a special meeting and ask everyone not to leave until I've had a chance to talk to them. I'm sure the police will want to question everyone, too."

Ryan squared her shoulders. The thought of Jared questioning all of her fellow employees didn't help her already frayed nerves. He'd be suspicious of everyone. This was not helping her with her plan. She knew him well enough to know that when he was in the heat of a case that was all he could focus on, and that's not what she wanted. She wanted him naked, not in the middle of an investigation.

She shivered, wondering how her stepfather could have hired someone to do such a despicable thing. All during the trial, George swore he'd get her for ruining his life. This had to be him. Nothing else made sense.

The tires on Jared's patrol car squealed when he pulled into the parking lot of the hotel. The hair on the back of his neck stood at attention. How could he leave Ryan alone now? This was the third incident, and he didn't believe it would be the last. But he swore he'd never let anything stand in his way again, especially with regard to this promotion. Second chances didn't come along very often.

He'd just have to make sure he took care of it before his two weeks were up.

With his hand planted on his weapon, he pushed back the doors and entered the main lobby. He removed his sunglasses even though the sun shone brightly through all the incredibly tall windows. The plush red carpet sank under his work boots.

"Officer, this way." A young girl waved to him.

He nodded and followed her down the hallway lined with beautiful picturesque paintings of the lake. Any other day, he might stop and enjoy the pictures, but not when someone was hell-bent on terrorizing Ryan and making both their lives miserable.

"Jared," Ryan said. "Thanks for coming."

He tipped the brim of his hat, unable to take his eyes off her. She seemed so in control. So capable. She was very much a woman, not a little girl who needed protecting. "That's what I'm here for." Being the first on the scene gave him lots of wiggle room to check things out before the sheriff's office and local PD showed up. There was always that manly pounding of chests where different law enforcement agencies were concerned. But this was personal; he wasn't about to let anyone else handle Ryan.

He scanned the inside of Ryan's office. The small space barely housed a desk and a few filing cabinets, but Ryan had put in all her finishing touches, giving the space a cozy feel. Her degree and a few awards hung neatly on the wall. Her spotless desk had plenty of room for a few pictures. He looked at one taken at a party last summer.

"We left the drawer open," Rick said.

"Who else has been in here?" Jared questioned.

"Just Ryan and her assistant."

Jared peered over the desk and caught sight of the furry critter covered in blood. "Any rat problems lately?"

"We have monthly checks by an exterminator, and the health department is in here on a regular basis," Rick offered.

"I take it that's a no." Jared checked over the desk before kneeling so he could get a better look at the rascal. The fuzzy brown animal appeared tacky from the half-dried blood. It looked as if the poor thing had been mutilated for effect, then shoved into the drawer. "Ryan have any issues with other employees?"

"Not really."

Jared lifted his gaze and stood. "What does that mean?"

"She's a pretty girl. Half the male staff has probably

asked her out," Rick said. "She's well-liked by everyone."

Ryan's wholesome good looks only intensified her girl-next-door persona. "Know of anyone who might want to get back at her for something?" Jared rubbed the back of his neck and took a peek out in the hallway. "This isn't the first incident."

"Someone's done something like this to her before?" Shock registered on Rick's face.

Jared only nodded. He couldn't give up the details, even to one of his closest friends.

"Excuse me." A woman peered through the doorway. "There's another officer here."

Officer Jenkins and Detective Walter Kent rounded the corner into Ryan's office. Nick Jenkins no longer sported the standard blue uniform.

"Jared." Nick held his hand out. "I think you know Detective Kent."

"You move up the ranks?" Jared asked.

"Yeah, well, got tired of driving around in a patrol car for hours," Nick said. "Didn't want to do undercover stuff, so detective seemed like the next best thing."

"Will you excuse us?" Walter eyed Rick.

"I'll be in my office if you need me." Rick stepped into the hallway.

Jared pointed to the drawer.

"Nice." Walter shook his head. "And this isn't the first calling card she's gotten?"

"Dead rose on her birthday with a threatening note, then someone broke into her home and stole all her undergarments," Nick added.

"She break up with a boyfriend lately?" Walter asked while Nick picked up the rodent and dropped it into an evidence bag.

"Last long-term relationship she had that I know of was about six months ago, but I think that was a mutual split."

"What about men she's turned down? Or a woman who might be jealous of her?" Nick asked.

"I don't keep track of her boyfriends." Jared felt an unwanted surge of anger course through his veins. He wasn't sure where it came from, or why. And he sure as hell wouldn't deal with it, either.

"Well, let's go talk to her and get a list," Nick said, sealing the bag.

Jared stood next to Ryan while she answered Nick and Walter's questions. She downplayed any problems she might have had with past boyfriends and jealous friends, but cooperated fully. Jared promised to fax them a list of anyone who'd had contact with her stepfather on the inside. He wouldn't rule out George hiring an old friend to scare her. Or worse.

"Want me to drive you home?" Jared asked after the two detectives had left.

"I've got some errands to run." Her usual happy-go-lucky demeanor had been replaced with a sudden sadness in her eyes.

"Please be careful. Call me if something seems out of the ordinary. You'll probably beat me home, so let yourself into the main house." Placing his hand on the small of her back, he edged her toward the main doors. "I bet you'd enjoy a nice bath."

The sun hit his face, along with a gust of warm air that carried her fresh rosy scent as he opened the lobby doors. Lifting his sunglasses from his pocket, he glanced out over the lake. This would be the first summer in years he wouldn't be working the lake patrol. It would be the first summer since he'd been a small boy that he wouldn't be fishing on a Saturday morning.

"I'd love a long hot bath," Ryan said, snapping him out of his trance.

Mentally, he reminded himself that his new job would more than make up for losing the scenic beauty of Lake George. Besides, Rochester had a couple of Finger Lakes, and Lake Ontario.

Maybe he could find a nice place on Canandaigua Lake.

"I'll pick up some steaks for dinner." He opened her car door. "Call me as soon as you get home. Make sure you lock the doors, and don't open them for anyone but me."

"I don't like being scared. And I don't like you telling me what to do." She slammed the door shut, rolling down the window. "I spent the first year George went to jail afraid of my own shadow. I refuse to live like that again." She squinted at him. "And I'm perfectly capable of taking care of myself, thank you."

"I'm only asking you to be safe, babe." He ran his hand across the back of his neck.

"And don't call me that. I'm not your *babe.*" She turned the key and rammed the gearshift into drive, jerking the SUV.

He reached over her, put the car in park, then opened the door and yanked her into his arms.

Shock registered in her eyes. "Let me go." She struggled to break free.

"This isn't a joke," he said, cupping her chin.

The determination he read in her eyes only heightened his awareness of her as a woman. A woman he desired, and that just pissed him off. "I don't know what the hell I did, but don't push my buttons, *babe.*"

"Push your buttons?" She gaped at him. "Don't treat me like a child."

"I'm just reminding you to use good judgment. You have to take these threats seriously."

"You think I don't know how to lock the doors after everything that's happened? I'm not stupid." She managed to shrug herself from his grasp.

"You wouldn't come with me the night George decided to snap." Jared clenched his fists. "I know he raped your mother, but she wouldn't press charges. She wouldn't let me take him in and when I got back, his dirty hands were all over you." Bile seeped to the back of his throat. Every time he thought about that night, uncontrollable rage boiled in his bloodstream.

"Your clothes were torn and he was touching you," Jared said. "You were just a kid." He blinked, trying to force the pictures from his mind, but it never failed. The memory of her kicking and screaming, struggling for life, always crashed with visions of his son lying lifeless in his crib. Two very separate incidents, but both were his fault. "I should've made you come with me."

Soft fingers glided across his jaw. "I couldn't leave Mom. Things were out of control, but I knew you'd be back." She palmed his cheeks, forcing him to look at her. "I'm not sixteen anymore."

"I know that." Taking her wrists in his hands, he kissed the soft swell of her palm. "But being an adult doesn't make you less vulnerable to some psycho."

"I'll lock the doors, okay?"

"And call me."

She nodded and pulled the seat belt across her lap.

He watched as she waved, then pulled out of the parking lot. Moments later, he got in his patrol car and headed back to his office. He needed to gather information, but more importantly, get her, and the effect she had on him, off his mind.

Once he'd settled behind his desk, he started going through the files Frank had collected on every man who'd served with George and had since been released. One name jumped out at him. A sex offender named

Rudy Martin, who now resided in Troy, New York, just an hour south of Lake George. It seemed Rudy got his jollies picking up unsuspecting women in bars, tying them up, and then jerking off. "Now that's just sick. Harmon, get your ass in here."

"Yes, sir. What can I do for you, sir?" Once again, Harmon stood at attention.

"This isn't the damn military." Jared closed the file, but kept the rap sheet out.

"No, sir. We're Triple A with guns."

Jared coughed. "That's not funny. Don't ever refer to state troopers as anything less than the highest form of police protection. Unless you want to find yourself hog-tied to the back of my pickup with 'honk if you think I'm a moron' tattooed on your ass." The Triple A with guns was such an old jab that it was almost funny, especially when a pimple-faced kid used it wearing the trooper uniform.

"Sorry, sir. My friend at the sheriff's office said that once, and it sounded funny at the time." Harmon stiffened even more, if that was possible.

"You can tell your friend he's a volunteer firefighter with a badge."

"I'll remember that one."

Jared went to the copy machine, slid the paper in, and pushed three. "I want you to get hold of our contact in the Troy office. Have him pick this guy up for routine questioning. Or have his parole officer do it."

"What are we questioning him about?"

"I want to know how well he knew George McIntosh, and if he's been in this area at all in the last few weeks. Has he been to the florist? What kind of car he drives. Where he works. Does he like rats?"

"Sir?"

"What?"

"You want to call the contact? Seems like you got a lot of specific questions." Harmon hadn't moved a muscle since he walked into Jared's office.

"Was your father a military man?"

"Marines, sir."

Jared chuckled. "And you didn't follow in his footsteps?"

"Did you follow yours?" Harmon's eyes grew wide but never broke contact. The kid did have some spunk. Jared had to give him that.

"Retired senator."

Harmon smiled. "You'd make a good politician."

Jared couldn't stand it anymore and let out a roar of laughter. "You're okay, kid. Now just make those phone calls."

"Sergeant Blake?" Harmon questioned as Jared made his way out to the hallway. "Does this have anything to do with what's been happening to Ryan O'Connor?"

Jared stopped and turned; his heart raced wildly at the mention of her name. "What do you know about that?"

"I know about the rose." Harmon stuttered a bit.

"And I heard about what happened today at the hotel. She's a really nice girl."

"You know Ryan?" Jared stared at the kid, giving him a once-over. "How old are you?"

"Twenty-two. I've met her a few times."

"Stay away from her, you got it?" He poked Frank in the chest. Damn kid didn't flinch, which annoyed Jared even more. Not to mention that he'd poked rock-solid muscle. "You're not her type."

"Yes, sir. Understand, sir."

Jared could've sworn the little bastard cracked a smile. "Get back to work."

"Should I call you as soon as I find something?"

"Sure." Jared stomped out of his office and down the hallway, wiggling his fingers. It had to be the stress of moving that had been affecting his usual good judgment. His parents hadn't been thrilled when he'd decided to put the house on the market, but his sister Karen and her husband Tim hadn't wanted to buy it. What other choice did he have?

Come hell or high water, he was taking this transfer.

Chapter Four

"Thanks for coming." Ryan pulled back the tab on a Diet Coke and handed it to Penny before grabbing another one for herself. "Want to take this in the family room?"

"God, I wish I could afford this place." Penny ran her fingers across the almond-colored granite countertops. "I would love to live here."

Ryan gripped her soda can. She had known she'd have to move someday; she just thought it would be when she was ready. "Me, too. I asked Jared if he would consider being the bank so I could buy this place, but he didn't go for it. Said something about he wasn't that rich."

"You could have ten kids, and this kitchen would still seem huge." Penny opened a few cabinets. "There's enough dishware in here to serve an army." She took a big swig of her soda. "How big is this place, anyway?"

"Here." Ryan grabbed the fact sheet and shoved it at Penny. "Five thousand square feet, five bedrooms, five and a half baths, and a partridge in a pear tree."

"Testy." Penny wrinkled her nose and then headed down the short hallway toward the family room, which was really more of a great room housing two oversized sofas, two recliners, a love seat and ottoman, and a large screen plasma television. Of course, one couldn't disregard all the expensive artwork and decorations. She couldn't help but wonder what Jared was going to do with all this stuff.

"I started looking for a new apartment." Ryan flipped the switch and the light flickered, illuminating the soft creamy walls, accentuating the chocolate-colored couches. "Not much out there."

"But this sheet says there's already a moneymaking tenant."

Ryan snatched the listing. "It says the servants' quarters have been converted to a carriage house which makes a great rental. And do you know what old man Foster gets for his little shack he rents out?" When she flopped onto the sofa, a pillow bounced to the floor.

"Can't say that I do." Penny joined her, tucking her feet under her butt.

"Fifteen hundred a month, and it's nothing like the carriage house. Not even close. I can't afford anything that high. Besides, I should move over to Bolton. It's closer to work, and these roads get really nasty in the winter. But I'm going to sleep here tonight. With Jared."

Penny coughed, then sputtered. "Did you just say what I think you said?" Penny wiped up the soda that had fizzed out of her mouth and landed in her lap. "Don't say stuff like that when I'm drinking."

"I'm serious, Pen. The man doesn't know how to have a relationship and that suits me just fine. I'm not ready for a lifetime of love, just one freaking night. That's all I'm asking for." Ryan let out a slow breath, trying to keep her erratic heartbeat under control.

"You can't handle it." Penny snorted. "He'll break your heart into tiny little pieces, and I doubt you'll be able to recover. I think you need to stay the hell away from him."

"Thanks for the vote of confidence," Ryan muttered.

"You want me to lie to you? Tell you that I think you should go for it? Come on, Ry. I've known you since we were in preschool. You've had it bad for Jared since you knew how to say his name. Being with him in the biblical sense will only hurt you, and you know it."

Wasn't that the truth? But Ryan still wanted to know what it would be like to make love to him, no matter the cost. She'd get over it. Her brother's first wife had run out on him for another man, and he'd survived. He'd found Marci, and now they were expecting their first baby. All was well in his world. So, she'd survive it, if she could get "it" to happen.

The kitchen door slammed shut. Ryan leaped to her feet and gasped. "Jared?"

His sexy drawl came from the kitchen. "Yep. Got your brother with me, too."

"Great." Ryan rolled her eyes. Just what she needed, her big brother. And knowing him, he'd demand she come and stay at his place, making up some story that Marci needed her help. Right. Dumbass brother.

"I'm going to go surprise Chuck." Penny gave her a sisterly hug. "I got him all hot and bothered on the phone, so I guess I should go put the poor man out of his misery."

"Are things going well?" Ryan asked.

"Well enough." Penny lowered her chin. "Be careful, okay? I love you lots."

"Yeah, yeah. Now get lost." Ryan shoved Penny toward the kitchen. "And keep your trap shut on the way out. The last thing I need is you and your mouth."

Penny dragged Ryan into the kitchen. "You love my mouth." Penny squeezed Ryan's cheeks together. "You've got such a face." She smacked her lips against Ryan's.

"Gross." Ryan wiped her mouth. "Save it for the boyfriend."

"God, I love a man in uniform." Penny patted Jared's arm. "See ya around."

"Goodbye, Pen." Ryan shook her head, watching Penny give a good hip walk to her car. That girl loved to put on a show. Chuck was in for a wicked night.

"That's one interesting girl." Jared laughed.

"Did you get stuff to fix my door?" Ryan asked and then landed a quick kiss on her brother's cheek.

"Didn't have time; you can just crash here for now." Jared ducked his head into the pantry and pulled out a cutting board and some seasonings. "Want a beer, Pat?"

"I think Ryan should come back to my place," Pat said, his lips drawn into a tight line.

"She's fine here." Jared clunked the wooden board down on the table and removed his gun belt, setting it on the counter in what seemed like one swift movement.

Ryan bit her tongue and looked between the two men who were acting as if she wasn't even in the room. No point in adding fuel to the fire. They never listened to her anyway.

"Marci could use the help, and I'd feel better if Ryan were with me, under the circumstances." Pat leaned against the counter with his hands braced on either side. His face was tight, and his blue eyes filled with determination. But not once did he glance her way.

Jared tilted his head and tapped his badge. "She's safer with me."

"I'm her brother."

Ryan blinked. The gorilla chest pounding would begin at any moment. "Look, fellas. I think I've got this under control. I'm going down to the village to find myself some hot guy, go home with him, and have hot, wild sex. A package of condoms is all the protection I'll need, so enjoy your steaks."

"Ryan. That's not funny." Pat contorted his face even more, if that was possible. He had this look in his eyes, like he had when he used to scold her as a child.

"What bar?" Jared asked with a devilish twinkle in his eye.

"Don't encourage her," Pat said, taking a step toward Jared.

"Hey, if she's going to pick up some guy, it might as well be me. I just want to know where she's going so I can go too." Jared winked.

"Get your things, Ryan; you're coming home with me," Pat said.

"Save the parenting for the new baby, big bro. I'm a grown-up."

"She looks like a grown-up to me," Jared said, checking her out.

His roaming eyes sent a hot shiver up her spine. "Oh, for crying out loud. I can't believe the two of you have the balls to talk to each other like I'm not even in the room."

Jared cocked his head and lifted a brow.

"Don't say it." She glared at him. "And don't tell me what to do, either." The only way to deal with a Neanderthal was to act like one.

"Ryan." Jared's fingers swept across the back of her neck, then squeezed gently. "I have plenty of room, and

I think it would be safer if you stayed here. With me. A cop."

Ryan swallowed as she stared into his intense blue-green eyes. His thumb still lingered on her neck, rubbing softly in small circles, sending signals to places that might make someone think the temperature had escalated to an all-time high. "Thanks. Now don't let this go to your head, but I'd have to agree."

Jared leaned over and brushed his lips across her temple. Her heart pounded so heavily, she thought it might thump right up her throat.

She took a deep breath and stepped away. "So, have you found out anything?"

"I've got a lead on a guy who was in prison with George, and I've got someone looking into it right now."

"I'd feel better if you were looking into it," Pat said, still scowling, but thankfully not fighting her on where she chose to stay. It was her choice after all.

Overprotective brothers could be a pain right in the petunia. "I'm sure he's on top of it, Pat." She grabbed the bag she'd left on the kitchen chair with some stuff she'd packed, in hopes of having to spend the night. "Do you care what room I take?" she asked Jared, tossing her hair in what had to be the worst attempt at being sexy.

"You can join me in mine," Jared teased.

"Keep dreaming there, big fella." She flung her bag over her shoulder, trying to act as if that would never happen when in reality that was exactly what she planned on doing. "Pat, you joining us for dinner?" Might as well be nice, even though she secretly hoped her dear sweet brother would take a hike, and soon.

"I've got to get back to the bar. My new manager isn't all that wonderful," Pat said behind a clenched jaw, seething in her direction.

Direct hit. "Catch ya later." Without looking back, she flew up the stairs and took the first bedroom on the right. Her brother would never learn that pushing her buttons would only make her push back. She dumped her bag on the blue comforter, then flung herself on the bed. Staring up at the ceiling, she began to devise her plan. She had nothing to lose. Even if the jerk turned her down, her humiliation wouldn't last that long. Two weeks, to be exact.

"Man, if looks could kill, I would have died five times by now." Jared coughed, knowing he'd pushed the line. But hell, Pat was such an easy target, especially when it came to Ryan.

"I don't like you flirting with my kid sister."

"She's not a kid." Boy, didn't Jared know it. He'd had a hard time sleeping last night because of ridiculous fantasies racing around inside his mind. If she kept this up, he knew exactly what would happen. Of course, part of him wanted it to happen, but he had to pull back. He cared for her; therefore, he didn't want to hurt her, and if he slept with her, well, that was the only possible outcome.

"She has some kind of hero worship going on with you, and then you encourage her."

"We're just friends with a long history. We've always been kind of flirty with each other. It's nothing." An electric pulse shot through his chest. It was more than nothing and he knew it.

"I have eyes." With both hands on his hips, Pat glared at Jared. "You find her attractive."

"And I find your wife attractive, too." Jared ripped open the paper the steaks were in.

"We're talking about my sister."

"Who happens to be my friend, age difference and all." Jared rinsed the steak before tossing it on the cutting board he'd already sprinkled with seasonings. Even when she'd been a teenager, Jared had considered her a friend. He'd been there for her, and she'd done her share of being there for him when his ex-wife had left.

Pat ran a hand across his jaw. "I'm worried about Ryan."

Jared pounded at the steak. "Me, too." He grabbed a dishtowel and wiped his hands, then flung the towel on the counter. "One of the guys George was in prison with is a sex offender, and he lives in Troy." Opening the refrigerator, he slammed the cutting board on top of some soda cans.

"Jesus." Pat rubbed his jaw. "Rapist or something?"

"Or something, but that's not my only angle on this one." Jared turned a chair, then straddled it when he sat down. "You know Tom Grady?"

Pat looked at the ceiling, then mumbled the name.

"He's the moron she went out with the other night. She also works with him. Something about him rubs me the wrong way." Jared fiddled with his badge. "So you see, the closer I keep her to me, the closer I get to finding out who's behind all this. Anyone tries anything, I'm there."

"What if you don't find this guy before you move?" Pat pulled the chair out to sit.

"I should be able to clear this up before I move, I promise."

"You can't promise that," Pat said.

Before he left, Jared would do everything in his power to make sure whoever was behind these crimes would be punished. "Let me do my job. I'm kind of good at it." Jared lifted his beer in a toast, then took a gulp. "What brought you by, anyway?"

"To check on my sister. And to let you know that you're going to be the godfather of my baby."

"Negative." Jared stood, then guzzled half his beer. Him, a godfather? Never. "You've got a lot of nerve to ask me that this week." Jared's heart raced, shooting adrenaline throughout his system. He slammed his beer on the counter.

"You didn't kill your son," Pat whispered.

"I'm not having this conversation with you," Jared bellowed. "Please leave."

"Let it go," Pat said.

Jared gripped the counter until his knuckles turned white.

"Lisa didn't love you or Johnny. She didn't leave you any choice," Pat said softly. "Think about it, okay?" The door rattled as Pat tugged it closed.

Pat had been right about one thing. Lisa hadn't given Jared a choice. She'd threatened to leave town, with his child, if he didn't toss seventeen-year-old Ryan to the streets. So he took legal action, making sure Johnny would stay with him.

And now Johnny was dead.

"I'm going to jump in the lake," Jared yelled to Ryan as he jogged up the stairs. His body trembled. He had the strong urge to grab his favorite stash and get lost in the darkness of a bottle.

Moments later, he stood at the end of the dock and contemplated jumping into the cold lake, butt naked. "What the hell." He stripped from his jeans and ripped off his shirt. Standing at the edge like he was king of the mountain, he took in a deep breath, then…

Splash!

He dove fifteen feet, making sure his hand squished in the muck before shifting his body and surging to the top. "Damn, that's cold." He hoisted himself onto the dock, then shook the frigid water from his naked body and wrapped a towel around his waist. He stared out over the moonbeams dancing across the dark-blue water.

He snatched up his clothes and headed toward the lounge chair on the lawn, ignoring the goose bumps climbing up his numb body.

"Nice show." Ryan's voice rang out soft and sexy in his ears.

The towel slid an inch or two as blood rushed to places it shouldn't. "How long have you been sitting there?"

"Long enough. And you're nuts. That water couldn't be more than fifty-five degrees." She'd stretched out across a lounge chair with her hands clasped behind her head and a warm smile plastered on her angelic face. Damn woman was too beautiful for her own good.

"Tell me something I don't know." He waved to her, flashing his clothes.

"All of a sudden shy?" she teased, seductively crossing her legs.

"No." He cleared his throat. "Turn around, unless you want a front row seat for the next showing." He released the tucked in corner of the towel and chuckled when she went scarlet and turned away.

Given the opportunity, he eyed her with appreciation. Her lean body had all the necessary curves to drive a man insane, but her legs—well, *wow*, was all he could come up with. "Do you always sneak up on skinny-dippers?"

She laughed. "That was a repeat performance."

"Excuse me?" He pulled his shirt over his head. "You can turn around now."

"Do you even own a bathing suit?" Her sultry tone warmed his chilled body.

He sat down on the edge of her lounge chair and propped his elbow on her knee. He inhaled and smelled her fresh rosy scent. "Of course. But I prefer my birthday suit."

"Once, Penny and I watched you and Randy stumble to the dock, strip, and dive in. We stole your clothes and towel and had to stick cold pizza in our mouths to stop from laughing when you two hightailed it to the house, nudie."

"So, you're the scoundrel who stole my trooper sweats." He dropped his chin, squeezing her thigh. The heat from her body rippled to his hand.

"Penny hoped she'd have to go rescue one of you."

"And you?"

"I would've let you both drown." Her playful smile told him otherwise.

He chuckled, then turned sullen. "Your idiot brother wants me to be a godfather. You have to talk to him."

She traced a path down his jaw with her finger and leaned closer. "It's time, Jared. It's been too long to hold on to this kind of pain." Her soft lips pressed against his unshaven cheek and melted away some of the heartache.

"I can't." He shifted her legs to the side, then rested

his head on her firm, flat stomach. Wrapping his arms around her, he closed his eyes. "I didn't know how hard it would be."

"Lisa made it hard," Ryan whispered, running her fingers across his buzz cut.

"I didn't make it easy for her."

"That's not true."

He tilted his head and caught her tear-filled gaze. "You were just a kid back then. What do you know?" He had wanted to push her away both back then and now, but for some godforsaken reason, she never left.

"Lisa didn't love you."

"You don't know the whole story." He dropped his chin down, slipping his hand under her shirt and across her warm skin. She gave him comfort and offered so much more.

"Stop making excuses for her. She took off, plain and simple."

"I pushed her away, and then Johnny died."

"He died of SIDS," she whispered, holding him tight. "You couldn't have known that would happen, and it would have happened whether or not Lisa had stayed." Ryan tugged at his head, forcing him to lock teary gazes with her.

"Had I been a better father, I would've known what was going on."

"Why do you do this to yourself?"

He let out a long breath. "I can't be a godfather to Pat's baby. I need you to tell him that."

"I won't do that and yes, you can." Her loving eyes pierced deep into his soul. "Loving someone doesn't kill them."

But if you don't love, you don't get hurt. That had been his motto since Lisa ran out. He still had love in his life. He loved his parents and sister. He didn't need anything else. "I can't help the way I feel."

Her breath hitched when he traced a path with his finger where her low-cut shirt met her soft, supple skin. "You can try," she whispered. "It means a lot to Pat."

Staring down at her perfectly shaped breasts, he moistened his lips and kissed the exposed skin. She tasted like honey. He continued to lose himself in her. Her hands splayed across his shoulders, neck, and back, easing the tension built up by years of not letting anyone know he cared.

He cupped her breast over her thin shirt, pinching the hard nipple between his thumb and forefinger. She let out a passionate moan. Kissing his way to her luscious mouth, he gently bit down on her lower lip.

Her eyes fluttered open, and he searched them for a reason to stop. But all he found was a woman who knew exactly what she wanted, and she wanted him.

His heart beat so fast it drowned out the world around him. He sucked in a quick gasp when her tongue darted out to meet his. A low rumble coming from deep in his throat rippled out in a groan of desire.

With trembling hands, he clasped his fingers around

her tiny wrists, and in desperation pried his lips from hers. She stared back at him, a hint of fear looming behind her glossy blue eyes.

"Ryan." He sucked in a ragged breath.

"Don't tell me you want to stop."

He shook his head. "I don't want to use you. At least a bottle of Jack Daniels doesn't have any feelings I'd have to worry about."

"You need to let yourself feel something other than anger and self-loathing." She swiped at a single tear that rolled down her cheek. "You're not the only one who lost someone."

"I don't want you to reduce yourself to a one-night stand because you feel sorry for me."

"I don't pity you. I feel empathy for you." Anger flashed in her eyes. "But if you'd prefer getting drunk to spending the night with me, someone who cares very deeply for you, well, I'll just go collect my things and go to my brother's. I won't hang out here and watch you slowly destroy yourself."

For a long moment she glared at him, not saying anything. He opened his mouth, but no sound came out. For the first time in a long while, he didn't know what to do. "I don't want to hurt you."

"You'd have to lie to me to hurt me. I know exactly what this would be and I still want it."

Her lips quivered when he traced them with his thumb, then pushed himself up to a sitting position in front of her. "You're suggesting that I use you—"

Her hand covered his mouth. "That we console each other instead of wallowing in self-pity. We both hurt, and having human contact might help."

He lifted a brow. "I've tried that before, but it didn't help."

"That's because they didn't understand you and what you're going through. They were nameless one-night stands."

"That's exactly what this would be." He stood and raked a hand across his head. She wanted him to be her knight in shining armor. She wanted more than just sex, and he couldn't give her that, ever. "You really need to get over this fascination with me."

She rolled her legs to the side and rose with style and grace. Standing before him, she lifted her hand and rested it against his thumping heart. "I'm not twelve. My eyes are wide open and I'm not looking for anything other than..." Cracking a smile, she said, "One night."

"You left out the *stand* part." Caving to her, he drew her body close. Her tender touch felt better than the best liquor gliding down his throat.

The other women he'd slept with following his son's death had been nameless girls who meant nothing to him. No matter how many times he'd tried in the past, this week he'd always ended up doing everything he could to keep himself from completely falling apart, yet that was exactly what happened.

Ryan had always tried to be there for him, offering him nights of soft whispers and caring words. She'd put up with shouting matches, name-calling, then she'd finally give up and let him drown. He didn't feel like drowning now. Somehow he owed it to her.

Had he just rationalized taking her to bed?

Her eyes brightened when he smiled. Shaking his head, he let out a throaty chuckle.

"Dare I ask what's so funny?" She tilted her head.

"I wouldn't if I were you." He brushed her hair back and his look turned serious. "Are you taking the pill?"

"I have condoms in the carriage house." Her voice cracked when she answered.

He arched his brow. "Really?"

"A girl's got to be prepared."

"Come on." He took her by the hand and tugged her toward the main house. "I've got a box by my bed."

"Really?"

"A guy's got to be prepared." He looped his arm around her and forgot about all the reasons why sleeping with her was wrong.

Very wrong.

Chapter Five

Ryan took in a slow, calming breath, hoping her hand didn't tremble as she slid it into Jared's back pocket. His hard buns pressed firmly against her palm, sending her pulse into a dangerous beat, but one she welcomed. No turning back now.

The walk from the front lawn to the main house seemed to go on forever. The longer it took to get inside and in bed, the greater the risk one of them would come to their senses and call the whole thing off. She wouldn't let that happen. Not this time.

"Would you like a glass of wine?" Jared asked, pushing back the kitchen door.

"Sure." She leaned against the doorjamb near the hallway to the family room. Sipping wine on the floor in front of a fire certainly would set the mood.

"Why don't you go put some music on," he

suggested as he pulled down a bottle and two glasses. "I'll be right in."

She made her way into the large family room, turned on a light near the stereo, and then ran her trembling fingers across his selection of CDs. After settling on a case labeled 'soft rock,' she sat down on the hearth and entertained her own second thoughts.

I'm not in love with him, she thought as she lit the long match and turned the switch to the gas starter.

A quick poof, then the fire began to take hold of the wood. She settled herself on the floor with a pillow against the couch. She liked him a whole lot and had lusted after him since she knew what sex was. But love didn't, and wouldn't, enter the equation. At least not the forever kind of love.

"You read my mind," he drawled, entering the room. Feet had never been a fetish of hers, but when he sauntered into the room with his T-shirt, jeans, and bare feet, sexy took on a whole new meaning. He handed her a glass and sat down next to her. The heat from his body was unmistakably inviting.

She took a long, slow sip, hoping the wine would go straight to her head. Her heart pounded so loudly she could barely hear the music playing in the background.

He tossed back the rest of his wine like it was a beer, then set the glass aside and stared out into the darkened room. He cleared his throat as if he might say something, but no words followed. Only a deafening silence.

A rush of adrenaline shot through her already shocked body. She couldn't let him change his mind. She had to get him out of her system once and for all. Following his lead, she finished her wine in a quick gulp, then threw her leg over his body and straddled him, making sure she positioned herself over the part that mattered.

"Ryan."

She touched her finger to his mouth. "Shh." She adjusted herself, knowing she had affected the right part of his body when he groaned and gripped her thighs. Framing his face, she lowered her eyelids and pressed her lips against his.

At first he barely participated, his lips merely responding to the movement of her mouth. The fire crackled in the background but didn't drown out the pounding of her heart. She rolled her tongue across his lips, catching his soft moan as it rumbled through her body.

He squeezed her thighs tight, massaging her quivering muscles. Slowly, he took control of the kiss as his hands made their way up her legs, over her hips, and across to her behind. His fingers dug in hard as he thrust his hot tongue into her mouth. Unable to keep up, she pried her mouth away, grabbing the hem of her shirt.

She looked down at him. His mouth gaped open, then shut tight as he swallowed. His eyes focused directly on her chest. She wiggled as she whipped off her shirt, exposing the most pathetic excuse for a bra. She had bought a bunch of plain white ones to replace the ones that got stolen. Sexy bra or not, he still stared. She reached for the front clasp.

"Don't," he whispered.

Fighting back the tears that had begun to well in her eyes, she inhaled a sharp breath. If he refused her now, it would be worse than waking up alone.

He shifted underneath her but didn't ask her to move. She scowled, not understanding what he wanted. The lump in her throat prevented her from forming any words.

His gaze lifted to her eyes as his fingers tingled up her spine. She arched like a cat while he danced his fingers across her skin.

A wide grin that showed off his perfectly straight teeth damn near knocked the wind out of her. He tapped his finger against the small of her back, one of the most sensitive spots on her body.

"That tickles," she said.

His hands slid down her skin, applying pressure at her hips. With ease, he shifted her off his lap and laid her down on the rug in front of the fireplace. Kneeling over her, he lifted his T-shirt over his head and tossed it to the side.

His magnificent torso glowed in the firelight. The perfect amount of hair lined his upper chest. She reached up to run her fingers through the coarse curls and let her inhibitions fade away.

Completely lost in the moment, she lowered her head and pressed her lips against his rock-hard abs. The muscles in his stomach twitched when she flicked her tongue out and traced a path around his navel. She continued on her exploration of his glorious body right up to his nipple.

"Ryan," he said with a ragged breath. "Slow down." Moist lips pressed into her neck, then glided down her collarbone. "I want to enjoy you."

"I was enjoying you."

Hot breath panted against her skin when he chuckled. "I go first." With nimble fingers, he unhooked her bra, sliding the thin straps down her shoulders, letting the garment fall to the floor.

"Why?" The calluses on his hands tickled when he ran his fingers up the side of her breast, brushing his thumb over her taut nipple. When he lifted his gaze, his lids were heavy and his stare full of desire.

"Please don't make me answer that."

The CD changer clicked, then clanked, as it changed from one artist to the next. She hadn't really been paying attention, and now she didn't care. The depth in his deep-green eyes commanded her to gaze intently at him.

She'd been with other men before, but nothing she'd experienced had come close to his gentle caresses and passionate kisses. No one had ever put her pleasure before their own. "Why?" she asked again, needing to know and understand his desires.

He drew her near. "I want to please you."

"Touching you would please me."

A deep groan rumbled in his chest. He ran his fingers through her hair, letting it fall at her shoulders. "I want to discover what makes you..." He traced a circle with his finger around her breast.

"Oh, God," she mumbled, closing her eyes.

"I want you thoroughly satisfied before I lose myself in you," he whispered.

She forced her lids open just as his tongue darted out of his mouth and drew her nipple inside. Instantly, her entire body ignited into a burst of fiery flames. Before she had a chance to come up for air, he pressed her back to the floor. He pried her jeans down her legs.

"Beautiful." He ran his hands up and down her legs. "You're a beautiful woman, Ryan."

The way her name fell from his lips sent a shiver from her toes to her fingertips. She cupped his head, feeling the softness of his buzzed hair on her palms. He laced her stomach with wet kisses before slipping off her panties in one swift motion.

In awe, she watched him lift her leg and plant an erotic kiss on her big toe. He moved his mouth to her ankle, and then worked his way across her knee, finally landing on her inner thigh. Her most vivid dreams didn't hold a candle to reality.

"Ja...red." She moaned, tossing her head on the floor and arching her back when his hand rubbed across her dark curls, then separated her legs more. His long fingers slipped inside her. She jerked at the intensity of his touch.

"Did I hurt you?" He stopped the most exquisite sensation she'd ever experienced.

She shook her head, gasping for breath. "Don't." She moistened her lips. "Don't stop."

"You like this," he said, moving his hand inside her once again. Hot breath tickled her skin right before he kissed her intimately.

"Oh, God." Her body flew into flames like a spark given just enough oxygen to explode into something more.

When he lifted his head, locking gazes with her, her breath hitched at the passion filling his sea-like eyes. A seductive smile broadened his face.

Her pulse raced out of control and her chest heaved up and down with her short, choppy breaths. The outside world disappeared like a ship sailing over the horizon. She rolled her hips in rhythm with his hand. The blood in her veins raced like a wildfire following the oxygen it needed to survive.

He nestled himself between her legs, his soft mouth stroking her to the point of sheer madness. Deep groans rumbled up to her throat and escaped her lips in a passionate sigh. Electric pulses pounded through her heart and spread to every inch of her body. Every muscle tensed when she reached her limit and convulsed over and over again, crying out Jared's name.

Sexually, she'd been thoroughly satisfied. Emotionally, she'd experienced something beyond her craziest dream. And with a man who was only capable of giving his body.

This didn't help get him out of her system, but made her system demand more.

Jared pressed his hand against Ryan's stomach. A complete sense of fulfillment washed over him. Hearing his name fall from her lips while her body reached the glorious pleasure he'd given to her gave him complete satisfaction.

If she wanted to curl up in his arms and go to sleep, he'd sleep as if he just had the best sex of his life.

"Up here," she whispered, cupping his face and drawing him closer.

His chest tightened when he looked into her bright-blue eyes. Just getting through the pain, he reminded himself. Ryan offered her warm body instead of the loneliness of a cheap bottle of whiskey. This was their way of saying goodbye to this part of their lives and moving on to something else.

He soothed her skin with his hands as he made his way to her perfect breasts. Taking a puckered nipple into his mouth and swirling his tongue around it, he lost himself completely. No one had ever responded to him the way she did.

Not wanting to let any part of her go untouched, he

switched his affections to her other breast while moving his hands everywhere he could manage on her quaking body.

"Jared," she called, tugging at his head.

Seconds after he lifted his mouth from her skin, her lips locked with his and her tongue thrust into his mouth with feverish intent. Before he could manage a quick gasp, she had him lying flat on his back and her lips were dancing down his neck.

"Sweet Jesus," he grumbled when his nipple got sucked into her hot mouth. Her teeth scraped against the sensitive nub when she began her descent. "Ryan." He breathed deeply. "You don't have to do this."

Her hands trembled with the button to his jeans; his erection pressing against the tight fabric wasn't helping the process. Ending his own misery, he swatted her hands away and began sliding his pants over his hips.

"These have to go." She toyed with the elastic to his boxers. Her bright smile electrified the room as she shoved them down to his ankles.

He groaned. Her hands massaged his thighs, then glided over him. Everything in the room blurred into a mass of nothing. She brought her mouth to him, sending him into the abyss. The way she touched and explored his body humbled him. No one had ever cared this much about how he felt. Hell, *he'd* never cared that much.

Sex had always been about instant gratification. The

release of tension and mutual satisfaction had been the sole purpose. But something in the way she caressed him and responded intuitively to his body's signals, made this experience something more.

"Stop," he said, pushing the insane thoughts from his mind.

"Why?" she asked.

He rolled to his side, pulling her next to him, holding her close, and enjoying the goose bumps her flesh created when he ran his fingers up and down her arm. "Because."

"Because why?"

"You ask too many damn questions."

"I asked one and you haven't answered it. Why do you want me to stop?"

He laughed, giving himself the time he needed to calm down. Damn woman had him unglued. "Because if you kept doing that, well, this would be over before we even got going."

"Oh." She kissed his chin. "So, you liked that."

Unglued was putting it mildly. Slipping his thumb under her chin, he tilted her head and brushed his lips across hers. "Yeah," he whispered, then a low moan grew inside him, releasing his deepest desire. "I like."

Rolling her onto her back, he took his time touching and probing, bringing her to the brink of pure passion, barely holding back his own primal needs. The fire crackled in the background, sending an outdoor smell that, when mixed with her rosy scent, acted as an aphrodisiac.

"I'll never forget this," he forced out with strangled breath. She was a sponge that soaked up all the pain he'd buried deep inside. He was finally allowed to have a single night of peace on the anniversary of the worst night of his life.

Her fingers splayed across his back, encouraging him to finish what they'd started. He pressed his hands against the floor so he could admire her precious face. He planted tiny kisses on her eyelids, cheeks, and lips before he entered her in one long, intense stroke.

Her body accepted him as if she'd been created for him to fill, savor, and please. His muscles shook like he'd been lifting weights beyond his abilities. He blinked his eyes shut, trying to distance himself from any real emotion. This was just sex, an act every adult human being craved, and it had nothing to do with happily ever after.

"Oh, Jared," she whispered. Her feet slipped to his inner thighs and her hips rocked in perfect motion with his body. Her hands massaged his back, chest, and shoulders while she moaned the most exotic noises.

He tried to ignore his need to make sure a second orgasm ripped through her body. He found himself caring too much for an experience that would never be repeated, couldn't be repeated. And shouldn't have happened in the first place.

Unable to rid himself of the deep-seated need to

fulfill her, he dipped his head, lifting her breast to his lips. Her gasp gratified him, dissolving any grief that might have intruded into his body. "Tell me when," he whispered.

Immediately, she tensed and thrust her hips upward, her insides gripping him to the point of undeniable passion. Nails dug into his rear end as her body quivered out of control.

"Ryan..." He thrust into her one last time, arching his back, his own release spilling from his shaking body. "Beautiful, Ryan." He kissed her temple, tasting the salty perspiration that beaded on her skin.

He eased himself down, adjusting slightly to the side, careful not to put his full weight on her, but keeping their bodies intertwined. He whispered sweet words in her ear and pressed his lips against her heated skin.

For the first time since his son had died, Jared felt a moment of peace. He still hurt and missed what could've been, but he didn't want to push the world away and disappear into the depths of hell. Instead, he wanted to hold the warm body that allowed him this freedom and give her everything she deserved, everything she desired.

When he opened his eyes, she stared back at him with a soft smile. His chest tightened to a painful heartache. He couldn't give her anything because he had nothing to offer. Ryan was the kind of woman who deserved a man to stand by her side and support her. A man who could give her love and family. Jared wasn't that man.

He traced her cheekbone with his thumb. True, he cared very deeply for her. Probably more than any other person in his life, but caring for someone was very different from sharing one's life. That was something he couldn't do. No matter how amazing the sex could be.

"Are you cold?" He rolled to the side and grabbed the throw blanket from the couch and covered their bare bodies, leaving her beautiful breasts exposed. He'd seen his share of naked women, but she made them all pale in comparison.

She pressed her cheek against his chest, snuggling in the crook of his arm. "I'm thoroughly satisfied, not cold."

He forced a chuckle, because while her body might be satisfied, he knew she didn't sleep around. She might have had some experiences with men, but the Ryan he knew wouldn't go to bed with just anyone, unless she had true feelings for him.

"So am I." He pulled her close. He could give her one night. He could make her feel like a woman should for a brief moment in time. One he'd never forget.

One that hopefully she would.

Chapter Six

A sudden chill rustled Ryan from her light sleep. She rolled, stretching her arm, but Jared wasn't in the bed. Wiping the sleep from her eyes, she brushed away the hair that had fallen across her face and looked around the dimly lit bedroom.

The promise of morning glistened through an open window, bringing with it a cool breeze. The sun peeking over the mountains shone on Jared's bare chest, casting a tall, muscular shadow across the room. He wore nothing but the tightness of his naked body. She couldn't have conjured up a better image if she tried. But that did nothing to ease her fears.

He'd been more than a fantasy, and she wouldn't deny her body would be forever changed. But she refused to deal with the change in her heart.

She wrapped herself in the disheveled sheet and tiptoed across the room.

He didn't flinch when she touched his back, but he raised his arm, pulling her to his chest. "Did you sleep okay?" He patted her shoulder awkwardly, as if he didn't know how to handle the morning after. His tender lips kissed the top of her head.

"Do you want to talk about him?" she asked and bit her lower lip. Only once had he ever spilled his guts about the morning he'd found his son dead. When he had finished his tale, he chugged half a bottle of Jack Daniels, then proceeded to throw a bunch of nasty insults her way. She'd finally taken the hint and left him to wallow.

"Would you come with me to the cemetery today?" he asked with an emotionless voice.

She blinked in surprise. "I would." She'd do just about anything to help him get through the next twenty-four hours. "Are you working today?"

"First year since he died." He tilted his head, dropping his gaze to meet hers. His eyes were sad and worn, and he looked as if he had aged ten years.

Her heart ached for him, knowing last night couldn't erase the pain etched forever in his heart. Tears stung behind her eyes.

"I don't know what to say." His hands trembled when he touched her cheeks.

"Then don't say anything at all."

A single tear rolled down his face, then dropped to

the floor. "He was cold when I went to check on him. I didn't even hear him cry."

"He may not have cried at all." How did she comfort him? Jared spent his life saving people. The world he'd created existed for the sole purpose of protecting those he cared about. Protecting the world from harm, yet he'd never been able to protect himself.

He couldn't protect his son, and he hadn't been able to save Ryan's mother. But no matter what Ryan told him, he always blamed himself. He tried to use those so-called failures to protect his heart, but she knew his heart had been shattered.

"I'm hungry." He wiped his face. "Would you like some of my famous chocolate chip pancakes?" He smiled, but she could tell it was forced.

"I would love some. Coffee, too?"

"You got it, babe." He patted her shoulder again in the same awkward motion as a moment ago. He kissed her temple as if he were fully clothed. When he turned from her, he slipped on his boxers, pulled up his jeans, and left the room as if they'd never had sex.

While showering, she kept trying to tell herself that her brother had been right all along. That she had Jared on a pedestal and this was simply infatuation. The young victim who had fallen for her hero. It wasn't love, just the inability to let go. Soon, she'd be given no choice but to let him walk out of her life for good.

After towel drying her hair and slipping into the clothes she'd brought over for work, she glanced at herself in the mirror. The pain behind her eyes was unmistakable. She'd watched her stepfather rape and beat her mother, then he'd turned on her. Between not remembering her real father and her brother taking off when things went from bad to worse, she realized Jared had a point about the men she'd chosen to date. They were safe. They were weak, both physically and mentally, making sure she'd always have the upper hand. Ensuring she was the one in charge.

Then why was she so drawn to Jared? He always had to be in control. No one dared tell him what to do or how to do it. He was the kind of man that people asked to make their decisions for them. And he was closed up emotionally like a bank vault.

She had hoped being with Jared would release her silly schoolgirl crush and allow the woman she knew existed to surface. That maybe she could move past the fantasy to live her life and fall in love with a man. A real man. Someone who'd be her equal, not someone who put her on a pedestal, or someone she feared would push her down into the depths of insecurity.

But now she'd had a taste of what it could be like with Jared, and she wanted more. In her heart, she knew there was more between them than a silly crush. But he would never give her anything more than a brotherly kiss on the temple, or a meaningless blending of two bodies to ease old wounds. He wasn't capable of anything more, and he'd made that perfectly clear. And she'd accepted it. She had to.

'Faking it' took on a whole new meaning.

She pulled out her eyelash curler and primed her lashes to make them appear longer. Her daily routine was the only way to keep her emotions in check. No way could she ever allow him to know how much she loved him. That would only make it harder for him to leave. Something she knew he had to do if he was ever going to move beyond his own past. With a steady hand, she applied her mascara, telling herself that she'd get through watching him walk out of her life.

She puckered her lips and brushed on some lip gloss, then headed down the hallway toward the stairs. She sniffed but didn't smell anything. Not even coffee. She shrugged, reminding herself that this house was at least eight times the size of her place. Lingering smells didn't carry themselves that far. But she couldn't ignore the prickly feeling that something wasn't right. When she reached the bottom step, she knew she should be smelling something by now.

Instead, she heard voices.

"Whoever this sick bastard is, he's messed with the wrong man," Jared said, slamming his fist on the table. "I want to put the pressure on that guy from Troy, and I want a court order to open Tom's record."

When Jared had opened the kitchen door and saw the newspaper stained with tacky blood, anger surged through every muscle in his body. But when he walked into Ryan's house, just to make sure everything was okay, his heart sank. No way would he ever let anyone hurt her again. He'd failed her when her mother died. And he failed her last night. Making love to her had been a mistake. He didn't love her, not the way a man should love a woman, and she deserved a man who could give her the world.

"This really doesn't fit with Rudy Martin's MO," Sergeant Harmon said.

"If it's Martin, he's not pulling the strings, just getting paid to deliver the message." Jared glanced out the kitchen window at the carriage house. The CSI unit was still inside, and he knew he'd have to go and get Ryan soon.

"That makes more sense than some pencil-pushing geek who might have done something stupid like steal his parents' car and get busted," Harmon said.

"Find a way to make the court order happen, okay?" Jared glanced at Frank, who was rubbing his jaw. "What's on your mind, kid?" Frank might be green and a little rigid, but he was a damn good cop, and Jared trusted him with his life.

"Sergeant Bower from Troy spoke with Rudy and said the guy's definitely weird. But he's a Jesus freak now. Born again, and doesn't put any chemicals in his system, lives in some kind of compound with a bunch of other religious nuts."

"Just because someone lives like a monk or believes

in God, doesn't mean he's not capable of hurting another person."

"Jared?" Ryan's soft voice filled the room. "Frank? What's going on? Why are all those cars here?"

"Sit down, Ryan." Jared wasn't sure he'd be able to explain what had happened without scaring the crap out of her. Then again, she should be scared. Hell, he was scared.

"I'll meet you outside," Harmon said, nodding to Ryan.

"You're frightening me." She gripped the chair but didn't sit.

He held his hand out to her. "Come here," he whispered, taking a single step toward her. "I promise I'll catch whoever is doing this." He'd sworn to himself this morning that he'd keep his distance, but under the circumstances, she needed him.

"Doing what?" Her eyes were wide with fear.

Taking her trembling body into his arms, he held her steady, trying to absorb her fear as she did his pain. "My newspaper was covered in blood this morning."

"Huh?" She pushed herself from his clutches, bumping into a chair. "Blood?"

"Someone ransacked the carriage house. Whoever it was took a knife to your bed and ripped it to shreds." Jared swallowed the bile rising in his throat. "They doused it with blood."

"Oh, my God," she muttered, covering her mouth and stumbling backward. "Why?"

"I don't know, babe. But we need to sit down and think about who might want to hurt you."

Her eyes narrowed. "Could it be you they're after?"

That thought had certainly crossed his mind. He'd made a few enemies over the years. There were criminals out there who wished him dead. But he also knew this particular criminal had focused on Ryan. "They left you a note."

"A note? What kind of note?" She fumbled about the kitchen, opening and closing cabinets until she found the coffee. It slipped from her trembling fingers and the grounds spilled out onto the counter.

He raked a hand across the back of his neck, letting her continue on her mission. She needed to keep her body moving. He knew the drill better than anyone. "A threat." With her back to him, he approached her, gently running his hands up and down her shaking arms. "A threat, made in blood, on your walls."

Her body jerked, then she whipped around. Her eyes were full of anger. Well, that was better than fear. He hated seeing her afraid.

"We're going to have to go over there, and you'll need to make a statement."

"A statement? About what?"

"Who might want to do this to you. Other than George. You have to consider other possibilities. I need you to consider other possibilities."

She jumped when Frank tapped on the door, then poked his head in. "I think you need to get over there."

"Give me five," Jared said, not hiding his impatience. He needed a few more minutes to help Ryan with what she'd be facing when she walked into the place she'd been calling home for years.

"Jared," Frank said, waving him over.

"What?"

"They found another note." Frank's eyes darted to Ryan, then back to Jared.

"Where?"

"By the kitchen sink," Frank said softly.

"Please, just tell me what it said." Ryan wiped the tears from her face. "I need to know."

Frank removed his trooper hat, fiddled with the rim, and looked at Jared. "Something about how he saw you last night, what you were doing, and how he'd get you for betraying him like that. Not the exact words, but close enough."

"Shit." Jared cursed under his breath, knowing the family room blinds had never been drawn. If anyone had been sneaking around, they would've been able to see in. "We'll be over in a few minutes." He grabbed Ryan by the hand and yanked her toward the stairs. Thank goodness she didn't fight him, because he would've thrown her over his shoulder and carried her away.

Once safely in his bedroom, he grabbed a shirt and tossed it over his head. "I was in the carriage house this morning. You need to be prepared." His own words sounded harsh and resentful. "It's pretty ugly."

Blackness smudged down her face while soft sobs echoed from her lips. "I can't imagine even George doing something like this."

"That's because you think everyone has a good side. You even defended that bastard."

"I did not." She sat down on the bed and stared at him. "But he didn't have an ea—"

"Easy life. Dirt poor, no job, and abusive parents. Like I said, you think everyone has a good side." He glared at her. "Who else besides Tom have you turned down lately? Or might have a grudge against you? Girls that might be jealous, guys that look at you funny."

"Eddy might hold a grudge." She winced.

"The dipshit you dated last summer?" He remembered Eddy, and the guy was a total moron. Okay, not a moron, but a nerd. "Why would he hold a grudge?"

Bolting from the bed, she began to pace. "God, this is so embarrassing."

Embarrassing? She had no reason to be embarrassed. Shocked, afraid, angry, livid, and a whole list of other emotions he could think of, but embarrassed? Circling his arm around her middle, he lifted her chin. "Why would Eddy hold a grudge? Of all the morons you've gone out with, he was actually a nice guy."

She swallowed. "I can't believe I'm going to tell you this."

He arched a brow.

"When we, well...oh God, I called out someone else's name instead of his, okay?"

"Whose name?" he heard himself ask. A pang of jealousy filtered through his body, followed by rage. Not just because she'd been with other men, but if it hadn't been his name, he'd be pissed. Something he had no right to be, considering their affair had already ended. He had no claims to her, and he didn't want any. He tightened his grip around her and stared into her eyes.

"Yours," she said so quietly he could barely hear her.

But he did. And he couldn't tell if he was flattered, horrified, or thrilled. "You'll have to tell the detectives about Eddy." His hands betrayed his better judgment and cupped her face. "They don't have to know all the details, but enough to question him about where he might have been last night." He had told himself this morning it would be best to just pretend last night had never happened. He told himself they could go back to being friends.

He reminded himself of that when he kissed her nose, then tucked her head into his chest. The erratic pounding of his heart echoed in his ears. A sudden rush of desperation clamped down on his emotions. Regardless of the cost, he'd do anything to make sure she was protected against any harm.

A thought he tried to keep at the forefront of his mind when he tilted her head and dropped his lips to hers. He let his body take over and slammed his tongue into her mouth on a search and destroy mission. Lost in the softness of her mouth, he forgot about the CSI unit and the two detectives waiting for them, until she had the presence of mind to pull away.

Stunned, he rubbed the back of his neck. "I'm sorry. I have no idea where that came from."

"It's okay. This whole thing's got us both on edge." She wrapped her arms around her chest. "I feel violated. Someone may have been watching us."

The idea that someone had seen them infuriated Jared. He'd always been a private man and kept his affairs discreet. His life was no one's business. "We'd better get over there." He strapped his weapon belt on and took her by the elbow. "I'll catch this guy, I promise."

And he meant it.

Ryan's stomach gurgled and pitched toward her throat as Jared walked her toward the carriage house. Two sheriff's cars, a state trooper car, an unmarked car, and a sheriff's van were parked in the driveway and on the street, lights flashing for the world to see. Some of her neighbors had come out to watch.

Mr. Thompson scurried across the road. "If I can do anything? Help out in any way?"

"Just keep your eye out and lock your doors," Jared said with a polite smile. His hand firmly planted on the small of her back. "Are you ready?"

A breeze kicked up off the lake and swished her hair across her face. She brushed it away and adjusted her long bangs as if looking her best would help the situation. The smell of rotten meat filled her nostrils when a police officer pushed back the screen door. Swallowing the horrible vomit taste in her mouth, she nodded.

Jared kept his hand on her spine. Had he removed it, her knees would have buckled. Her kitchen floor had droplets of blood scattered about the black-and-white linoleum. She had to sidestep them to the sink where a folded piece of paper with the number six sat on the countertop like it would at a wedding reception.

"Don't touch anything, ma'am," the cop said, the same cop who opened the door for them.

Ryan glanced at Jared, then back to the note. It read: *My sweet Ryan, not so sweet. I saw you betraying me, you whore. I will get you for what you and your cop friend have been doing. Don't you worry, you will pay.*

"George accused Mom of cheating on him." Memories of her stepfather ranting and raving in a drunken state flashed before her eyes. She blinked them away.

"Isn't this George character in prison?" said a man in plain clothes. She looked toward the voice and recognized the man but couldn't place him or remember his name.

"Hey, Nick." Jared thrust his hand forward. "Ryan, you remember Detective Jenkins from the rat incident?"

A vision of the fanged little bugger hanging in her

desk drawer popped into her head. "Yes." She rubbed her shaking hands on her slacks.

"I'm sorry to have to put you through this, but after you look around, I need to question you both."

"Question?" Ryan leaned closer to Jared.

"Standard procedure. He just needs to find out where we were last night and rule us out before he goes forward with this investigation."

"Why would I do this to my own house?" The anger in her voice caught her off guard. Last night was supposed to be special. Something shared only between Jared and her, not on display for the whole world to judge.

"He's not implying anything. But he has to go by the book."

"The book sucks." She shivered, crossing her arms across her chest as they made their way to her bedroom, following the trail of blood. Every piece of furniture in her home had been turned upside down and stabbed with some sharp object.

Clicking noises sounded in her bedroom and flashes of light danced across the hallway, hitting the wall.

"Take a deep breath," Jared whispered in her ear.

She swallowed, then peered around the corner. Her heart pulsed before it stopped for a brief moment. She took in a deep calming breath as her pulse began to flutter in inconsistent beats. Both of her hands instinctively clamped down over her gaping mouth, muffling her scream.

Blood was smeared across what remained of her bed. The mattress had been pulled to the side, half sitting on the floor with the insides exposed by each tear. Four men, all with gloves and masks on, stopped what they were doing and stared at her, then went back to taking samples and pictures.

"Where did the blood"—she gagged—"come from?" Jared's bicep didn't even flinch when she grabbed it for support.

"We don't think it's human," someone said.

"Little Jimmy Henderson said his dog didn't come home last night." Jared looped his arms around her, but it didn't stop her body from trembling. "But we don't know anything right now."

She turned her head, not wanting to look at the horrifying scene anymore. A bright redness on her wall caught her attention. "What is..." She blinked a few times to gain focus and realized she was looking at words. The letters were dripping like the title in the book *Helter Skelter*. "Oh, God." She stared at the words "Die Bitch." Her stomach lurched into her throat. "I'm going to be sick."

A thud followed by a few curses fell faint in her ears as she pushed aside everyone and anything that stood in her path. The bathroom seemed so far away. Not bothering to shut the door, she dropped to her knees and gagged. Then gagged again. But the only thing that came up was a foul taste.

Her entire body broke out in a cold sweat. Shaking

her hands out, she stood up, panic overriding her good judgment. Her pulse hurt as it pounded loudly in her head. She paced in the tiny bathroom, unaware of her surroundings. Unable to cope. "Damn it!" She swept her hand across the countertop, knocking everything to the floor. "I won't be afraid!"

"You have to be afraid." Jared's voice rang out strong and confident. He yanked her by the shoulders and heaved her to his chest with steady arms. "This guy, whoever he is, has snapped. We need to believe he'll stop at nothing—"

"To kill me?" She pounded on Jared's chest. "Why me? What the hell did I ever do?" She'd spent her life making sure she treated people better than she'd been treated as a child. After her father had died, her mother slowly began to rot in a bottle of whiskey. Her brother up and married the first woman who could guarantee his freedom from the hell of poverty, only to get a good dose of hell in another form.

Then her stepfather entered the picture, turning her already turbulent world upside down. He belittled her and her mother. He used his strength and power to keep them down. She swore when that man had been put behind bars that she'd never let another soul dictate her life.

She'd make sure everyone in her world knew they were loved and cared for. Every chance she had, she found a way to praise the people around her. Things as simple as helping the elderly across the street, or bringing a neighbor you barely knew dinner when they'd broken their leg, were the rules she lived by. Do unto others as you would have them do unto you.

That rule just bit her in the ass. She felt violated and now distrusted the world. Everyone around her was suspect, even Jared, according to the cops. Although she could certainly vouch for his whereabouts last night.

"If not you, it would be some other unsuspecting victim."

She glared at him, shoving from his embrace. "It's got to be George. He's the only one who makes sense. These are things he used to say."

Jared rubbed his unshaven jaw. "George is in jail, and he doesn't have a lot of money."

"What does that have to do with anything?"

"Most criminals of this nature need a payoff of some kind. Either a personal one, like a vendetta, or money. If George was behind this, either someone owed him big or George gave him money. Money he doesn't have."

Fear gripped her as she stared into Jared's blue-green eyes. Eyes that told her being afraid would be the smart thing to do. Doing everything she could to protect herself from some psycho would be her only possible chance at survival. "Eddy had a fetish for underwear."

"Excuse me?" Jared narrowed his eyes.

"He bought me sexy underwear all the time. He had

a weird thing going on with them."

"How weird? I mean, I like to see women in their underwear."

"Oh, how do I say this?"

"Just say it," Jared said impatiently.

"Eddy seemed more interested in the underwear than me."

"I still don't follow." Jared smoothed a hand across his head. "Sexy underwear is something every guy likes to see on a woman."

She looked around and took in a deep breath. "I caught him once...well, the day we broke up..." How did she say this without making herself look like a fool? She closed her eyes, then said, "He started...masturbating. He'd rather do that than actually have sex." She squeezed her eyes tighter.

"Did you make fun of him?" Jared asked.

She opened her eyes slowly. "I wouldn't say I made fun of him. But it kind of wigged me out. Then he reminded me of the time I used the wrong name. He was jealous."

"Of me." Jared shook his head. "Damn it." He grabbed her hand and pulled her through the house while barking orders.

Before she knew what hit her, she was sitting in front of Detective Jenkins, filling him in on the details of her short-lived relationship with Eddy Houser. All the while, Jared paced behind her, uttering numerous profanities. And giving her the evil eye.

Chapter Seven

Jared spent the morning in his office, even though he couldn't concentrate or get much paperwork done. Nick had decided that it would be better if Jared kept a low profile. Basically, he'd been told to stay out of it. Nick Jenkins had even gone to Jared's superior and asked him to make sure Jared didn't fly off the handle.

Jared didn't care that Nick was a damn good cop; he wanted his hands wet on this one. He had less than two weeks to close this case. Less than two weeks to make sure Ryan was safe so he could move without any ties to her or Lake George.

Nick had called around ten and gave Jared permission to come down and watch them question Eddy. Watch? If Eddy was the perp, Jared wanted to throttle the guy. But the cop in Jared had to consider all the possibilities. George did make more sense.

Jared maneuvered his patrol car in and out of traffic, heading toward the sheriff's office. It seemed that Eddy Houser had been picked up once before for downloading pornography of the illegal variety. This gave the cops a little more leeway in their questioning.

The idea had been to scare the crap out of him and get him to confess to trashing Ryan's place. Nick was good at confessions. He was good at playing the cop you could trust. Tell him what he wanted to know, and he'd make sure you got a good deal. He had that "I'm a nice guy" look that made the bad guys spill the beans and the girls fall at his feet.

But Nick was taken. Married three years now, with a kid on the way. Jared took in a deep calming breath as he turned into the parking lot. A detective shouldn't have a family. They didn't mix well with police work. Jared had learned that firsthand. Not a mistake he ever planned on repeating.

Jared rolled his car to a stop, barely turning the key before leaping out the door. He took long strides toward the station house.

A few prisoners in orange suits sat against the wall, and a desk deputy held a phone to his ear. He pointed down the hall when he eyed Jared.

"In here," Jenkins said, waving him down. "Houser's in there; you can watch from the two-way room."

"I want to talk to him." Jared knew they wouldn't let him. His property had been damaged. And since he and Ryan had admitted to spending the night together, they viewed him as the boyfriend. Not a very comfortable feeling for him.

"You're lucky I invited you." Nick opened the door and waited. "This guy's really nervous."

"Does he have an alibi for last night?" Jared asked.

"We haven't even gone down that road." Nick pushed his suit coat back when he planted his hands on his hips and stared through the two-way mirror. "The college has some pretty strict rules regarding the use of the internet. Eddy was marked by the FBI about a month ago when a few coeds who ran webcams got harassed. One girl was raped."

"Get to the point." Jared stared into the interrogation room. Eddy sat at a metal table with three chairs. His knee bounced uncontrollably while he picked at his nail.

"The Feds brought him down because he had naked pictures on his computer of the girl who'd been raped." Nick turned and made direct eye contact.

Jared had known about the porn but hadn't heard this latest development. "You mean to tell me the FBI had already picked him up? And he's been accused of rape?"

"He was questioned and then released. The victim said she got a good look at the guy who raped her, and he wasn't Eddy. But we know he goes to these girls' websites and watches them parade around in their underwear." Nick stepped across the room, then stopped at the door. "Let's see what he's got to say."

Jared stared through the glass. His pulse elevated. Nick and his partner Walter marched into the small room with freshly painted white walls. These rooms were always stripped bare, making sure there were no distractions.

Nick began by repeating the Miranda rights to Eddy, asking him if he understood.

"The FBI said if I cooperated, they wouldn't press charges. Why am I here now? It's not like the girls didn't know what they were doing and who was watching."

"Some of them were underage." Walter lifted a brow.

"I didn't know. Most girls on campus are over the age of eighteen." Eddy dropped his gaze to his lap. "It's not like I touched any of them. Just watched."

Jared slammed his hand against the table, rage coursing through his veins like a hot rod blazing down the racetrack. Eddy had touched Ryan. Now Jared wanted to wrap his fingers around Eddy's slimy little neck and squeeze the breath out of him.

"Eddy, would you mind letting us know where you spent last night? We've got this little problem, and we really want to just rule you out." Nick sat down on the edge of the table and smiled.

"Last night?" Eddy's voice cracked. "Oh, God. I'm going to lose my job."

"Just answer the question," Walter snapped.

"What is it that you think I might have done?" Eddy looked up at Nick. Fear radiated from his eyes. "I don't want to get the girls in trouble."

"What girls?" Walker asked.

"The college girls I was with last night." Eddy picked at the skin on his thumb.

Jared narrowed his eyes, peering through the glass, and focused on Eddy's facial features. Something told him while this guy was a bona fide pervert, he wasn't the guy they were looking for. "Come on, Nick, mention her name."

"You were with college girls?" Nick asked. "Not spying on an ex-girlfriend?"

"I wasn't spying on anyone, why?" Eddy's eyes widened.

"You know Ryan O'Connor, right?"

"Good job, Nick." Jared shook his trembling hands.

"Ry…Ryan? What the hell does she have to do with this?"

"Were you with her last night?" Nick asked. His tone was still calm and considerate.

Eddy shook his head vigorously. "I wouldn't give that woman the time of day."

"Don't like her much, huh?" Nick shifted to the side, putting his hand on his thigh. "She a bitch or something?"

"Or something," Eddy muttered. "But I don't care

what she's doing these days. We broke up a while ago, and I haven't seen her since."

"Okay, then where exactly were you last night?" Nick stood, staring down at Eddy.

"There's a group of girls on campus. They call themselves The Relievers. I was with them."

"Doing what?" Nick asked.

"Watching. They do striptease, lap dances, stuff like that. I didn't do anything wrong."

"We'll need to verify this."

"I have the pictures on my PC. I can prove I was with them. They were all of age. We were consenting adults." Eddy's voice pitched up an octave. "I didn't do anything wrong."

"Who's Ryan seeing these days?" Walter asked.

"I have no idea," Eddy said, obviously shaken. "I honestly haven't seen her or talked to her since we broke up."

"Why did you and Ryan break up?" Nick asked politely.

"Same reason most girls dump me. I've got a little problem with watching." Eddy drew his hands to his face. "Why must you people humiliate me like this?"

"Not trying to humiliate you but get to the bottom of a little situation I've got," Nick said.

"You prefer watching people get it on, do you?" Walter asked.

Jared's breath caught. He knew what they were doing, and he knew it was necessary, but he didn't like them reducing Ryan to a woman who was just getting it on.

"I think I'll invoke my Miranda rights now."

Jared flipped open his phone and called Harmon. He'd put his own guys on this campus call girl stuff and do a little digging of his own. In the process, he'd find out if George had been bragging in prison, and what good old Rudy had been up to the last few days. Too many unknowns.

Harmon didn't pick up his cell phone, so Jared left a message. He could only hope Frank was onto something. The annoying kid was turning out to be one damn good cop. Jared pushed back the door and met Nick in the hallway.

"He'll be out by nightfall. The FBI has already ruled him out as a suspect in the college rape," Nick said. "I'll keep pressing for information, but my gut tells me this guy isn't the man you're looking for."

Jared raked a hand across his head, then slid his hat on. "Make sure someone is tailing him when he does leave."

"You got it."

Jared pulled his sunglasses out, slipped them on, and then stepped out into the parking lot. He ducked into his patrol car and headed toward the hotel.

Eddy was a wacko, and Ryan had known it. He rammed his foot on the gas pedal and the patrol car lurched forward. He whizzed by a car that had slowed below the speed limit.

He really wanted to give Ryan a piece of his mind. She should have told him long ago about Eddy's little underwear fetish. He glanced at his watch, knowing he might already be a few minutes late to pick Ryan up so they could go to the cemetery, but he needed to calm himself before he did or said something really stupid. He rolled the window down and took in a good dose of fresh, cool air rolling in off the lake.

He knew his emotions weren't all tied up by Eddy and his perverted ways, but by the visit to the cemetery. In years past, he'd visited with a bottle of Jack Daniels. And two years ago, he'd even slept at the cemetery. This year everything was different, and he wasn't quite sure how to handle it. But he'd made his bed, now he'd have to lie in it.

Ryan pushed open the main doors to the hotel and waited in the cool spring air for Jared. Her eyes shifted around the front lawn, fear always prickling at her neck, even in the scenic beauty of bright colorful bushes lining the walkway to the crystal-clear waters of Lake George. The plush green mountains surrounding the lake only added to the breathtaking view, except today it did nothing to ease her growing tension. Every time her phone rang or someone tapped on her door, she practically jumped out of her skin.

Rick had offered to let her take the day off, but

where would she go? She didn't feel safe at home, not after what happened. She didn't feel comfortable staying at Jared's since someone had been watching them. Her brother was already at the bar, and she really didn't feel like hanging out there.

As much as she wanted to blow the whole thing off, she couldn't.

"Ryan."

She whipped around, unable to breathe.

"Oh, sorry. I didn't mean to scare you." Tom had stopped a few feet away from her. "I sort of heard what happened. If you need anything, if I can help in any way, let me know."

"I'm okay. Jared's on the case."

"You guys an item or something?" Tom asked, taking a step closer.

She swallowed, but didn't back away. Tom seemed genuinely concerned. He might be a little odd, but he wasn't a psycho. She'd leave that to her stepfather. "Jared and I are close friends." Her heart skipped a beat, but only because it wasn't a lie.

"If you're not seeing him, I'd like a second chance. I think you're a nice girl." He smiled, placing his hand on her arm. "I like you."

Trying like hell not to tremble or pull away, she forced a slight grin and said, "I'm sorry if I led you on. It's nothing personal, but right now I can't afford to complicate my life with a relationship, especially one at work."

His smile faded and his eyes narrowed. They appeared to change color. To darken. When his hand fell from her arm, she saw a coldness in his gaze that frightened her. She took in a breath and chalked it up to being paranoid.

"I guess I understand." He continued to stare at her.

"Thanks, Tom." From the corner of her eye, she could see Jared sauntering down the pathway, hand on his gun.

"I've got to go," she muttered, then scurried toward Jared. The last thing she needed was for him to go off half-cocked. She figured his nerves were frayed right about now. Jared didn't drink much, except for the week of his son's death. Then the bottle became his best friend. A friend she'd taken away from him when she'd decided to let him get lost in her body instead. Except she was the one who was lost now. She hoped she hadn't made a mistake.

"You okay?" He took her by the elbow, but glanced back at Tom. "I'm still waiting to find out what he's hiding."

"Did anyone find Jimmy's dog?"

Jared's body tensed, giving her the answer she didn't want to hear. "Oh, God, no."

"I spoke with Mr. Stevens, and when the time is right, I'll get Jimmy a new puppy."

"That poor little boy." She slid into the passenger seat of her SUV. "Has anyone talked with Eddy yet?"

He slammed her door, scowled, and then jogged

around the front of her Honda Pilot. He didn't say anything when he got in, just started the engine and headed out to Route 9 North.

"You sure know how to pick them," he finally said about a mile from the cemetery.

"I didn't date him long, and I only slept with him once, sort of, which was more than enough." She blinked. What a ridiculous thing to say.

Jared groaned like someone had just sucker punched him in the gut. "I didn't need to know that."

"Look, I don't sleep around. He'd taken me out seven or eight times, bought me all sorts of nice things. I thought he liked me, but he only liked the underwear he bought me, so I broke up with him. End of story."

"How the hell did my name end up coming out of your mouth when you were with the likes of him?" He put the SUV in park and stared at her.

"I guess my life can't get any more embarrassing." She fixed her hair and looked at him dead-on. She'd made love to him; this shouldn't be that hard. "If you must know, I was bored, so I did a little pretending."

He rubbed the back of his neck. "I have no idea how to respond to that."

"It's a compliment." She pushed back her door and stepped out, taking in a small breath. Cemeteries always smelled a little off to her. Even though there were flowers everywhere, sadness filled the air instead of the pretty scents of the living.

"I was there when Nick questioned him, but my gut

tells me he's just a pervert who gets his rocks off by watching girls strip."

"I'll buy that. I practically had to throw myself at him. He seemed more interested in me undressing than any kind of intimacy. It was like once the underwear was off, so was he."

"You should've seen the writing on the wall." His fingers laced between hers, and they made their way down a path of tombstones covered with flowers.

"Like I said, we went out a few times. The first time I was at his place, I found my underwear. He must have swiped them when I cooked him dinner, but I was actually flattered."

Jared glared at her. "That's just plain weird."

"Yeah, I know."

His fingers tightened as he led her across a dirt road to the section where Johnny was buried. "What about that guy Tom? He have any weird traits you haven't shared with me?"

"He's just cocky and boring. He really thinks he's something special, and he's very persistent. He actually asked me out again." Her steps became slower, following Jared's. Only three stones and they'd be where Johnny had been laid to rest.

"We've got three solid leads. I have a good feeling this will be over in a few days. Until that time…" He paused, tilting her head with his thumb. "You are not to be alone, you got it?"

"I'm not moving in with my brother. Maybe I can crash at Penny's place."

"You'll crash at my place. If I have to work late, you can hang out at the bar with Pat or at Penny's; otherwise, you will be with me."

The sun had settled high in the sky and forced her to squint, barely able to make out the intensity of his face. But she read him loud and clear by the tone of his voice and the pressure of his fingers on her chin.

She clenched her jaw. She hated it when anyone told her what to do and how to do it. Especially guys like Jared. He thought he had all the answers. But under the present circumstances, she had to admit that being alone would be stupid. "I don't know if I can stay at your house knowing someone was watching us."

"I'm not real thrilled about that either, babe. But you're still safer with me."

His head shifted, blocking the sun. Her pulse beat wildly as she looked at the intent gaze in his eyes. "About last night..." Pressure from his soft finger hushed her lips.

"Last night was just what I needed, what we needed. I won't let anyone take that away from us." He leaned forward and kissed her temple. "For the first time since Johnny died, I think I can get through today without feeling like I've let down the world."

"Oh, Jared." She cupped his face. "You've never let anyone down."

"Yeah, right," came a female voice. "Don't you two make a lovely couple?"

Ryan blinked a few times, then shook her head, making sure her eyes weren't playing tricks on her.

"Lisa? What the hell are you doing here?" Jared said, not hiding the venom in his tone. He hadn't seen his ex-wife since the day she walked out on him and their son.

"Visiting Johnny." She glared at him. "Or did you forget he was mine too."

His body went rigid as he took a step away from Ryan and jammed his hands into his pockets. "Have you ever been here?"

"None of your damned business," Lisa said, gripping a small teddy bear. "Would you mind giving me a minute? I've got someone waiting for me."

"Oh, I mind all right." Jared's hands came flying out of his pockets as he lunged toward Lisa.

"Jared," Ryan whispered, stepping in his way. His chest muscles tensed at her touch. "We've got time. Let her have a moment."

"She doesn't deserve a moment since she didn't care enough when he was alive," he snapped.

"Judge me all you want. I don't care." Lisa wiped her face, then approached the stone where Johnny rested.

"Come on." Ryan tugged at Jared's arm, pulling him away. "I left my purse in my SUV, and I've got a toy car for Johnny anyway."

Jared glared at Ryan, then looked over his shoulder. "I don't think she's been back here since—since she ran out."

Ryan patted his arm, forcing her stare forward. She wanted to know why too, but she wouldn't dare ask it. Lisa hadn't been a very nice neighbor, at least not to Ryan.

When they reached the car, Ryan grabbed her purse, and by the time they started back toward the grave, Lisa was on her way toward them. She wore a shiny black trench coat, hiding her clothes, but Ryan noticed the expensive shoes that matched the designer purse. Ryan also noticed the limo waiting for her. Seems Lisa had elevated herself from white trailer trash.

Ryan mentally slapped herself. What a horrible thing to think. Besides, Ryan had grown up in that same little strip of houses known as The Under Developers, a nice way of calling their run-down, old rented trailers, shacks.

"Thank you," Lisa said, holding out a card.

Jared took it in his steady hand, then stuffed it in his pocket without looking at it.

Ryan wanted to fish it out and see what it said.

"I'm living in Saratoga now," Lisa began. "I plan on coming here often."

"Thanks for the warning," Jared said.

"What are you doing in Saratoga?" Ryan's curiosity was going to get her in trouble based on the daggers Jared just threw her with his eyes.

"My husband owns a horse farm there." Lisa adjusted her coat. "I must be going."

"Nice to see you." Ryan winced when both Lisa and Jared glared at her. "Goodbye?"

Lisa slipped past them without another word. Ryan couldn't help it; she had to keep peering over her shoulder. A gray-haired man got out of the limo and kissed her cheek, then they both disappeared into the car.

"I want a check on Lisa Madden. At least, Madden is her maiden name," Jared bellowed.

"What are you doing?" Ryan whipped around and stared at him, cell phone to his ear.

He arched his brow, then turned his back. "She's married to some horse farmer—wait." He dug into his pockets. "Lisa Stillman is the name now, lives in Saratoga, and I want a full check on her, her farm, and her husband."

"Why?" Ryan asked.

Jared moved his phone from his ear and stared at it for a moment before he lifted it and began speaking. "She's a suspect in the case involving Ryan O'Connor."

"Jared Jonathon Blake, what the hell are you talking about?" Ryan grabbed his arm.

Shrugging it off, he didn't turn. "Just get on it, okay? I'll explain everything this afternoon."

"Explain it to me now." She glared at him. Lisa was a lot of things, but she hadn't been around for years. She had no reason to hurt Ryan.

"There's nothing to explain." He took a step toward the tombstone.

"Jared, *now*." She leaped in front of him. "Either you are just using your police power to get back at her, or there's something else going on. I have a right to know."

He ran a hand across his head and glared up into the sky. "After your father's trial, right before she gave birth." He dipped his gaze and caught her eyes. "She gave me an ultimatum."

"What kind of ultimatum?"

"If I didn't stop helping you out, she threatened to leave. I told her if she left, she couldn't take Johnny with her."

"So she just left you? The baby? Because of me?"

Chapter Eight

Jared had never planned on having this conversation with anyone, much less Ryan. But so much was changing. "Right before Lisa told me she was pregnant, I'd been offered the job I'm taking now." Jared lowered himself onto the soft green grass next to Johnny's grave, unable to look at Ryan. "I turned it down."

"Why?" Ryan questioned.

"You, the trial, the baby. Lots of reasons." He lifted his gaze to meet her shocked expression. "Pat was in L.A. and going through hell. He counted on me to help take care of things with you, considering everything. You were only sixteen. And alone."

"Oh, God, no," she mumbled, shaking her head.

"I told Lisa as soon as you got into college, I'd be free to leave."

"Free? To leave?"

"That's not what I meant," Jared said, knowing that Ryan would think he allowed himself to be tied to her somehow. That taking care of her had been a hardship, but it hadn't.

"I didn't realize what a burden I've been to you all these years." She tilted her head and stared into the soft-blue sky. A few clouds rumbled in. "I knew about the possible transfer, but I thought you stayed because of Lisa."

"Come here." He held out his hand.

"No," she said, pacing on the narrow path. "I can't believe this. You turned down that job because of me? Did Lisa want you to take it?"

"Lisa trapped me," Jared admitted. "She got pregnant on purpose and used Johnny to try to force me to move. She didn't think she'd be happy staying here."

Ryan stopped and stared at him with questioning eyes. "You let your marriage fall apart to stay and help me?"

He took a deep breath, choosing his words carefully. "My marriage was doomed long before I got married." He reached out again, gently lacing his fingers in hers, but she yanked her hand away. "I don't regret turning the position down back then. I wanted Johnny to be raised here. Besides, moving wouldn't have done anything but prolong the inevitable." He held out his hand again. "Please, come sit here with me."

She scowled, but complied, seating herself down next to him. She toyed with the Matchbox car before resting it next to the small, sandy-brown bear. "Jared, I'm sorry. I didn't realize."

He touched the soft curves of her lips, hushing her silly words. "I made a decision, one that I'm proud of. I know I have nothing to do with who you've become, but I like knowing I helped pay for your education and gave you a chance you might not have gotten otherwise."

"I'm not a charity case." She glared at him. "You should've moved. Everything would be different."

"Maybe, but I'm glad Lisa and I divorced. I was miserable, and honestly, so was she."

"Do you ever wonder if things would've been different for you and Lisa had I not gotten in the way?"

He let out an exasperated sigh. "You didn't get in the way."

"You just said she didn't want you helping me out."

"Because *you* were a threat to her." Jared wanted to laugh out loud at the absurdity of his words. At the time, Lisa was about Ryan's age now, and Ryan was just a teenager. But the words were true, and years later, Lisa's premonition was materializing.

"Me? That doesn't make any sense."

"I paid more attention to the teenager living in my carriage house than I did her." He drew Ryan back between his legs, resting her head on his chest. She hesitated before giving in.

"Lisa wanted money and respect, and thought they'd come to her in that order. When being with me didn't get her the respect in this community she thought she deserved, she ran."

"Look who thinks there's a good side to someone now?" Ryan said, shifting from his embrace. "Next you're going to tell me she was misunderstood."

He laughed. It wasn't funny, but it was true. "I couldn't forgive Lisa if I tried, but..." He tucked some of Ryan's sun-warmed hair behind her ear. "If I'm being honest, I was part of the problem."

Ryan rolled her eyes. "You didn't do anything wrong."

"Maybe not, but I didn't do anything right, either." He leaned back on his hands and glanced at Jonathon Mitchell Blake's grave, at the words "Cherished Son" etched in the hard stone. "I didn't want to get married, but she was pregnant."

"Such the noble man," she muttered. "Women have kids out of wedlock all the time."

Stretching his legs and crossing his ankles, he studied Ryan's face. Her eyes lit up from the bright sun. Beauty that defied all reason. "Not with my kid, they don't."

"You don't want kids." She stared at him with a sudden harshness in her eyes.

He ripped a blade of grass from the ground and rolled it between his fingers. "I wanted Johnny." Jared never admitted to anyone how much he'd wanted Johnny. But he'd never allow himself to go through that kind of hurt again. "From the moment Lisa told me, I loved him."

Ryan shifted, tucking her feet off to the side and leaning on one hand. "I know you loved him," she whispered.

A single cloud shifted in front of the sun and the wind kicked up. He glanced out toward the direction of the lake and could almost smell the rain coming. Gray clouds collided in the darkening sky.

He ran a hand across his unshaven face. The stubble scratched at his calloused hands. "Lisa wanted to start over where no one knew her. She resented you, because the world seemed to ignore the fact that you grew up—"

"Dirt poor, and my parents were trailer trash." She shook her head. "I just ignored the whispers, the little jabs here and there. I still do."

"That's not how she saw it. She saw that you were somehow better than her. Adding the unwanted pregnancy and the constant gossip of her being a gold digger, well, she lost it. And her sudden return has me wondering."

"That's the most ridiculous thing I've ever heard." As the sun peered out again, she shifted to her feet and brushed her hands across her fanny. "So, because the woman was insecure, you now think she's out to get me?"

He chuckled. "I'm suspicious of anyone who might've

said something negative about you, even if it was five years ago." He rose, dusting off his uniform before he adjusted the bear and car in front of Johnny's grave.

"Do you really think Lisa could've done something like that?"

He took her by the hand, noticing his own hand didn't tremble. He looked down at the grave and patted his heart. "I never thought I'd be able to come here like this; thank you."

"You're welcome." She leaned into him and planted a moist kiss on his cheek. "But you didn't answer my question." Their hands swayed back and forth as they strolled to her SUV.

No. He hadn't answered her question because he honestly didn't know the answer. Not only was Lisa an insecure, vindictive woman, but she had some other issues, too. She'd been known to let her temper fly out of control. She'd tossed a few objects at him during heated arguments, and right before she left, she'd belted him a good one.

"I think Eddy has some real serious sexual issues. Not sure he'd actually harm anyone, but he definitely needs help."

She shook her head. "You're still not answering my question."

"I'm running all the usual suspects through my mind. Let me do this my way. Okay?"

"Fine," she said, not sounding convinced.

"Tom's got a record that's sealed. It could be something; it could be nothing. George still wants to hurt you, so I'm sure he'd do whatever it took." Standing about ten feet from the car, he turned to face her and shifted his sunglasses up to his forehead. "Lisa looks like she's got the kind of life she's always wanted. A rich husband and money to burn. But I'd be a bad cop if I didn't look at every angle."

Her lower lip quivered as she bit down on the glossy flesh. She stared into his eyes, but fear loomed behind her pupils.

"What?" he asked.

"I hope you don't regret last night."

A surge of unknown emotions choked him. He didn't regret it, but he didn't know how he felt about it. He wasn't supposed to feel anything. "I regret nothing. But I don't want to hurt you."

She smiled, easing some of his fear, but not all of it. "You can't hurt me, Jared. And while last night was amazing, I know it wasn't about us, or…I don't know how to say this."

"It wasn't about romance," he said. "It wasn't about a beginning, but an ending."

"No, not ending. A change. There's a difference."

"Okay, a change." Not wanting to pass up the opportunity to hold her one more time, he cupped her face and drew her lips to his. One tender kiss, nothing romantic, nothing sexual. Just lips against moist lips. Then he slipped his arms around her and tucked her head to his chest.

"I hired a contractor to fix up the carriage house." Unable to resist her soft skin, he glided his hands under her light jacket, lifting her blouse from her slacks in search of warmth. "I think it's best for you to stay with me." Inhaling her soft hair that still held the scent of peach shampoo, he closed his eyes. "You would be safer with me."

"I hate inflating your ego, but I have to agree." Her hair blew into his face. He didn't bother to brush it away.

"It sucks being right all the time." He laughed, forcing the serious edge of his emotions from his voice. He didn't have feelings for Ryan, not that kind anyway. He was just caught up in the case, dealing with his son in a new way, and moving.

Ryan could tell that Jared was holding something back, but that was okay. He'd come farther this week than ever before. Every year, she'd begin her crusade to save him from the depths of despair. And every year, she made it so far, only to watch him spend at least two days in the pits of hell.

The car ride back to the hotel was quiet and uneventful. She watched the clouds roll across the sky, bringing the promise of cold rain. The wind swirled in a howling cry, and empty tree branches pitched and snapped, until the wind died down to a whisper.

Storms like this were a dime a dozen around Lake George, but they could still be devastating.

"Go straight to my place and call me before you go into the house," Jared said, unlocking his patrol car.

"Don't you think that's being a little paranoid?" She slammed her door, frustrated with having to look over her shoulder. When she went to college, she'd always race across the parking lot to her classroom, glancing around at every shadow. It took her years to be able to sit alone in the carriage house, in the dark, and not jump at the icemaker.

"I've got leads, but nothing else, babe. Even I get paranoid." He ducked his head, then slid into the driver's seat. "Or you could get Penny and Chuck to meet us at your brother's bar for dinner." The window hummed as it rolled down. He flashed a pearly white smile and winked before he dropped his sunglasses from his forehead to cover his crystal clear, blue-green eyes.

"That's a fine thought. I'll call your cell."

He saluted and then pulled out of his parking space. "Go." He waved her toward the hotel lobby doors. "I'll wait here until you're safely tucked inside."

She rolled her eyes and adjusted her purse on her shoulder. "Not necessary." She turned on her heel and headed for the lobby doors. She didn't bother looking back when she pulled back the door, because Jared wouldn't leave for at least five minutes.

She strolled to her office, trying to tell herself that

he was just doing his job. That it had nothing to do with him being an overbearing pain in the butt.

She closed her door and slumped into her chair. Dropping her elbows to the desk with a loud thud, she rested her cheeks in the palms of her hands.

A loud buzz from her phone startled her, making her jump. She hit the intercom button. "What is it, Cheryl?"

"You've got several messages regarding the golf tournament, and Tom said he needed to see you."

"Great," she mumbled. "Call Tom and tell him I'm in my office." She swiped at her face, running her index finger under her eyes and checking for mascara marks. "I'm in no mood to go chasing after him." Satisfied she was put together enough, she rose and opened her door.

"Oh," she gasped. "Tom, I didn't expect you this quickly."

He glared at her. "We need to talk."

"Is there a problem?" Ryan asked, stepping aside and letting him in her cramped space.

"Shut the door," he snapped.

"I don't think so." With her heart pounding, she rubbed her hands against her pleats. "Now, what's the problem?" She fought the urge to pray for one of Jared's surprise visits. Seems he always showed up when she needed him. But those days were gone.

"This is personal," he whispered, then eyed the hallway. "Please."

Considering Jared's warning words and all the suspects, Tom was really not high on her list. "You've got five minutes."

He sucked in his lips as if totally disgusted with her statement. "So you did sic the cops on me?"

"Excuse me?" A tight breath caught in her throat. She gripped the doorknob just as it clicked shut. "What is that supposed to mean?"

"Some trooper came to work this morning asking me if I had ever committed a crime, even when I was a kid." He lifted his arms as though he were ready for a fight. "Why would anyone care?"

Trying not to shake, she collected her thoughts. "As you know, there have been some threats made against me." She swallowed. "I'm sure the cops are just checking around the hotel."

"So why pick on me? I took you out, bought you a nice dinner, and what did I get in return?"

Careful not to make a noise, she twisted the knob. An eerie darkness seeped from his stare. "I'm sorry you feel that way. But like I said before—"

"You're only interested in friendship. But I guess you're certainly interested in that trooper friend of yours."

"What do you mean by that?" The cops knew about her and Jared. They wouldn't go around telling the world that they were having sex while someone ransacked her apartment. The only other person who would know, would be the person who'd been watching.

"I mean it's obvious that the two of you are an item, which makes no sense since he just took a job transfer." His chest heaved up and down, while his fingers trembled. "I didn't put that rat in your drawer, and I resent you implying that I did."

"First." She swung the door open. "I didn't imply anything. Honestly, the thought never crossed my mind." Needing to get the upper hand, she looked him directly in the eyes. Damn jerk didn't back down. "As far as whom I choose to date, or not date, it's none of your business."

"I see the nice girl-next-door façade has finally cracked." He arched a single brow. "Call off the hounds, or else," he ground out before bolting from her office.

Shaking out her trembling hands, she reached for her purse with the intention of calling Jared, but it seemed someone had decided to call her. Without looking at the caller ID, she flipped open her phone and answered with a shaky breath.

"Ryan, how could you? I trusted you."

"Eddy?" She couldn't believe her ears. It had been months since she'd spoken to the man. Her rump hit the corner of her desk, and she let out a little yelp.

"You said you understood."

"I never said I understood." The throbbing in her temples pulsed, shooting pain to other parts of her body.

"I don't like getting badgered by the cops. At least your boyfriend had the decency to hide behind a two-way mirror."

"I don't have a boyfriend." Eyeing her office, she wanted to kick herself. It wasn't as if Eddy was hiding in some corner. "Crap," she mumbled, looking under the desk. "Where are you?" She moved to the hallway and looked in both directions.

"Basically under house arrest, no thanks to you."

"Why'd you call me?"

Silence, followed by muffled voices in the background, then Eddy spoke softly, too softly. "You'll get what's coming to you."

The phone went dead. "Damn it." She punched Penny's number. She tapped her wristwatch. Hopefully Penny could slip out of work and meet her at her brother's bar. Jared would be the next phone call, and she was sure he'd demand she leave and go to the station or her brother's or something. She decided to set up her own plan and make Jared deal with it.

But being alone wasn't an option.

Chapter Nine

Ryan pulled into the parking lot of her brother's bar. She glanced around for a spot just as Pat ran from the door. She winced, knowing he wasn't rushing to her side because the rain was coming down in buckets.

"Do you think anyone followed you?" He opened the door, offering a hand. She took it and then nudged the door closed with her hip.

She hurried toward the well-lit entrance with Pat's arms tight around her. He constantly looked over his shoulder.

Her brother might have meant well, but this kind of treatment would drive her wacko. "I take it Jared called." Water sloshed onto her already soaked feet when she shook her coat. "Are Penny and Chuck here?"

"They're in the back corner." Pat grabbed her by the shoulders. "This is serious shit, ya know."

She wanted to stuff her fist in the man's mouth. "That's why I called Jared."

Pat narrowed his eyes. "Is something going on with you two?"

She opened her mouth, but then shut it tight, knowing she'd just given him the answer he'd been looking for.

"I'll kill him," he grumbled.

"Why? What the hell did he do?"

"I don't know. You tell me." Someone called Pat's name, but he just put his hand up and stared her down like she was a child.

"What I do with my life is my business. But if you must know, we went to visit Johnny together and, well, he's different, that's all. I think he's finally going to be able to move past all this."

"And on to Rochester." Pat arched a brow. "Can you move past this?"

"I think I'm a little more concerned with who's stealing my underwear, sticking dead animals in my desk, and ripping my bed to shreds, than Jared's move."

"I'm sorry. I'm scared for you."

"Me, too," she admitted, accepting his overpowering hug. Sometimes it was like he forgot she was half his size.

Ryan shook out the water on her coat, then hung it up on the rack before making her way to the back of the bar. She spotted Penny, who was practically sitting on Chuck's lap. Chuck was all smiles, while he batted Penny's nose with his finger. *Must be nice to be in love,* Ryan thought, trying not to be jealous as hell of her friend.

Normally Penny's love life didn't affect her one way or another because it wasn't a love life, just sex. Penny caught her eye and jumped up, waving frantically, calling out her name. At least Ryan knew she'd always be a part of Penny's life no matter who stole Penny's heart.

"Thanks for meeting me." Ryan wrapped her arms around Penny, getting almost all the comfort she needed.

"Anytime."

"But I'm sure you and Chuck had other plans." Ryan dropped her purse over the chair, then planted her butt in it.

Chuck smiled politely. "Not really. Besides, Jared said someone was stalking you? You really shouldn't be alone."

Oh, yeah. This guy was a keeper. It appeared his world revolved around Penny. His brown eyes conveyed a genuine empathy. No one could fake that.

"I can't say the prospect of being alone right now is all that appealing." As much as Ryan tried, she couldn't shake the feeling that someone was watching her. All the time.

She lifted the water glass to her lips, then swallowed the lemon-flavored liquid. The hairs on the back of her neck stood at attention.

"Jared will figure all this out," Penny said with hopeful eyes.

"He's moving, Pen."

"When he does, you'll stay with me." Penny patted her shoulder.

The chatter in the background only added to Ryan's already frayed nerves. Laughter boomed at one table, sparring words echoed at another, and still other muffled words sounded in her ears, only adding to her confusion. "I just might take you up on that."

"Jared told me his new job doesn't really start for a few weeks." Chuck folded his menu, then set it on the table. "But when he does finally leave, maybe both of you should stay with me."

Ryan could barely bite back her smile. Chuck's protective tone and the way he slipped his hand into Penny's could only be viewed as true love. "I could also stay with my brother." Ryan took another sip of water. She'd be a third wheel no matter where she went. At least if Marci had the baby soon, Ryan would have something to do. "And I do have to find a new apartment."

"Jared's here," Penny whispered.

When Jared strolled into Ryan's view, she almost forgot all her problems. His eyes locked with hers and didn't shift until he took her by the hand and lifted her from her seat. "Hey, babe."

She blinked, then blinked again, trying to pull herself together as he bent and brushed his lips across her temple.

"Any news?" she asked.

He settled himself down, resting his arm on the back of her chair. "Nothing concrete."

"This sucks," Penny said. "I mean, I can't believe anyone other than George would do such a horrible thing to Ryan."

"Honey, some people are just psycho," Chuck said. "You up for a game of pool before dinner?" he asked Jared.

"Sure." Jared rose. "Order me a beer and maybe some nachos."

"Same for me." Chuck planted a kiss on Penny's cheek, then strode away with Jared.

"If you don't want to stay with Jared, you know you can stay with me." Penny leaned in, taking Ryan's hands. "I know how you feel, and it's got to be hard staying in the room next door."

"I stayed in his bed last night."

"With him in it?" Penny asked with a shocked expression. "Don't mess with me."

"I'm not."

"Was it bad?"

"Oh, good God, no." Ryan laughed, then smiled. "It was amazing. I never knew sex could be that great."

"Then why do you look…never mind." Penny

scowled, tossing her napkin on the table. "You shouldn't have slept with him."

"Hey, weren't you the one giving me pointers last year?"

"That was different."

"How so?" Ryan asked, folding her arms across her chest. "It's not like he was any more emotionally available a year ago. The only thing that's changed is he's moving."

"And you think you're in love with him." Penny glanced over her shoulder.

"I'm not in love with him." How could someone be in love with a man who had nothing emotional to give? "We had sex, that's it."

"I hope you used protection."

"I'm not an idiot."

"Glad to hear one of us isn't." Penny glanced at Ryan, then dropped her gaze to her lap. "I'm pregnant."

"What?" Ryan knocked over a glass, sending water all over the table. "Did you say preg—"

"Shush, I don't want people to know." Penny's eyes shot around the room. "I haven't even told Chuck yet."

"Are you sure?"

"What am I going to do?" Penny wiped her face. "He told me he loved me."

"That's a start." Ryan finished cleaning the table, thankful for the change in subject. "Do you want to spend the rest of your life with Chuck?"

"God, Ry. I never thought I wanted all of this. I mean, a husband, a baby. But damn it, I do."

Ryan looked over at the pool table. A smitten Chuck waved and then winked. Jared, on the other hand, took the blue chalk and fiddled with his cue stick, giving Ryan only a half-smile. He might have told her he didn't regret last night, but his actions spoke louder than his words. "Do you want the baby?"

"I want it all," Penny admitted.

"Then go for it." Ryan shifted her gaze to Penny. "Tell him how you feel, what you want, and tell him about the baby. If he loves you, things will work themselves out."

Penny smiled. "He did say he wanted to get married someday and have a couple of kids."

"When did he say that?" Ryan felt her purse vibrate on the back of her chair.

"The other day. We're so great together, and I think he really loves me, but I'm scared."

Ryan glanced at her cell. It was a blocked number. Her forehead beaded with perspiration. She tossed the phone back in her purse. Determined not to deal with it, she turned her attention to Penny. "I know you're scared, but you have to tell him tonight."

"I will. Who called?"

"Probably a wrong number." Her chair jerked. "Hey!" she yelled, looking over her shoulder.

Jared yanked her purse from the chair, then dug his hand deep inside, rummaging around.

"What are you doing?" She tried to grab it back.

He didn't answer, just snatched up her phone and flipped it open. "Damn it, Ryan. You really need to call me over when this happens."

"When what happens?" She plopped against the back of her chair, folding her arms. "Control freak."

"Is this the only blocked call you've gotten today? I checked out the phone call from Eddy; he actually had the nerve to call you from the police station. This isn't a game." Jared's tone could only be described as condescending.

She knew it wasn't a game, and she was damn scared. But she didn't like her lover treating her like a child. *Lover?* No, Jared wasn't her lover. He was still the overbearing protector he'd always been. "I got two hang-ups at work, but I already told you that."

"If it happens again, wave me over and then answer it. We might be able to get a lead that way." He rested his hand on her shoulder. "I'm just trying to nail this guy before something really bad happens, okay?"

"Yeah, like having her home gutted isn't bad enough," Penny said.

"I'm doing the best I can," Jared said behind his clenched jaw.

Ryan kicked Penny under the table. Jared didn't need to be reminded of what he thought were his failures in life.

"Fine, but I'm worried about her." Penny grabbed Chuck's hand when he sat down beside her.

"*Her* is sitting right here." Ryan waved to everyone.

"We're all on edge about what's happening." Chuck's calm voice rang out. "Let's all just try and have a good time."

Ryan wasn't sure if that was possible. Between some sicko successfully scaring the crap out of her and dealing with the consequences of sleeping with Jared, she wasn't sure a good time could be had.

"Give me your keys. It's still pouring." Jared held his hand out to Ryan. "I'll drive your car to the door." He peered out the small window in the restaurant's door, doing his best to remain indifferent.

"What about your truck?" Ryan asked.

"You'll drive me to it, then I'll follow you home." And then he'd go straight to bed, without her.

"What are you going to do about the carriage house?" She plopped her keys in his hand.

"I hired a buddy of mine, Rory, to fix it. He starts tomorrow. I'll have him store your belongings in the garage." He pushed open the door, then turned back to look at her. "I spoke with the real-estate agent. She actually thinks it's a good idea if you live in the main house until it sells. I'd pay you."

Her already annoyed expression turned deadly.

"I didn't mean it like it sounded," he said softly.

"What exactly did you mean?" She glared.

"It's going to take at least a month for the carriage house to be completed. You need a place to live, and after I move, I'll need someone to take care of the place until it sells." Had he not taken her to bed last night, he supposed his words wouldn't have felt so cold. But the harsh reality was last night shouldn't have happened, and it would never happen again.

"I told you I'd help with the sale of the house." She huffed. "I'm tired and I want to go to bed."

"I'll be right back." He charged out into the wind and rain. Lightning flashed in the sky, followed by a big bang. The raging storm matched the fried emotions he didn't know how to handle.

Not to mention the broken condom. He didn't know if she knew about it or not. Part of him didn't want to say anything. The likelihood he'd gotten her pregnant...hell, he should know better than anyone it only took one time.

He hoped he hadn't gotten her pregnant. He wouldn't be able to live with himself if he had. He'd thought about having a vasectomy but just never got around to it. Maybe he should. Having a kid would ruin his life. And hers.

The rain came down so hard and fast it didn't matter how close to the door he got her SUV, she was drenched by the time she scooted into the driver's seat.

"So much for having a great hair day." She ran her fingers through her luscious hair, dripping water in her lap.

"I like it wet." He reached in his pocket for his keys, then looked over at her. Mascara smudged under her eyes, and when lightning flashed across the sky, her face brightened. Never before had he seen such a beautiful sight. "You've got an umbrella?"

She shook her head. "I always lose the suckers."

"I guess we're gonna get even wetter." He bolted to his truck, then followed her the half mile home.

The rain didn't appear to be letting up at all, even though the wind had died down. After snatching the mail, he took Ryan by the hand and raced to the porch.

"Crap," she muttered. "I need a change of clothes from the carriage house."

He pushed back the door, then flicked on the kitchen lights. "Pack up your clothes in the morning and Rory will bring them over here. And anything else you might need." He shook off his coat, then kicked off his shoes. "Damn socks are soaked."

"I'm not moving in with you." She folded her arms across her chest.

"I'm not asking you to." He glared at her. "But until this bastard is caught, you're stuck with me, babe."

"I don't need a damn bodyguard." She tossed her purse on the kitchen table, then pulled back a chair. Once settled in the seat, she kicked off her black pumps and rubbed her feet.

He enjoyed watching just about anything she did. He rubbed the back of his neck. Nothing about his thoughts made much sense. He wouldn't deny he cared, but he didn't like the feeling that he cared beyond protecting her from bodily harm. "I spoke with Rick today, and he said he could give you Friday off."

Her shoe fell to the floor, then she looked up at him with wide eyes. "Why would you do that?"

"I have to go to Rochester, and I don't want to leave you alone."

"Oh, no, you don't, buster." She bolted upright, sending the chair tumbling backward. "You've got some nerve going behind my back like that. What gives you the right to tell me where to go? Or to use your friendship with my boss to manipulate me?"

"You're not staying here alone while there's some lunatic out to get you," he said. Letting out a breath, he tried to rip his gaze from her angry eyes hurling daggers at him. Heck, he was just trying to be a nice guy.

"Not the point."

He laced his fingers around her upper arm and shot a few daggers back of his own. She could be too damn stubborn for her own good. "Exactly the point."

She looked down at his hand. "I'm not a child, nor your property. I will not be dictated to." She yanked her arm free from his grasp.

Blinking his eyes, he tried to calm his frustration before he said or did something he'd really regret. "I'll see if I can postpone my meeting."

"Damn it, Jared." She threw her arms wide. "I don't want you forfeiting your career once again out of your own guilt or sense of duty you have toward me. I appreciate your diligence and dedication to your job and to my case, but I will not bear the responsibility of your losing out on this opportunity. And I won't let you tell me what to do, either."

A flash of lightning brightened the sky, followed by a loud clap of thunder. The lights flickered on and off. A deafening silence followed. The wind hurtled around outside, creating a faint whistle, and a few tree limbs smacked against the house, breaking the silence.

Jared glanced around the kitchen, then locked gazes with her. Her eyes were hard, and her lips pressed in a determined line. For a brief moment, his heart pulsed out of control and he held his breath. Even angry, she had a way of sending his good senses out the window. Her sheer determination should be admired and respected. But he wouldn't give her that, not today.

"You're coming with me."

Her nose flared. "Like hell. I'll stay with my brother." She turned, ducked her head into the refrigerator, then came up with a beer. When she twisted off the cap, a loud pop drowned out the hiss of fizz.

Instincts kicking in, Jared lunged forward and tossed Ryan to the floor, the beer bottle landing with a thud and spraying its foamy contents everywhere.

"Stay put," he whispered, reaching for his weapon. He crept toward the door, then flicked off the lights.

"What was—"

"Shhhh." He pressed his finger to his lips, then pushed back the door.

"Oh, no."

He turned when he felt warm hands pressed on his back. "Ryan, get back in the house."

"Like you said, I shouldn't be alone."

Holding his weapon in one hand, he looped his free hand around her waist and pulled her to his back. "Stay close and behind me."

"Yes, sir."

He chuckled. "Now you're willing to follow orders."

"Was that an order?" She pulled back.

"Please." He glanced over his shoulder, tugging her closer. "This isn't a game. That sounded like a gunshot."

"Sounded like Mr. Thompson's car."

The trees swayed with the wind, and the rain pelted his body as he made his way toward the road. "Grab my cell from my hip."

He scanned the area as best he could and hoped for some lightning to help him, but no such luck. When he reached the side of Ryan's SUV, he saw the shattered window. "Shit."

"Ouch," Ryan said as her hands left his body. "I cut my foot."

"Don't move." Jared lifted her into his arms, tiptoed across the driveway, and dropped her down onto the grass. "Your window's broken." As he glanced over his shoulder, the weather decided to cooperate and a flash of lightning lit up the sky, providing enough light to do a quick scan. "Come on." He lifted her back into his arms and carried her toward the house.

"What happened?"

"Not sure. But I'm about to find out." He pushed back the door, then sat her down on the table. "Let's look at that foot first." He lifted her leg at the same time he flipped open his phone. He wanted to get some help to sweep the area, especially if it wasn't the elements that took out her window. That pop could have been anything in a storm like this one, but he wasn't about to take any chances.

Blood dripped from her big toe to his hand. "We need to wash this out and make sure there isn't any glass in there."

"What about your foot?" She pointed.

A trail of blood followed his footsteps. "I guess we do the same thing to me."

"Harmon here," Frank said over the speakerphone.

"Get your ass to my house pronto."

"Why? Sir?"

"Because when I say jump, you don't question it, you just do it. Get Jenkins too."

"On my way, sir."

Jared lifted Ryan into his arms once again, then placed her firm rump on the counter near the sink. When he looked up, she might as well have slapped him. Her eyes narrowed and her brow tightened.

"What now?"

"You're a bully."

"Am not." He grabbed her foot and shoved it under warm water.

"Ouch, that hurts," she yelped.

"Did you see that?" He pointed out the window.

"See what?" She turned her head with wide eyes. "What, see what?"

While she was distracted, he plucked out a wedged piece of glass in her big toe and then one on the ball of her foot. "Oooouch!" She tried to yank her foot away.

"Got it." He tossed the glass in the trash.

"Jerk."

"Thought I was a bully." He winked.

"Damn it, you're both." Grabbing a paper towel, she swiveled her hips and dabbed her wound. "Why can't you just ask nicely?"

"What?" He hoisted his own foot up over the sink and yanked out a small piece of glass.

"Why do you have to order everyone around? It just annoys the hell out of us." She hobbled off the counter and dropped her adorable ass on a kitchen chair. Her hair dripped down on her white shirt, nipples puckering through both her wet bra and blouse.

A wave of desire rippled across his body. "As far as Harmon goes, it's his job to do as he's told. It's my job to train him. Part of the territory."

"Well, I'm not some rookie cop. I'm..." She glanced toward the ceiling.

His own gaze followed hers in search of what she

was to him at this point. "My friend," he offered. "And at present, a case." Opening a cabinet, he reached for the first aid kit. "And someone may have just shot at your car for their own personal jollies, which just plain pisses me off." He held out a couple of Band-Aids for her. "And the reason you're coming with me to Rochester."

"Jared," she said with a stern tone.

"What?" He stared at her as if he'd just been scolded.

"I'll stay with Pat."

He slammed his fist on the table. "He'll be working late, which means you and a very pregnant Marci will be sitting ducks for some psycho to attack."

Her stubborn blue eyes narrowed. "I'll have Penny come over, too. It'll be like old times, or we'll hang out at the bar after work. I promise not to be stupid, okay?"

He sat down and took her hand in his. She accepted his touch, and a sense of doom overwhelmed him. Why did he care so much? "I'm not worried that you'll do something stupid; I'm worried that some sicko will hurt you, or worse." Because it was his job to care.

A warm but simple smile softened her determined face. She laced her fingers through his and slid off her chair into his lap. Her lips pressed gently against his, and he could taste the cool rainwater. Unable to blink his eyes closed, he stared into a pair of hypnotic blue pools.

She glided her lips across his scruffy face, unaffected

by the coarseness of his stubble, then whispered, "Thank you for caring, but—"

Snapping his head back, he glared at her. "No buts."

Her forehead thumped against the side of his head. "You're not responsible for me. I can take care of myself."

His hand trembled when he hooked his fingers around her wrists. "If that were the case, people wouldn't need cops."

"Cops, yes. You, not so much."

"What the hell is that supposed to mean?" But he knew exactly what she meant.

"If this happened after you moved, I'd be on my own."

"But I'm here," he protested, not wanting her to give up what he could offer her, because he didn't have much.

"And I'm grateful for everything you've done for me. But it's time you let go of this sense of duty you have toward me and do what you want. I hate knowing you didn't take that job in the first place because of me."

"I told you before, that wasn't the only reason, and I'm taking it now."

"Then don't screw it up."

"I don't plan on it." He slid his hands over her wet sleeves, across her shoulders, and through her glorious wet hair. "Can we come to a compromise?"

"What kind of compromise?"

"I'll try to arrange my meetings so I'm only gone

one night, and you promise never to be alone." He fisted his hand in her thick hair, water dripping on his lap. "And you let me have Frank check on you."

"Fine," she said.

Emotions he'd never felt before swelled inside his gut.

She clasped her fingers behind his neck. "I'm freezing. Mind if I take a bath in that huge tub of yours?"

Flashing lights filled the kitchen window. "Not at all. I'll take care of your car."

"Crap," she muttered, circling her arms around her middle as she rose. "I need my car."

"Take my truck until it gets fixed."

"And what will you drive?"

He chuckled. "I just got the BMW ready for summer. I had planned on taking it to Rochester anyway." He patted her wet bottom, letting his hand smooth across the firm muscle. "Go get warm."

He raked a hand across his head and glanced out toward the driveway. Jenkins had already pulled out his flashlight and was looking around Ryan's car. "She doesn't need me," he whispered, knowing it was the truth and exactly what he wanted. He didn't want to be needed by any individual, nor did he want to need anyone in particular.

Chapter Ten

After the tow truck pulled away with Ryan's SUV, Jared jogged up the path, then shook like a dog on the back porch. Soaked to the core, he had only one thought, to slide into the hot bubbles next to Ryan, with vanilla-scented candles burning in the background.

"Why the hell not." He kicked off his shoes and raced up the stairs, his blood boiling over with lust. The door to his bedroom wasn't locked, and he could already smell her soapy rose scent.

Glancing around the room, he peeled off his soaked shirt, then rid himself of his binding jeans. Hopefully the bathroom door wasn't locked, even though he'd have to give her a good lecture about safety.

His heart pounded against his chest. The door slipped open and he peered in. She lay in a tub full of bubbles. Her arms stretched out along the sides of the tub and one leg lifted, exposing her knee. The foam hid the rest of her as it sloshed about in an exotic dance.

As he tiptoed across the bathroom floor, he tried not to laugh. This would be a lesson he enjoyed.

Just then, her hand shot up, making a fake gun, and one eye peeped open. "Don't move or I'll shoo...shit... you're naked." She jerked in the tub, sending water to the floor. Her eyes were wide with shock.

He stepped into the warm water and settled down, enjoying the way she tried to arrange the bubbles over her naked body. "People generally take their baths that way." He dunked his head under, then came up for air. "Thank God my parents like things big."

"This isn't a public hot tub." She scowled, holding her knees to her chest.

"It's definitely private, but it does have jets." He reached to the side in search of the buttons, pushing them to start the bubbly effect.

"Oh, good Lord." She jumped. More water sloshed out onto the floor.

"Now that's nice," he whispered, pulling her to his lap. "Did the jet get your rump?" He smoothed his hand over the soft curve.

"Something like that." She wiggled but seemed to settle herself nicely against his thighs. "This isn't a good idea." The bubbles melted across her chest, allowing the tight pink nubs to blossom in the cool air.

"Maybe not," he said between ragged breaths. Raising

his hand, he tilted her chin. "But it's not a bad one, either." He stopped breathing the moment her heavenly eyes caught his. Desire and passion and so much more lured him closer to giving in to his worst fear. Caring about other humans and putting their existence before your own only caused the kind of pain that changed your soul.

"This is crazy." She snuggled into his lap, letting her body relax in his arms. "Nothing can ever come of this."

"I know." He brushed his thumb across her lower lip. "We shouldn't, but I want to."

A slow smile spread across her face. "Yeah, I can tell."

"You're a very bad girl."

"So spank me." Her soft hands ran down his chest, tortured his nipples, then glided across his twitching stomach.

His vision blurred and everything around him faded in the background. She rolled her legs and straddled him. He cupped her face with trembling fingers and assaulted her mouth, nearly missing. Her tongue lashed out, catching his while she gently massaged him into madness.

Grabbing her thighs, he stood and stumbled out of the tub. He snatched a towel and began to wipe the bubbles dribbling down her soft, supple body. When he finished down by her feet, he worked his way back up her body with his mouth. Her hands roamed his head and shoulders, then finally she reached for a towel and started to dry his wet skin.

Unable to maintain his control, he tugged her to the bedroom, then pressed his body against hers as he dropped them both to the cotton sheets. "You're incredible," he murmured against her pearly skin. "More passionate than I imagined."

"You imagined?" She spoke softly.

He tilted his head and looked deep into her amazing eyes. "A few times."

Her face flushed, giving off a sexy glow. "When?"

"When what?" He scowled, annoyed he'd admitted such a thing.

"Just curious." She wrapped her legs around his body, grinding her hips against him. He rolled his eyes to the back of his head.

"I love it when you do that."

"You like to talk, too, don't you?" He forced his eyes open and adjusted his body as he reached for the condom beside the bed.

"Sex doesn't have to be silent."

"Thank God for small favors, Miss Noisy." He repositioned himself on top of her, spreading her legs and entering her inch by glorious inch.

"I'm not…oh, God." She moaned, tossing her head back. Her breath was heavy and long. "Yes." She tilted her hips, then shifted sideways. Her body seemed to know the exact way to touch him, respond to him, and drive him mad.

He lowered his mouth to her perky breast, sucking in her taut nipple. Her moans grew louder and her breath faster. Fingers dug into his back, then slid down to his ass and heaved him closer, forcing him fully inside.

Her hips swiveled and rocked, then repeated the motion. She cried out his name over and over again until her body shivered, sending a burst of adrenaline through his shocked system.

"Ryan," he moaned, giving in to his deepest passion. Never before had he been so lost in the moment, in the desire to feel connected to another soul, that he lost all sense of sound reasoning.

She squeezed her legs tight around his middle, then dropped them and her arms to the sides with a loud sigh. "Who knew?" Perspiration beaded against her glowing skin.

"Certainly not me." He brushed her damp hair aside and studied her face. The content smile on her lips let him know once again he'd thoroughly satisfied her. But this time it disturbed him.

"Oh, come on, Jared." Fingers pressed into his waist. Slowly she glided up his spine. "I'm sure you've had mind-blowing sex before."

"Nope." He kissed her nose. "The best I've ever had."

Her cheeks flushed. "How sweet." She cupped his face, smacking her lips against his. "And that was great, but—"

He hushed her with his finger. "I care about you. Hell, I like you a whole lot, but I'm taking that transfer."

"I'd hate you if you didn't." She narrowed her eyes.

He swallowed, unable to reply immediately. He'd expected her to try to talk him into staying in Lake George, giving a relationship a try. Feelings he didn't understand, didn't have words to describe, circled his mind, creating chaos. He hadn't had a relationship since Lisa, and he didn't want one now.

"I guess you won't have to hate me then. But I do need to talk to you about something." He scooted up the bed, ripped down the covers, hoisted her next to him, then drew the blanket back over their naked bodies.

"Oh, for crying out loud. I can move myself." The feather pillow formed to her head as she raised the covers, swishing the air and sending her intoxicating feminine smell across the room. "You figure out what happened to my car?"

The muscles in his neck tensed. "Sort of, but that's not what I wanted to talk about."

"I don't understand."

Rubbing his aching chest from the sudden onset of heartburn, he cleared his throat. "One of the condoms broke last night." A sudden rush of fear swelled in his mind.

"Shit," she whispered and held up her fingers and began to count.

"Just one broke." He gave her a puzzled look. "What are you doing?"

"Trying to figure out where I am in my cycle." The sparkle in her eyes faded.

"Bad?"

She counted a few more fingers, then said, "Shouldn't be a problem. Does that happen often?"

"Broken condoms?" he questioned, raising a brow.

"Well, it's never happened to me before."

"If it happened often, I would've had a vasectomy long ago." He shivered. Curling the covers in his hands, he wanted to reach for a bottle of good old Southern Comfort. Maybe being with her wasn't helping after all.

"I think it's great you know exactly what you want from life. I'm still not sure."

"I don't follow?" He turned to look at her.

She lay on her side, elbow digging into the pillow and her head rested in her hand. The covers draped across her curves, but left part of her perfect breast exposed. She looked confident and determined.

"I thought you wanted it all." He blinked. The pressure of moving and her problems must be getting to him. "The husband with a stable job, two point five kids, and a white picket fence."

"You left out the dog." She laughed. "But I'm not sure anymore. I love my job and I'm not willing to give it up for anyone, at least not anyone I've met yet."

"Having it all would include keeping your job."

"If you had a wife, you wouldn't want her to work."

Here we go, he thought. She's going to bring up him staying anyway. "I won't ever have a wife again."

"It was hypothetical." She adjusted herself higher on the bed. "It seems I know only two types of men: the boring, no fun, mousy guy who asks me how high to jump, or control freaks like you and Pat. I want an equal."

He chuckled. "Good luck with that."

"Exactly. Although, I think Penny found a good one in Chuck."

"He's a good guy, but he's of the controlling variety." Feeling uncomfortable about the topic, he settled down into the softness of the bed, then turned off his light. "I'm sure you'll find what you're looking for someday, babe." He rolled away, unable to take her in his arms.

"You're really worried about that condom, aren't you?"

"It would complicate things." Squeezing his eyes shut, he tried to ignore the comfort her roaming hands offered him. Never in his life had any woman ever made him feel so many conflicting emotions. "But we can't do anything about it until we know for sure." He sucked in his breath, waiting for her to attack.

"This is true." She sighed and molded her body against his, wrapping her arm around his middle and shoving her leg between his. "I should get my period by the middle of next week. If I don't, I guess we'll have to deal with it."

Deal with it? Cold perspiration beaded at his brow. Had she implied not having it? And how could she be so calm? Didn't she care one way or the other? A dull ache began to throb at the base of his skull. He couldn't believe the Ryan he knew would ever consider having an abortion, but he couldn't consider being a dad, much less the occasional weekend dad.

Unable to push her away, he clamped down on her knee, then covered her hand and pressed his lips against her fingertips. It seemed no matter what he said or did, she just wouldn't go away.

And right now, he didn't want her to.

The following morning, Ryan had successfully put on a forced smile and kept her manner light and carefree in front of Jared. She couldn't let him know how she really felt about the possibility of being pregnant. Not that she knew how she felt, other than scared shitless.

Now, sitting behind her desk, she closed her eyes, trying to keep the butterflies floating about her stomach from leaping up her throat. With her forefinger, she patted the sensitive, puffy skin under her eyes, annoyed that Jared had been able to fall asleep and snore the night away while she tossed and turned.

Rubbing her temples, she let her head dip forward. She still had a ton of paperwork, and then she needed to check on all the details for the upcoming golf tournament. The buzzer on her phone rang, making her jump. "Yes, Cheryl."

"There is a Lisa Stillman here to see you."

"Ohhh, okay. Send her in." Ryan swallowed, unable to force a coherent thought. Hearing footsteps, she rose from her desk, then greeted an unsmiling, very mature-looking Lisa. Nothing like the Lisa she remembered. "Mrs. Stillman," she said, deciding formalities were best.

Lisa's cold fingers slid into her hand, shook once, then pulled away.

Ryan stood still, ignoring the urge to recoil and hide under her desk. "What can I do for you?"

"First." Lisa stripped off her gloves, finger by finger before stuffing them into her purse and eyeing the chair next to Ryan's desk.

"Please, sit down." Ryan wedged herself behind her desk and squeezed her shaking knees.

"Thank you." A very stiff, doll-like Lisa crossed her legs at her ankles and rested her purse and hands on her lap. The woman screamed Stepford wife.

"My husband will be hosting a big horseracing event, and I need to book suites for the guests."

"How many rooms, and when do you want them?" Without shaking on the outside, Ryan opened her desk drawer and pulled out the scheduling and reservation papers she needed.

"June ninth through the thirteenth. I'll also need meeting rooms, a dinner, and I'd like to set up several rounds of golf." Lisa dug into her purse and pulled out a sheet of paper, handing it to Ryan.

Ryan tensed every muscle in her body to keep from looking like she was suffering from some dreadful disease as she took the yellow sheet in her hands.

"I'll want the best of everything, and money isn't an issue."

Ryan pressed the paper down on her desk, skimming over the details. Focusing on the task at hand, she shuffled some forms around, checked the booking schedule on her computer, then turned her head. "I can accommodate you. If you'd like, we can take a tour and I can show you a few different style rooms. I've got two meeting rooms to choose from, and we could even go meet the chef. I'll need a deposit."

"Just don't disappoint me," Lisa said, not looking at Ryan. "Give me the best of everything, and keep the food to my specifications, and we'll make it through this process like I don't despise you." She handed Ryan a credit card.

The credit card fell from Ryan's fingertips. She snapped her head toward a scowling Lisa, whose eyes were cold and loathing.

"If I could have avoided this meeting, I would have. But this is what my husband wants." Lisa leaned over, picked up the credit card, and placed it on the desk.

Blood drained from Ryan's face, fear cutting off her ability to think on her feet. With trembling hands, she ran the credit card through the machine.

"And since I'm here, you'd best tell Jared to call off his bloodhounds. If he wants to know something about my life or my husband's, he can ask himself." Lisa stood and smoothed out her bleach-blond hair.

A sudden rush of adrenaline coursed through Ryan's body, replacing the sullen child with an angry woman. "If you want to give Jared a message, call him yourself." Ryan ripped off the printed credit receipt, grabbed a pen, and handed it to Lisa, glaring at her. "I'm not his personal secretary."

"Whatever," Lisa muttered, signing the receipt. "If you do anything to undermine me or ruin this for my husband, I will have your job."

"If you'd prefer, I can have someone else handle all the details, and we won't need to have any contact. But if you still want me to handle this, you will treat me with respect or leave my office." Staring Lisa dead-on, Ryan squared her shoulders.

Lisa took a step forward and leaned in. Her face contorted as if she'd just eaten a lemon. "You're the reason my son died, and I'll never forgive you for that." Her eyes shifted toward the hallway, then back. "I'd like nothing more than to make sure you suffer the same pain, but I guess you'll get your due when Jared breaks your heart into tiny pieces."

"Impossible." Ryan took the credit slip and thrust it toward Lisa. "I feel sorry for you." She hit the intercom button. "Cheryl, please show Mrs. Stillman around the hotel." Ryan continued to glare at Lisa. "If you have any other questions, please either call my assistant or email me."

"You haven't changed one bit; you still don't know your place." Lisa slipped on her white gloves, then with a tilted chin, met a wide-eyed Cheryl in the hallway.

"Bitch." Ryan slammed down her fist on her desk, knocking over some papers.

"A little pissed?" Tom said.

She jumped, stubbing her toe on the bottom of her desk. "Damn it, you scared the crap out of me." She wiggled her nose at the overdone aftershave assaulting her senses.

"Are you okay? You look a little pale." His slimy hands rubbed up and down her arms.

"I'm fine," she said, stepping away from him. He was proving to be a roller coaster ride. One minute angry with her because of all the questions, the next minute hitting on her. The guy just couldn't take a hint. Then again, according to Penny, Ryan was too nice and never made guys understand when she just wasn't interested.

"Wasn't that Lance Stillman's wife?" Tom leaned around the door to look down the hall. "She's got to be twenty years younger than him."

"I think she's twenty-eight or so." Ryan rubbed her butt, then scooted back behind her desk. "What do you need?" She pulled out a folder, labeled it, then filed all of the paperwork for Lisa, ignoring the prickly feeling Tom gave her.

"I want to apologize for my outburst."

She lifted her lids like she was peering over reading glasses. "Okay." The shifting of his weight from one leg to another made her skin crawl, not to mention the way his eyes scanned her body like he was taking a mental picture of her or something. "Apology accepted."

As he shoved one hand in his pocket, he waved the other one in the air. "So, could I talk you into going out for a drink with the gang? Say, your brother's place?"

"Not tonight."

"But that's not a no, right?" He smiled, looking like a pathetic dog begging for food.

Her brother had always told her persistence was a good thing, but in this case, her brother was wrong. Dead wrong. "It's still a no, Tom."

"Can't blame a guy for trying." He turned on his heel, then marched proudly out of her office.

"I'm a loser," she muttered. Why couldn't she land herself a normal guy? One that was good-looking, interesting, emotionally available, and didn't try and control her every move? But that would be too easy. Nothing came easy to her.

Chapter Eleven

Jared pushed back his office chair. He rolled his neck and rubbed his aching shoulder. Research hadn't been his favorite aspect of his job, but the most necessary.

"Excuse me, sir." Harmon peeked his head in. "Special Agent Randy Garrison is here."

"Send him in and join us," Jared instructed.

"Yes, sir!"

Jared chuckled. Harmon might be green and young, but where instincts were concerned, the kid was one of the best. Jared would enjoy signing off on his request to join the scuba squad. Hell, if Jared had stayed in Lake George, with his own swimming abilities, he would have enjoyed going through the training with the kid.

"Good to see you," Randy said, stretching his hand out.

"Thanks for stopping by." Jared offered him a seat. "How's the FBI treating you?"

"Different from being a state trooper, but I'm glad I made the move."

"So, what do you have for me?" Jared motioned for Harmon to sit. Hopefully, the kid would learn to relax a bit.

"Eddy Houser has cooperated fully, but we're not going to pursue anything further regarding this 'Reliever' thing. We need to find out who's behind the disappearance of some of these college girls. We believe it's some kind of black market or human smuggling and these girls are being taken out of the country." Randy opened up his briefcase and took out some folders. "Honestly, we just stumbled onto Houser. But here's a complete history of the guy. Nothing out of the ordinary."

Jared flipped through some of the papers. The information seemed detailed, but as Randy said, Eddy seemed to be relatively normal, as perverts go. "What about Tom Grady?"

"I spoke with the arresting officer from his juvie file. He exposed himself to a bunch of girls."

"He got arrested for that?" Jared thought back to his streaking days. What teenage moron didn't flash himself at least once?

"The cop said he was wasted and hit one of the girls. He also resisted arrest. The judge sentenced him to community service and sealed his record." Randy tossed a few more papers toward Jared. "Rudy's a nutcase, but then again, I'm sure you knew that."

Jared wasn't quite sure what to make of Rudy Martin, but he wasn't on the up and up, no matter what the guy's parole officer said. "How about the Stillmans?" Jared pushed back his chair. He'd called in a big favor on this one, since Lisa and her husband didn't fit into the suspect list yet.

"She spent a few months going from town to town and doing drugs. She got picked up here and there, but nothing huge." Randy cracked his knuckles, then lifted a folder. "She ended up working for an escort service, where she met her husband."

"Oh, great," Jared muttered, swiveling his chair. What he'd ever seen in that woman was totally lost on him now. Then again, he certainly knew how to pick them.

"He had an exclusive contract with her, then married her about three years ago."

"How long has she been living in Saratoga?" Jared questioned, running a hand across his head.

"About as long as she's been married."

"That doesn't make sense." Jared stood and began to pace behind his desk. Why just show her face now?

"Sir?" Harmon spoke for the first time. "I think the old man owns land in Kentucky, too."

"Actually, that's his brother. Lance left the family business and moved here about ten years ago. Had a falling out with his dad, so he started his own farm.

Pretty successful, I might add." Randy remained in his chair, pulling more papers out and settling them on Jared's desk. "However, I got some credit card info and it seems she travels a lot, alone. And she isn't here much, just makes appearances."

"Marriage of convenience." Jared should've known. She'd always wanted money; guess she'd caved on the respect part.

"Probably. Except for her street days and possible prostitution, they're both clean. Not even an issue with taxes." Randy stood, collecting his briefcase.

"Doesn't mean she wouldn't hold a five-year-old grudge."

"I've held one for a lot longer," Randy admitted. "So have you."

Jared focused his gaze out the window, not wanting to admit Randy was right.

"I've got to get back to the office." Randy headed toward the door.

"Nice meeting you." Randy smacked Harmon on the back as he strolled through the door. "Chuck called and asked me to meet him at the Mason Jug. Did you know he's dating Penny?"

"Seen it with my own eyes. The guy's flipped his lid."

"Yeah, well, if Penny's there, then so is Ryan. I haven't seen her in a while, and she sure would be a sight for sore eyes."

Jared opened his mouth, then clamped it shut. He

had no right to say one word about Randy's comment. He had no claims on Ryan and didn't want any. Then again… "She's not your type."

"According to him, she not anyone's type," Harmon added.

"Don't you have work to do?" Jared said.

"If I didn't know you better, sir, I'd say you've got the hots for her." Harmon turned on his heel and practically jogged down the hallway.

Randy chuckled.

"What the hell is so funny?"

"Nothing." Randy cleared his throat. "Hell, you're so damned protective of her, I think you're missing out on what's really right in front of you."

"And you're chasing a ghost."

"Yes, I am. I'll see you later." Randy shook Jared's hand, then pushed back the main door and made his way to his truck.

The only thing Jared had ever missed out on, besides getting to know his son, was this promotion. He'd wanted to work for this unit since he'd joined State. Well, maybe not this particular unit, but something more exciting than what he did now. Nothing was going to stand in his way. Not this time.

Ryan glanced in her rearview mirror as she made the turn onto Mason Road, making sure no one followed her. The sun had started its descent behind the mountains, and the red glare forced her to squint, only intensifying her already paranoid feelings.

Damn Jared!

He had her so worked up she didn't trust a soul. Everyone was suspect in her eyes these days, and that drove her nuts. Tom was just annoying and in need of some attention from someone other than her. Eddy might have an odd fetish, but he was harmless, and Lisa was just a bitch.

George McIntosh, on the other hand, was behind bars for a reason, and he was the only one who had motive to cause Ryan bodily harm. She just had to get Jared, or maybe even Frank, to focus their attention on George and nail his ass. The sooner Jared left, the sooner Ryan would be able to move past him.

She shifted his truck into park, then slammed the steering wheel. Just because his BMW was in the garage, and he was home, shouldn't make her feel safe.

She stepped from the truck, taking a look around. Jared was probably watching from the kitchen, and she was in no mood for a lecture. How she could've ever thought he was some kind of dream man was beyond her. She couldn't imagine anyone wanting to be with a man like him.

Her body shivered, remembering his gentle kisses and soft caresses. "Oh, God." She could probably have a spontaneous orgasm just thinking about his lovemaking. Okay, so he had one redeeming quality, but the rest of him was damn annoying.

She flipped open her mailbox. "Jerk." He'd picked up her mail. Did he think she was completely incapable of taking care of herself? The back porch steps squeaked when her heels clunked against them. Tomorrow she'd be staying with her brother. She sighed. That wouldn't be much better. Maybe Penny wasn't staying at Chuck's place all the time and she'd be able to stay with her.

"Yeah, right," she muttered, using her foot to push back the kitchen door to the main house.

"What?" Jared crumpled the papers he'd been looking at and peered over them. "You okay?"

"Oh, I'm just ducky." She tossed her briefcase on the kitchen table, sending it tumbling across the ceramic top. It landed on the floor with a thud.

Jared's gaze followed the flying briefcase to the floor, then he glanced back to her with a lifted brow. "Bad day?"

"My life can't get any worse. And I owe it all to you." She plopped down in the chair, kicked off her heels, and wrinkled her toes.

"Care to tell me what I did?" He chuckled as he set his papers aside. He clasped his hands together and lifted them behind his head, like he was amused.

"Thanks to you, I'm paranoid, afraid of my own shadow, and I can't even have a conversation with someone without wondering if they're out to get me."

She gave him a nod, pursing her lips, then went back to rubbing her aching feet. "And you got my mail."

"I happened to be getting my mail and your box is right next to mine. Excuse me for being a gentleman."

"Trust me, you're no gentleman." She dropped her left foot to the floor, then lifted her right and started rubbing the ball of her foot.

"What happened that you're not telling me?" He asked in his usual commanding tone. The table shook when his hands landed on the top.

"You see?" She bolted upright. "You're such a control freak. I can't take it. I think I'm going to my brother's tonight."

"No, you're not." He glared at her.

"Oh, yes, I am, and don't try and do that thing with your eyes, then kiss me you know where, because I'm not sleeping with you again." Stomping to the refrigerator, she pulled back the door and grabbed a soda.

"Is that what this is all about? Us?" He rubbed the back of his neck like he always did when something bothered him.

"Relax, Jared. There *is* no us." She patted his shoulder. "I'm just annoyed by the way you try to control every aspect of my life. And now, having to come home to you? I miss living by myself."

"You're not living with me." He reminded her with a harsh tone. "And don't fret, because I think we've got some good info on Rudy. I wouldn't be surprised if we were able to make an arrest in a day or two, although that doesn't mean you can be lax about your safety." He stood and hovered over her, cupping her chin with a firm hand. "Rochester is hot for me to start, so don't sweat it. I won't be around to annoy you much longer."

She swallowed, staring into his angry eyes. "You really think it's George through Rudy?"

"Yeah." He dropped his hand and turned from her, taking slow steps toward the hallway. "Chuck called me this afternoon. He'd like us to be at the Mason Jug around seven. He's got a surprise for Penny, and he'd like you to be there." Jared paused and glanced over his shoulder with narrowed eyes.

"I think he's going to propose, and it would be nice if you were there for *your* best friend." He waved his finger at her. "But that's just a suggestion. I wouldn't want you to think I was controlling that aspect of your life. Hell, I'm sorry I ever cared." He smacked his hand against the doorframe. "Damn it," he muttered.

Ryan watched in shock as Jared walked away. She stood in the middle of the kitchen for what seemed like an eternity, just blinking and staring off into nothing. She'd been hard on him, yes, but she never dreamed he'd react like she'd actually hurt the man's feelings.

"Impossible." She shook out her trembling hands. That man was just impossible, and no one would ever be able to live with him. How could she have fallen in love with him? "Oh, God, no," she whispered, dropping her face into her hands. *I don't love him; I don't love him!* she tried to tell herself, but it was no use.

She loved him.

All of him.

Now what was she supposed to do? All of her toiletries were in the master bathroom, where he was probably changing from his uniform and jumping into the shower. "Don't even go there," she scolded herself.

Squaring her shoulders, she left the kitchen and made her way upstairs. Jared's words about Chuck rang out in her ears. She'd do anything for Penny. Even if it meant she had to face Jared at the moment.

She tapped on the door but got no response. She pushed it open. Thank goodness, she could hear the water running in the bathroom. She tiptoed toward her duffel bag, reached in, and grabbed her favorite jeans and the skimpiest top she could find. Anything to annoy the man.

Everything else was in the bathroom. Well, she figured one of the other bathrooms in this house had to have soap and towels. She'd survive. But could she survive the glorious smell of Irish Spring seeping from under the bathroom door?

"You can have it now." His dark sexy tone made her jump. "Sorry, didn't mean to scare you."

"I've been like that all day." She tried to scurry past him without noticing the towel draped low around his waist. But he stopped her by curling his fingers around her forearm.

"What happened? More hang-ups? Did someone threaten you?" He tilted her chin with his thumb. "I'm not trying to control you, but keep you safe, and do my job." His greenish eyes held her stare.

She swallowed the emotions leaping from her gut, screaming at her to throw herself at him. "Lisa visited me today, on business."

"Really." His brows shot up. "What kind of business, and why didn't..." He cleared his throat. "I wish you would've called me."

"She wanted to book some rooms for a business function for her husband, but she made it very clear she can't stand the sight of me."

Jared tightened his grip. His eyes reduced to narrow slits and his jaw clenched tight. "Did she threaten you?"

"Jared?"

"What?"

"You can't go off half-cocked because Lisa came to see me at work. I was the person she was directed to. She probably tried to avoid me."

"Are you going to accuse me of being controlling when I tell you that she's got her own set of problems and could be a possible suspect? Are you going to flip out on me because I'm trying to do my job?" He released her arm, but his face had turned flaming red.

"No, but I'm going to tell you that I'm in charge of my life, and you have no say in who, where, or what I do."

His chest heaved up and down with his ragged breath. His eyes had grown dark, a look she knew well.

However, the intensity of his stare carried a sense of passion she'd never seen before. His gaze dipped to her middle. "Two things I won't budge on." He raised his head and met her gaze head-on.

"Excuse me?" The muscles shaking in her legs caused her to falter and tumble into his arms. His tone had softened, but his words seemed harsh against her ears.

"You're to do things my way regarding your safety until I have someone in custody. And if you're pregnant, you will tell me, and we'll decide what to do together; got it?" His tone wasn't meant as a question, but an order. Not something she could live with, ever.

She cupped his face. "You are a big ogre. But—"

He opened his mouth to say something, but she tapped her finger against his lips and shook her head. She'd never lie to him, but she wouldn't cower from him either. No matter what happened or didn't happen in the future, he had to know she was her own woman. And a capable one at that. "I will trust you when it comes to my safety. I will take all the necessary precautions when I stay with Pat, and I won't do anything stupid. Heck, if you want me to call you five times a day, I will, if it will keep you off my back."

His lips formed a half-smile.

"As far as the whole baby thing goes, no point in talking about it until we know, and it would appear I'm going to get my period any day now, so no stress."

His smile faded for a moment. "What exactly does that mean?"

"If you must know the details, my body does certain things a few days before, like I gain five pounds and my breasts are swollen and tender."

"Really?" He cupped her breast and gave it a squeeze.

"Hey." She jumped back.

He chuckled as he adjusted his towel. "You're right. They are bigger."

"Oh, my, God. You are an impossible man." She appreciated how he tried to lighten the mood, or possibly change his attitude when it came to her, but sometimes she couldn't read him as well as she would like. Although she knew for certain Jared was not a family man. Not anymore.

"Yep." He turned and maneuvered toward his dresser. "Now, unless you want me naked and on top of you, you best get in the shower and..." He glanced at the clock. "And we have about forty-five minutes, which gives us plenty of time."

"Not." She slammed the door behind her, then locked it. The nerve of that man. The nerve of her stupid body aching to be filled by the most arrogant, self-centered, condescending, adorable, sexy, kind, and loving man. "Oh, God." She stepped into the shower, not allowing the tears to fall. Talk about falling for the wrong person.

Jared bit his tongue the moment Ryan entered the kitchen in a top that left nothing to the imagination. Not to mention the jeans that hugged her body showing every glorious curve. He knew if he said what he was thinking, she'd probably smack him. "You want a sweater? It's kind of cold out there."

She tilted her head and pursed her lips.

"Fine," he muttered, pulling back the door.

She laughed, then tossed her hair behind her shoulders and smiled as she walked out the door.

"Wonderful," he mumbled, resting his hand on the small of her back. "We walk or ride; you get to decide."

"Oh, how big of you." She crossed her arms around her middle and shivered. "Ride."

"I won't say I told you so."

"You just did." She opened her own door, scooted in, then slammed it shut without giving him a second glance. Why did he care so much? Why did she have to smell like peaches and roses?

He punched the gas, making the tires squeal, but didn't say a word. He slammed on the brakes as he pulled into a parking spot. Once again, she ignored him, getting out and jogging toward the door. "Fine, I quit." He tossed his hands wide and followed her in.

Ryan searched the room, and Pat pointed to the back corner. Penny and Chuck sat at a large table with Randy and a blonde.

Jared followed Ryan to the table, feeling like a puppy in tow. He went to pull back her chair, but she beat him to it and had the audacity to glare at him. Why was being a gentleman these days so taboo?

"Looks like she's pissed off." Randy leaned across the table, shoving a beer in front of Jared.

"I tend to have that effect on women these days." Jared sipped his beer and scanned his surroundings. "Damn." He eyed Tom and a few people he didn't know. Tom was taking a group photo with an expensive-looking camera. That guy was nothing but trouble, and Jared knew it.

"Isn't that the guy you had me run a check on?" Randy asked.

"One and the same." He glanced at Ryan, who actually acknowledged him. She nodded, signaling she was aware of Tom. At least she was living up to her end of the bargain and was aware of her surroundings.

Although the way she twirled her hair with her fingers and acted all sexy certainly didn't help the situation with Tom, much less Jared's own insane lust.

Jared adjusted his seat to check out what was going on behind her. "Oh, hell." He spotted Lisa at a table with a few women. Thank goodness her back was to him.

"I'm Tammy," the blonde next to Randy said, then thrust her hand in front of him.

"Crap, sorry. Jared, this is my date, Tammy Caulkins, Jared—"

"Yeah, yeah, nice to meet you, Tammy."

"I've heard a lot about you," she said, smiling, practically shoving her breasts forward for him to check out. Not going to happen. He kept his eyes above her neckline.

"I wouldn't believe a word of it." A flash caught his attention. Whipping his head around, he focused on Tom, what he was wearing, and whom he was with. Jared reached out and yanked Ryan's chair closer. He whispered, "Who's he with?"

She leaned into him, pressing her cheek against his. "Some people from work. I knew he might be here." Her breath was hot against his neck. "He invited me, too."

Blinking, he cocked his head. "I should've known that."

She patted his cheek. "Now you know. Who's with Lisa?" Without even trying, Ryan was the most radiant woman he'd ever known. She carried herself with such poise and confidence; he pitied the fool who fell in love with her.

He shook the bad thoughts away. Throwing his arm around her chair, he leaned forward and inhaled her intoxicating scent, then planted a kiss on her nose. "One of them is some chick she hung out with in high school. Bad news. Not sure about the other ones. But they don't look like the kind of women Mr. Stillman would like his wife socializing with."

"She seemed so mature and Stepford-like when she was at the hotel."

"Everything about her has always been an act. I don't trust her as far as I can spit."

"She blamed me for Johnny," Ryan whispered. "Why would she do that?"

"I don't know, babe." Forgetting about his surroundings, he lost himself in her warmth. "Jealous, I guess." The pounding of his heart echoed in his ears. His breathing grew labored, and the pressure of her hand against his thigh was more than he could manage under the circumstances. Tilting his head, he brushed his lips against hers, thrilled beyond comprehension when she closed her eyes and participated.

Until a flash interrupted the moment. "What the hell?" Jared blinked, pushing his chair back, wiping his eyes. "Are you nuts?"

"Sorry. Just wanted to get a picture of Ryan for the company picnic. She's fairly photogenic, ya know," Tom said with a phony smile.

Jared had half a mind to deck the guy right there. "I could arrest you for that."

"For taking a picture?" Tom chuckled but took two steps backward.

"If the lady doesn't want her picture taken, it's an invasion of privacy, and I sure as hell didn't want my picture taken." Jared fisted his hands.

"Jared." Ryan stood, placing a firm hand on his

chest. "Let it go." Then she turned to Tom. "If you need a picture, come by my office in the morning."

"Sure." Tom shrugged, then backed away, heading for the door.

"I see the two of you are causing quite a stir. Seems you're living up to your trashy reputation," Lisa said, standing behind Ryan.

"Why, you…" Ryan flew around, hand cocked, ready to strike.

"Whoa there, babe. Not worth it." Jared did his best not to laugh while he grabbed her flying fist. "Can we do something for you, Mrs. Stillman?"

"I should've never come here." She reached in her purse.

Jared moved his hand, ready to whip out his gun. He wouldn't put anything past this woman.

She pulled out a disposable camera and took a picture, sending the flash right in Ryan's face. "I'll ruin you if you do anything to make Lance or myself look bad." Lisa shoved the camera back into her purse and marched toward the door, never looking back.

"Okay, folks. Show's over." Jared glanced around the room at all the staring faces. "Go back to having a good time." He pushed Ryan back in her chair and then sat down himself. "So, why was it so important we meet you here tonight?" Jared lifted his glass in a toast. While his night might have been ruined by too many unanswered questions, that shouldn't ruin it for everyone else.

Chapter Twelve

Ryan lifted her glass. If Jared, Mr. Paranoid, could blow this whole thing off, so could she. "Hey, where are you going?" She glanced at Jared.

"Making sure they left. I'll be right back."

"You shouldn't go alone." She grabbed his hand. "I mean, if you think one of them could be dangerous."

"Fine." He rolled his eyes. "Randy?"

"Yeah, I'm on it." Randy stood up and walked away with Jared.

Ryan let out a sigh of relief, then a chuckle. Did she just dictate to Jared? Maybe he acted like a control freak because he could, and people tended to listen to him.

Stop. She chided herself. Making excuses for the man wouldn't change him. And regardless, he was moving. End of story.

She glanced around the restaurant. The familiar bacon and hamburger smell filled her senses. She loved a good cheeseburger, and she planned on having one tonight. Along with cheese fries.

"You okay?" Penny leaned in, squeezing her thigh. "And what was that all about?"

"Let's just say Jared thinks one of them could be behind all the bizarre things that have been happening to me lately."

"And what do you think?"

"I'd prefer not to think about it. Did you tell him?" Ryan lowered her head, keeping her eyes glued to Penny's.

"Tell who, what?" Penny tried to look like she didn't know what Ryan was talking about.

"To quote my best friend, 'it's me you're talking to.'"

Penny pursed her lips and cocked her head. "I'm scared."

"You've got to tell him."

"I know, I know."

Just then, Jared and Randy strolled in and took their seats. Jared rested his hand on Ryan's neck, making small circular motions with his thumb, sending her pulse soaring.

Chuck clanked his glass as he stood. "I'm not sure why I wanted to do this with all of you around, but here goes nothing." He got down on bended knee and took Penny's hand in his.

Ryan clutched the emerald necklace Jared had given her. A surge of joy, mixed with sadness, trembled inside her body. Penny was about to get it all. Ryan swallowed. She was truly happy for Penny, but part of her wanted to crawl in a hole and hide out for months. Her life would never be so perfect.

"I love you, Penny. Will you marry me?" Chuck wiped his eyes, then pulled out a ring from his pocket. His hand shook while he slid the ring on Penny's finger.

As if on cue, every female at the table let out an "Aww," followed by a sniffle.

Penny just sat there with her mouth gaping open and her chocolate eyes welled with tears.

"Say something, honey, anything." He wiggled her hand.

"You want to marry me?" Penny's voice cracked.

"Penny, I've been in love with you long before I ever had the courage to ask you for a date. I can't imagine spending my life with anyone other than you."

"You loved me before we started dating?" She blinked.

He dropped his head to her hand. "Yeah. Will you please answer my question?"

Penny pulled her hand away and looked at the ring on her finger. "You need to know something first." She took in a deep breath and leaned over and whispered in Chuck's ear.

Chuck fell over onto his butt with a thud. His eyes

were wide with shock, but the smile plastered on his face said it all.

"Did she say no?" Jared whispered in Ryan's ear.

"You're an idiot," Ryan said.

"A baby?" Chuck swallowed. "Oh, my." He blinked a few times, then shifted back to his knees. "The only thing this changes is the reaction my mother's going to have."

"Will it be bad?" Penny asked.

"Not if you think getting pampered and being treated like a queen for the next nine months is bad."

Tears rolled down Penny's cheeks, taking globs of mascara with them. "I thought you'd be upset."

Chuck laughed. "I might be if you don't answer my question." He raised a brow. "So?"

"Yes! Yes! I love you." Penny cupped his face and gave him a kiss that should only be done in private.

Everyone just looked the other way for a few moments until Randy cleared his throat. "Let me be the first to congratulate you." He tossed an ice cube at Chuck. "Now stop that or get a room."

"Hey." Chuck wiped his lips, then sat in his chair, looping a protective arm around the soon-to-be blushing bride.

"You needed a little cooling off. Your public display of affection bordered on lewd behavior." Randy chuckled.

"Oh, please." Penny admired her ring. "This is beautiful. I love it."

"I'm glad," Chuck whispered. He pressed his lips against her forehead.

"Let me see it." Ryan snagged Penny's hand. "Wow." Ryan gazed at the sparkling diamond, her heart hammering in her chest. The ring itself was simple, but the round diamond gave off a colorful glow. Perfect.

"Any morning sickness?" Tammy asked.

"Not yet." Penny slipped her free hand under the table, giving Ryan a gentle squeeze. "I haven't even gone to the doctor yet."

"We should do that soon, right?" Chuck's voice rose.

"We? I like the sound of that." Penny's smile brightened the room.

Ryan glanced over at Jared. His body was rigid, and his smile forced. He'd never been a big supporter of the happily-ever-after life. Never thought it mixed well with his choice of career. She was sure the baby thing had rubbed him the wrong way, considering the broken condom and all. Anytime anyone got married after the fact, he always assumed the woman had trapped the man.

"I can't believe bratty little Pen is going to be a mother. Amazing," Randy said, snapping Ryan out of her trance.

"Thanks a lot." Penny guzzled her water as the waiter brought their appetizers.

Over the course of the next hour, the topic of conversation consisted of babies and weddings. Jared didn't say much, and Ryan could feel the tension in his body. But to his credit, he didn't let anyone else know how uncomfortable the whole thing had to be for him.

After the bill had been paid, Penny said, "I think I want to go home now." She held up her finger and admired her new rock. "This is not something I want to celebrate with the likes of you people anymore."

"Works for me." Chuck jumped up from the table. "Thanks for coming, Randy. Don't stay away so long."

"Anything for you, man. Good luck."

Ryan turned and watched the happy couple sway their way through the crowd, wiping her own tears from her face.

"I'm still hungry. Up for sharing some chocolate cake?" Ryan asked Tammy, not wanting to go home just yet.

"Oh, God. I'd love to."

If Ryan had to rate the evening, she'd give it a ten, as long as she kept the focus off herself and on everyone else.

Randy was working his dream job and doing everything in life he'd set out to do, including getting over a broken heart. Jared laughed and joked with Randy all night and talked about how great this transfer would be for his career. Tammy even piped in about her so-called modeling.

Ryan forced herself to contribute to the conversation. Waving to her brother, she had to admit it felt good to brag about her life, even if it was incomplete.

She wanted more; she wanted it all, and she wanted it with Jared.

Never going to happen.

Lightning filled the sky when Ryan took the coat that Jared offered her as they made their way to his car. The moon danced behind light-gray clouds, but no rain threatened to fall. A clap of thunder echoed behind the mountains.

"I love nights like this," Jared said, sliding his arm under her shirt. His fingers tingled across the small of her back, only adding to the bleakness of her emotions. "Do you think she might have done that on purpose? I mean, she doesn't seem the type."

Ryan glared at him. "I can't believe you." She ducked into the sporty BMW.

"There is such a thing called birth control." Jared got in, then revved the engine, popping the clutch and peeling out of the parking lot. In seconds the car was safely tucked away in the garage, and they were walking toward the main house.

"Which can break," she mumbled.

"You trying to tell me something?" The kitchen light flickered once before illuminating the room. Jared locked the door before kicking off his boots.

"No worries." She swallowed her breath, wishing she could take back her words. Her period wasn't due for a few days.

"Good to know." He rubbed his jaw. "I hope they make it. They do seem like they love each other."

"So, you do believe in love." She closed her eyes. When would she learn?

"Never said I didn't." He stretched and leaned his arm against the doorjamb to the family room, crossing his ankles. "My parents have a great marriage, and they still love each other to the point of being embarrassing."

Love would never happen for him. He was too closed off, no matter what anyone, including her, felt for him.

"They are smitten, aren't they? I miss having them around. I wish they hadn't moved so far away."

"It was time to join the rest of the retirees. They love Arizona, but they're still pissed as hell at me for selling this place."

Ryan tossed her purse over the kitchen chair before looking at the man standing in her way. She really wanted to go upstairs and settle into a bed that didn't belong to him. "Have you thought about renting it?"

"Too much work." He looked around the room. "Besides, this place needs a family."

"So, you believe in family, too." She bit down on her tongue.

"Of course I do." He scowled.

"But not for yourself." She took a tentative step toward him, throwing her insecurities to the lake. "Why?"

He turned his gaze from her and glanced toward the ceiling. "There are a thousand reasons. Mostly because

I don't want to have to answer to anyone. My new job will be dangerous, and I just don't want to have to think about how what I'm doing might affect someone else."

"You're afraid."

He lowered his head and met her eyes with severe coldness.

"Love doesn't have to hurt," she whispered, gliding her hand up his muscled chest. "Not everyone dies."

"Yes, they do." He grabbed her wrist. "And love has nothing to do with my decision." Glaring at her, he pushed her back.

"Bullshit," she said boldly. "But you're right about one thing." She raised a mocking brow. "That kind of life wouldn't mix with you." She turned from him, lifting her mail in her hands.

"Don't walk away from this conversation." His hostile tone startled her, and her mail tumbled to the floor.

"There's no conversation. You've made your choices."

"What the hell is that supposed to mean?"

Filling her lungs, she turned to him. "One has to be willing to put his own heart and insecurities on the line in order to find true love with someone. Not something you're capable of."

His eyes narrowed while his hand rubbed his scruffy face. His inability to come up with a retort told her she had hit the nail on the head.

She lifted the manila envelope and eyed it suspiciously. It was marked "Fragile, Don't Bend," but she hadn't ordered anything recently. She flipped it over and looked back at the postmark. No return address, but it had been mailed from Lake George.

A lump formed in her throat, and fear gripped her heart. She chalked it up to damn paranoia and ripped open the envelope. She peered inside, then reached in and pulled out a photograph. "Oh, my God," she mumbled, staring down at a picture of her and Jared in front of the fireplace in his family room with the words *'I'll get you'* scribbled across her face and "He'll die" over Jared's.

A sudden flash of lightning filled the room followed by a loud clap of thunder. She leaped toward Jared, tossing the pictures to the floor.

"Jesus. What's gotten into...shit." His arms circled her body.

She could feel his body flex with tension as hers trembled out of control. "Why," she cried. "Why me?"

He hugged her so tightly she thought she might suffocate. But she didn't care. If he were to let go, she'd fall to the floor in a heap of nothing. She struggled to contain her tears as he held her in his strong, comforting arms.

"Shhh, now," he whispered, kissing her temple. His hands cupped her cheeks as he drew her face from his neck. "I'll take care of everything."

His eyes bored into her core so deeply she felt for

one brief second they'd become one, then anger surged up into his pupils.

"I'll enjoy beating whoever is behind this within inches of his life, then stuffing his sorry ass in jail." His jaw clenched tight. "I need to call Detective Jenkins. Can you handle this?"

"Do I have a choice?" She glanced back at the scattered pictures. Their moment of pure passion and healing reduced to something dirty. "I'll wait in the family room with some whiskey."

"Stay away from the bottle." He flipped open his cell phone, then pressed his lips against her cheek. "Think about coming to Rochester with me."

Ryan walked mindlessly into the family room, flopped onto the sofa, and turned on the television. Under the circumstances, she didn't have the energy to fight with him.

She blinked as she flipped through the channels and tried to find something interesting to watch while she waited for Detective Jenkins to come and confiscate those nasty pictures. "Oh, my God!" She gasped.

"What?" Jared's footsteps vibrated the floor as he stomped into the family room. "What now?" he said, breathing heavily.

"The cameras." She shook her head, remembering Lisa snapping the stupid thing in her face.

"Already on it, babe."

"Don't call me that!"

He narrowed his eyes. "Is something else bothering you?"

"Does something else need to be bothering me? Isn't it enough that someone has taken dirty pictures of me, stolen my underwear—"

"I get it. Sorry."

A single siren rang out in the background. Jared glanced over his shoulder, then back at her with confusion looming behind his usually confident eyes. "Nick's here."

"Do we really have to show him those pictures?"

"I'm not too keen on the idea, but yeah." He stuffed his hands deep in his pockets and turned. "I'll go let him in."

"My mistakes always come back and bite my ass," she muttered, but watched him pause mid-step and knew he'd heard her. She opened her mouth to say something, but by the time she'd conjured up the nerve, he was gone.

A roll of thunder rumbled through the night air. Lightning flashed in the distance. Still no rain, but the wind howled and the waters of Lake George rushed the shore, hurling its waves over the concrete breakwalls and onto the land.

Jared secured the front porch door and made sure all the windows were locked tight. Glancing out into the swirling dark lake, he rubbed his neck, trying to release the built-up tension from the night's events.

Seeing his and Ryan's private moment captured for some wacko's perversion only intensified his need to protect her. A feeling he wholeheartedly resented. He didn't want to care, but he couldn't leave knowing the moment he turned his back, someone would reach out from behind the shadows and possibly cause her bodily harm.

Yet, if he screwed up this transfer, he'd never be offered a job like this again.

The lights flickered in and out as the tree limbs scratched across the windows. The dark yard appeared to be secure. Nothing out of place. Jared tucked his gun in his jeans and headed up the stairs for the night. He knew full well that Ryan wouldn't be in his bed.

A large boom echoed in the house. It rattled the shutters before the humming of the heater faded and the house went pitch-black.

"Damn," he cursed, then turned and tiptoed to the family room to grab the flashlight. On the way, he checked outside to make sure the other houses had also suffered the same fate. He couldn't help the prickle in the back of his brain from thinking something more sinister was going on. But the street was darker than the night sky.

He slammed the flashlight against his hand and twisted the top. "Great," he muttered. With the help of another bolt of lightning, he fished out some new batteries, then changed them in the dark.

He'd never been afraid of the dark or scared of the boogeyman, but tonight, the eeriness of his own home haunted his soul. A shadow scurried across the top of the stairs. Goose bumps appeared on his arms for the first time in years.

Pressing his back against the wall, he reached for his weapon. With silent steps, he crept toward the top. A faint glow emanated from his bedroom. Staying on the opposite wall, he kept his gun pointed toward the ceiling as he stepped in front of the doorway.

The sexiest set of legs this side of the Mississippi graced his eyes. "Damn it, Ryan." He chuckled when she gasped and fumbled with the candle in her hands. Her chestnut hair bounced wildly against her shoulders.

"Damn me? Geez, put that thing down." Her doe-like eyes danced in the flicker of the orange glow. "If I were a cat, all of my lives would've been used up in one swoop."

He stepped into his room, rested his gun on the nightstand, and turned to her. "Aren't you cold?" The oversized shirt she wore didn't hide her curves in the semidarkness of the room. Her puckered nipples begged for his attention.

"Not really." She rubbed her temple. "I've always been afraid of the dark."

"Me, too."

She laughed. "Right."

"Come on." He reached out and took the candle.

"I'm not sleeping with you." She dug her heels into the floorboards.

"Who knows how long the power will be out, and it's damn cold. No sex, just sleep. Besides, you came looking for me."

She let out a loud breath. "I'm serious."

"I'm cold. Now come on." He nudged her.

"You stay on your side, got it?" She leaped across the bed, her shirttail flipping up in the air, showing off her...his... "Hey, those are my boxers." He set the candle down and reached out for an ankle but pulled back as she tucked her legs under the blanket.

"Your shirt, too."

"Really?" Slipping off his clothes, he glided between the sheets, careful not to touch her.

"I stole it from you years ago."

"That's weird." He rolled toward her, tucking his hands under his cheek.

"Not so weird. But I suppose it's a little odd that I still have it. Honestly, it's my favorite nightshirt, and not because it belonged to you. So don't go getting a swelled head or anything."

"That could never happen." He cleared his throat. "I'm really sorry about those pictures and having to show them to Nick."

Her finger traced a path down his cheek and jawline before landing on his chest. "You didn't take them."

"I still feel responsible." The blood pounding in his ears drowned out his own good judgment. Her fingers moved through his chest hair, driving him insane. He couldn't be held accountable for anything with her teasing him like this.

"Just catch the asshole."

"I'm working on it, ba—Ryan."

"Thanks." Her hand dropped to the mattress. He could barely see her eyes, but the crisp blue color would be forever imprinted on his brain. "You're not going to be able to stay over there, are you?"

"Sure I can." He swallowed, trying to slow his racing pulse. "But you can't."

"Oh, yes, I can." For the next few minutes she tossed and turned while he remained still.

He couldn't make the first move. It wouldn't be right. Besides, if she came to him, he could justify it like he always did. It was just sex, and she'd asked for it, not him. Somehow he thought that might make it better.

"Damn you," she whispered, slipping into his arms. "Why do I want you? I don't even like you."

"Excuse me?" He brushed back her silky hair, letting the strands tangle in his fingers.

"You are so not my type. You're arrogant, cocky, controlling, and overbearing. Besides, you don't like me that way, either."

In the darkness, his eyes met her gaze. Fear of the unknown loomed behind her usual confident stare.

"You're right, I don't." He continued to search her eyes, forcing the decision on her. "I think you're a beautiful woman and an amazing person, but I don't want anything other than physical satisfaction. If you don't want that, roll over and go to sleep."

"You won't think badly of me if I choose not to sleep?" The heat of her body sent his heart thumping against his chest as she snuggled in next to him. Her hands glided across his body, touching all the places she knew drove him insane with passion.

"I just want you to know where we stand." He kept his hands to himself in a desperate act to keep from completely ravishing her body.

She cupped his face and leaned in. Her breath smelled like wintergreen. "I'd really hate you if you stayed here because of me, again."

Unable to contain his desire anymore, he grabbed her butt and heaved her to him. "Nothing." He narrowed his eyes, hoping to drive the point home. "And I mean *nothing* will stand in my way of this promotion."

His pulse stopped momentarily when she smiled. He had expected her to falter, gasp, or try to hide her emotions. Not react as if all the pressure had been taken off her, like she'd actually been worried he might be falling for her.

Never, he chided himself, before roughly taking her mouth with his. "Whoa," he said as she flipped him on his back, removing his boxers in a matter of seconds.

Somewhere in the midst of passion, he realized she was no different than him, using his body for her self-fulfillment. Somehow, it changed the experience for him.

She wasn't going to try to change his mind. She didn't want anything other than sex.

Later, he shifted carefully in his bed, not wanting to disturb the naked beauty tangled between his legs and arms. Staring at the nothingness of the ceiling, he let his senses fill with her peachy smell. The softness of her supple skin felt like rose petals against his.

The red glow of the sun peeking from the mountaintops pushed through the windows. He'd have to put an end to this constant poor judgment. Nothing good could come from using her, even if she wanted to be used. Worse, she was using him.

The phone rang and Ryan jumped, bumping him in the face.

"Damn it. You got my nose again." His eyes watered while he fumbled for the phone.

"Oh, God." She chuckled. "I'm so sorry."

He lifted the phone from its cradle, then hit the talk button. "Yeah, right," he muttered. "Blake here."

"Oh, like I did it on purpose in my sleep," she said.

"Is that my sister?" Pat yelled.

Jared swallowed. "Pat? It's five in the morning. What's wrong?"

"Marci's in labor."

"Is she okay?" Jared rubbed the back of his neck. "Maybe Ryan should come with me to Rochester."

"No!" Ryan snapped. She covered her mouth with her hand.

Jared's heart stopped for a moment, silence on the other end. "Pat, you there?"

"I'll deal with you later. Put my sister on the phone."

Jared closed his eyes, then handed the phone to Ryan. "He wants to talk with you."

"Great." She yanked the phone from his hands. "What?"

For the first time since he was a kid, Jared felt like he just got caught with his hand in the cookie jar.

"You take care of your wife and I'll take care of myself. I'll let you know what I decide when I come see you at the hospital." She clicked the phone off and chucked it onto the bed. "Damn, I've got a loud mouth."

"Won't argue that point," Jared said.

She shot him a sideways glance. "What are your plans today?"

"I've got some paperwork, but otherwise I'm free until I leave for Rochester."

"I have to go in to work for a few hours, then do you mind if we stop at the hospital on the way out?" She threw back the covers and jumped from the bed, snatching his robe and tossing it around her naked body.

"Out of town? As in, you're coming with me?"

"Only because I refuse to horn in on Penny and Chuck since they just got engaged, and I can't listen to my brother's lectures. I guess you're the lesser of three evils."

"Oh, babe, I'm evil all right." He leaped from the bed and marched to the bathroom, trying to figure out why he was so mad. It wasn't like he should be upset. She was coming with him, but only for safety reasons. And that's all he cared about.

Chapter Thirteen

Ryan fisted her hands, then rolled them across her lower back, staring at the clutter she'd let collect on her desk. Nothing she did could ease her constant fear that someone was watching her. Or rid her of the memory of Jared's touch. Last night had been a true test of her acting ability. It honestly amazed her that she'd been able to pull it off.

Jared believed she didn't care about anything other than sex.

But she hadn't expected Marci to go into labor, tying up her brother for days. Last Ryan checked, Marci still hadn't given birth. Between the horrid pictures, three more hang-ups, and no real answers, the only smart choice would be to take a mini-vacation. With Jared. Wonderful.

Ryan tapped her pencil against some papers, but she

was unable to concentrate on anything other than those photographs and Tom and Lisa. Tom had been carrying an expensive camera and looked like he knew what he was doing. Lisa's camera was one of those disposable ones, but you could still blow up the negatives. Eddy owned a camera. Then again, so did just about everyone, including Jared. Her stepfather had a fascination for pornography, but she didn't ever remember him taking pictures.

A knock on her door startled her, sending her pencil tumbling to the floor. "Tom." Jared had warned her to stay clear of Tom. Jared went so far as to call Rick and ask him to keep tabs on Tom.

She'd been pissed and let Jared know it, but she knew he was right. She needed to be careful.

"I owe you an apology. I had a little too much to drink last night and I think it got the better of me," he said, his tone remorseful.

She kept her eyes from locking with his. "I didn't like you sneaking up on me like that."

"Again, I'm sorry." He remained in the doorway and looked genuine, but that didn't make the goose bumps on the back of her neck go away. "The camera is digital, so I deleted the ones I took of you."

"Well, thanks." She didn't believe him, but it didn't matter. "Do you take a lot of pictures?"

He smiled. "It's a hobby."

"What do you like to take pictures of?" She hoped her voice didn't sound panicked.

"Mostly people. I love action shots."

She studied the man standing before her. He wasn't very tall, nor was he muscular, but he did carry himself with a sense of confidence. He sort of looked like one of those successful dorks who'd made a million. He didn't look like some guy who went around lurking in the shadows.

Then again, Eddy didn't seem like a guy who liked to masturbate while he watched women parade around in their underwear.

"I heard about your car." He stepped into her office. "I can't believe someone actually shot at it."

"Me neither," she admitted.

"Some of us can't help but wonder if whoever is doing this is really after that trooper friend of yours. Cops make enemies all the time."

"I'm sure they do," she said, checking the time. "I can't imagine what I've ever done to make someone hate me that much." She prayed her voice didn't shake like her trembling legs.

"I know this isn't my place, but like I said, maybe it's the company you're keeping." He tossed his hands to the sides. "It's not just me. Other people think that, too."

"Great," she said under her breath. What would those people think if they saw those damn pictures? "I have to let the police handle it." She opened her middle drawer, searching for a pen, then slammed it shut. "I've got a lot of work to do before I take off today. Thanks for your concern."

"I heard you were taking some time off. Going anywhere?"

Her pulse hammered so fast spots danced around her head. Placing both hands on the desktop, she swallowed and forced her eyes to connect with his. "My free time isn't any of your business. But if you must know, I'm just going to be hanging out and working on getting my house back in order." Lying had never come easily to her, but lately she'd been the queen of falsehood.

"Well, I'm handy with a paintbrush and pretty good with a hammer." He winked. "If you want my help, just give a shout." He turned on his heel and in seconds was gone.

She blinked a few times, shaking out her hands. Hopefully she'd be able to relax a little in Rochester. Just then her cell phone buzzed. Her brother's number flashed across the caller ID.

"Hi, Pat! Did she have the baby?"

"It's a boy," he said. "A big one. Not sure Marci's talking to me right now."

"How big? And what did you name him? Come on, spill." All the tension she'd built up in her body over the course of the last few days melted away at the thought of a new life entering the world.

"Nine pounds, eight ounces, and his name is Nolan Jared O'Connor," Pat said proudly. "It was amazing. I was there the entire time, and Marci...God, I didn't think I could love her any more."

"I can't wait to meet my nephew." She relaxed back into her chair, letting the happy tears roll down her cheeks.

"I don't have to stay at the hospital the whole time."

"But you want to. And you should." And she should go to Rochester with Jared. She'd be safer and maybe it would give the police a chance to catch the guy sneaking around Jared's empty house. And no one besides her boss and brother knew she was leaving town. Not even Penny knew right now.

"Are you okay?"

She swiped the tears from her eyes. "I'm fine." Hearing footsteps down the hall, she squared her shoulders and tried to peer out of her office. "As soon as...speak of the devil. Jared's here." She waved Jared into her office, trying not to gawk at him. He wore a pink golf shirt and black dress pants, and he looked like a walking advertisement for the pro shop. "Marci had a boy."

"That's great," Jared said. A small smile appeared on his paling face.

"Can we come see the baby?" Ryan asked her brother.

"See you in a little while. I love you, sis."

"I love you too, big brother." She hooked the phone back on her hip, then looked up at Jared. "Let's hit the road." For the first time in a week, she didn't feel like the world had spun out of control, tossing her to the curb. "We don't have to stay long, but I have to go meet my nephew. They named him Nolan, and do you know what his middle name is?"

"I don't want to know," Jared muttered, then uttered a curse. "I thought he was joking."

"Let's go, Godfather." Ryan shook her head. Nothing could dampen her joy, not even a sour-faced Jared.

The entire ride to the hospital, Jared gripped the steering wheel. Over the years, he and Pat had been to hell and back together. Jared didn't begrudge the man his happiness or his child. But there was a small piece of Jared that couldn't help wondering where he'd be today if things had been different.

"What floor?" Jared asked as they got into the elevator. He hated hospitals. They smelled like death and sadness covered by antiseptic. Like having a clean environment where people fought for their lives would somehow make untimely death better.

"Five." Ryan reached out and poked the button a few times.

"That's not going to make the elevator go faster."

She rubbed her hands together while excitement sparkled in her eyes. "I can't help it." Her smile brightened the already well-lit space and melted his heart.

The elevator bounced at the fifth floor, then a bell rang as the doors began to push back. Ryan wiggled her way through the small opening, then took off in the direction of Marci's room as if she were running a marathon and the finish line was only inches ahead.

He shoved his hands deep in his pockets, following a few steps behind.

"Here." When she glanced back at him, her hair bounced playfully at her shoulders. "Pat? Marci?" She tapped the half-open door.

"Hey there." Pat greeted his sister with a big bear hug, then reached out to Jared, yanking him in the room with his handshake. "Get in here."

"I'm sure Marci doesn't want me here. I'll just hang out in the waiting room." Jared's pulse beat frantically at the sight of Marci holding her infant son.

"You will not," Marci said. "I can't believe how much he looks like Pat."

"I don't think Pat was that big." Ryan reached out and rubbed her hand across the baby's red hair. "And I think he was bald."

Jared's son had been bald, but he remembered the softness of his skin. The way he smelled and how fragile he looked. Those images he'd never be able to get rid of. No matter how hard he tried.

"Pat said the labor was..." Ryan began.

But Jared didn't hear the rest of the words. Visions

of a tiny casket being lowered into the ground engulfed his memory. His son's mother nowhere to be found. His body flexed, but he felt like his legs would buckle at any moment.

"Jared?" A firm squeeze of his bicep jolted him from his nightmare. "Marci asked you if you wanted to hold your godson."

"No," he said quickly.

"Damn you," Pat muttered, taking a step toward him.

"You can do this, Jared. Trust me," Ryan said in a soft tone.

"Trust you?" He glared at her.

"You expect me to trust you when it comes to my safety. Well, I expect you to trust me about this." She kicked the door closed with her foot, then glided across the room. With ease, she lifted the baby into her arms, kissed his forehead, and whispered something.

Jared stepped back, bumping into the wall.

He reached for the constricting button on the top of his shirt. Perspiration beaded across his forehead.

"Hey there, Nolan. Let's go meet your godfather. The man who gave you your middle name," Ryan said.

"Ryan, please don't," Jared whispered, rubbing his sweaty hands across his tense thighs. But she ignored his plea, lifting the baby up and pressing the tiny warm body against his chest.

Nolan's hands flew up in the air, whacking Jared in the chin.

"It's a startle reflex. He's fine." Ryan smiled widely, beaming with love and pride.

"I know what it is," he grumbled, raising his arms and nestling Nolan's head in the crook of his elbow.

Nolan sucked in his lower lip, then gasped a hearty breath and let it out with a whiney sigh.

Jared swallowed. He stared down at the precious bundle of life. He hadn't held a baby since Johnny passed, and while part of his heart soared with joy, another part died again. "He's…cute," he said, trying to relax.

"Like Pat," Marci laughed.

"Nothing cute about him." Jared breathed slowly, using his training to keep as calm as possible. Feeling all eyes on him, Jared glanced around the room.

Ryan wiped a tear that dribbled down her face. Pat had seated himself on the edge of the bed next to his wife, dipping his head against hers and looking back at him with brotherly admiration.

As if on cue, Nolan squirmed.

"Okay, here's your Auntie Ryan." Jared fumbled as he handed the baby back to Ryan.

"Oh, my, God. I can't believe he's here." Ryan snuggled Nolan in close. She deserved everything. Everything Jared couldn't give her.

For the next hour, Jared fetched water, soda, coffee, and junk food. Anything to get out of the room of happiness. He couldn't help but remember how different things were with Lisa when Johnny was born.

Jared hadn't been there when his son entered the world, but he was there when he left.

"I'm sorry, but we really should hit the road," he said, trying not to sound too impatient. "Can I have a word with you, Pat?" Jared turned and stepped into the hallway. "Rory's going to be working on the carriage house, along with his girlfriend."

"I heard she's some kind of private eye or something."

Jared chuckled. "Something like that. Anyway, we want to make it look like Ryan's there. Only her boss knows she's coming with me."

"I get to stay here at night, but tomorrow I've got to go to the bar for a few hours."

Jared rubbed his jaw, then slid his hand across his neck. He didn't think Marci and the baby would be in jeopardy. But if George was behind these attacks, who's to say he wouldn't turn on his other stepchild? Jared pulled out Frank Harmon's business card. "This kid's really good, and he'd do anything to help out. I've already asked him to keep an eye on things. He can come and plant himself here in the hallway while you're gone."

"Are you sure? I don't want to put anyone out." Pat shoved the card into his pocket. "But I'm worried."

"So am I," Jared admitted. "But Harmon's already got instructions to be at your beck and call. Let's go, Ry."

Anger quickly replaced Pat's concerned look. He gritted his teeth, then said, "That's my sister."

Jared nodded but couldn't form any words.

"You make sure nothing happens to her." Pat glanced over his shoulder, then back, taking a step closer. "I don't know what's going on with you two, and I don't want to know. But if you leave her heartbroken, I'll hunt you down."

"Oh, get over yourself," Ryan said, slapping her hand down on Pat's shoulder. "Not to be blunt, but I'd have to think of him as something other than a Neanderthal to have my heart broken. Now *Nolan* on the other hand." Patting her chest, she rolled her eyes. "He's a heartbreaker."

"Watch your back," Pat said.

"I'll see you in two days." Ryan planted a kiss on her brother's cheek, then looped her arm through Jared's.

Still seething over being pushed into things he didn't want and being called a Neanderthal, Jared continued to frown all the way to the parking garage.

"See, holding Nolan wasn't all that bad." She smiled at him, slipping into the car.

It had been damn near impossible. "Don't do anything like that to me again." He still felt the cold chill lingering in his bones from years ago.

"My God. What's wrong with you?" Tucking in her leg, she reached for the door handle. "Can't you just be happy for them?" She slammed the door.

Happy for them? They had nothing to do with it. “For the record, I’m not a Neanderthal.” He turned the key and revved the engine while adjusting the stereo. While he loved his truck, there was nothing like the feeling of a sports car.

She swatted his hand, turning the volume back down. “You can’t possibly be mad at me for that?”

“That and forcing Nolan in my arms when you know how I feel.” He popped the clutch and backed out. “I’m a big boy, and I can make my own decisions.”

She burst out laughing.

After paying the parking attendant, he glanced at her. She’d covered her mouth, but laughter still managed to seep out.

He shook his head, then headed for the highway. “I don’t see what’s so funny.”

“Welcome to my world.”

He shifted gears, then swerved out into the passing lane. “I didn’t appreciate you telling me what to do and how to handle my…oh.” He bit back a smile. “Well, I’m not a Neanderthal.”

She fidgeted in her seat, shifting her left leg behind her right. The knee-length skirt she’d worn rode high up on her bare thigh.

Resting his hand on the gearshift, he focused his eyes back on the road.

“You think women belong at home, in the kitchen, waiting on their man, doing as they’re told.”

"I do not." He furrowed his brow, giving her a quick glance.

"If you were to get married, you'd expect your wife to stay at home and do as you commanded."

Tapping his finger on her exposed skin, he said, "First, I'm never getting married again. Second, if I were, I wouldn't want a woman who was incapable of thinking for herself."

"That's such bull. You constantly bark out orders, expecting the world to do exactly what you say."

The softness of her skin was just too much to pass up. Opening his hand wide, he smoothed his palm across her thigh. "When it comes to my job, which I'm damn good at, well then, yes, I expect people to do it my way."

"I don't work with you or for you, and you expect me to do things your way."

"Because some psycho is threatening you." He squeezed her leg.

"What about when I went to buy my car? You got all controlling and forced your help on me." She gave him a playful poke.

"Car salesmen are the scum of the earth. I just didn't want you to get taken for a ride."

"Do you think I'm smart?"

He glanced out at the leafless trees swaying in the wind along the side of the thruway. Being smart had nothing to do with it. "Of course."

"Don't you think I'm capable of handling a simple negotiation?"

"Buying a car isn't simple," he mumbled, speeding out into the passing lane and flying by a few cars.

"If you do your research, check out pricing, and don't buy the first car you look at, it's not so hard. Besides, if you're aware that some salespeople are idiots who try to take advantage of you, then you learn to avoid them."

"Why are we talking about this?" Looping his finger in his shirt, he rolled his neck.

"Because you don't think you're a controlling shit."

"You're young and inexperienced."

"I've been living on my own since I was seventeen. I don't need you to handle things for me."

"There is nothing wrong with asking for help," he said, then blew out a breath. For the first time since arguing with his father, he felt like he was about to lose. He didn't like to lose.

"As I recall, I hadn't asked for help. Remember when you asked me why I date the type of guys that I do?"

Aware of the trooper stationed a few miles ahead, he slowed and moved to the right lane. Then he pushed the insane jealous thoughts from his head.

"I want to be with someone who will see me as his equal on all levels. I want someone who will ask for my opinion about things. Value my ideas, my career. I want respect."

"Are you implying I don't respect you?" he snapped.

"In some ways I suppose you don't."

The last thing Jared wanted was to get pulled over and then have to pull out his badge in front of Ryan. She'd just accuse him of using his power. He stifled his urge to hit the pedal and bring the car to ninety. "Then you don't know me very well." He pulled his hand from her thigh and gripped the steering wheel.

"I know you mean well, but it's just that it comes across like a dictatorship. No one will ever want to be with you when you act like that."

"That's a good thing," he said behind a clenched jaw. "I much prefer to be alone anyway."

"Wow," Ryan exclaimed, stepping into the lobby of the Rutherford Hotel. "This is beautiful."

"I was told it's one of the nicest in the area." Jared approached the front desk, glancing over his shoulder. "I only reserved one room. It's a suite with a sofa bed. I'll take the pullout, or I could get a second room if you'd prefer." His face showed no emotion, but his eyes carried the hurt she'd caused him.

"One room is fine," she said, turning from him. She'd never noticed the vulnerability behind his cool exterior before. She hadn't meant to insult him, just to show him she was a capable human being. And he wasn't always right.

"All set." He took both their bags in his hands.

Silently, she followed him to their room. When he pushed back the door, he stepped in, not giving her the option of going first. Not something she was used to from him. She didn't want him to stop being a gentleman, just from telling her what to do.

"Oh, my." She closed her eyes and inhaled. Any hotel she'd ever stayed in always smelled musty or like wet laundry. This room smelled like a mix of fresh-cut spring flowers and cinnamon swirl bread. She blinked, then kicked off her shoes, feeling the plush carpet on her bare feet. "This place is amazing. Nicer than the resort I work for."

He shrugged, then plopped down on the couch and reached for the remote. "I've got meetings all morning, then we've been invited to an early dinner with a guy I'll be doing some training with. His girlfriend will be joining us. I accepted because I thought it might be fun."

Ryan's stomach churned over. She stood in the middle of a magnificent room. She knew he wouldn't have made such extravagant arrangements if it weren't for her having to tag along. "It does sound like fun," she said, hoping to ease his sour mood.

He lifted his bag onto the couch, then pulled a pamphlet from it and tossed it on the coffee table, before propping up his feet. "I took the liberty of signing you up for a facial, massage, and some other spa treatments this hotel offers." He glanced at her with narrow eyes. "I was just trying to be nice because I'd be gone all day, but I suppose that gesture is just me being controlling."

"It's both," she said as she took a tentative step toward him when his feet hit the floor.

"I need a drink. You want to come?"

She shook her head.

"I won't be long." He marched past her without a second glance. The walls didn't rattle when he pulled the door shut with a slam.

"I might have been rude, but I didn't deserve that." Snatching the brochure from the table, she decided on a long hot bath.

The bathroom had to be twice as big as the one in Jared's house. She suspected the tile was marble, and it felt silky and expensive under her fingers. Silver faucets set off the creamy tan and brown swirl countertops, and beautiful paintings hung on the walls as if she were standing in a museum.

The bath soothed her aching body but did nothing for her aching heart. She loved Jared, even though he had to be in control of everything. Considering their relationship the last few days, she couldn't help but wonder if maybe she'd subconsciously tried to change him. But why would she want to change him? Was he really all that bad?

She'd keep the spa treatments, and somehow she'd find a way to make it up to him. She didn't want him to move under these circumstances. She didn't want him to move period.

"Oh, you stupid woman," she chided herself, tossing back the covers to the bed. She left the door open so she'd hear him when he came in. Not that she'd be able to sleep until she knew he'd returned anyway.

She shouldn't have forced him to hold Nolan. He'd hold him eventually, when he was ready. She tossed and turned but was unable to settle her body into sleep. She stiffened the moment she heard the main door click open.

Time to fake it.

Chapter Fourteen

Jared couldn't even manage getting drunk. He'd ordered a beer, but hadn't taken more than two sips. Since when did he care so much about what one person thought about his actions? He'd only been acting like a gentleman. Not to mention some of the incidents she'd mentioned on the car ride over hadn't even been his idea, but Pat's.

He leaned against the doorjamb to the bedroom, listening to her breathe. She definitely wasn't sleeping. "I'm sorry I acted like such an ass," he heard himself say. "I know you're not sleeping."

The form tucked under the sheets shifted. "I'm trying to."

"Will you at least let me apologize?" Hesitantly, he eased himself toward the bed. The firm mattress gave way to his weight. "I took out my issues with Johnny and his death on you."

Adjusting the pillow, punching it with her hand, she sat up and brushed her untamed hair from her face. "I shouldn't have pushed."

"You thought you were doing what was best for me. I can't fault you for that since I do the same thing to you." Feeling a little more confident, he scooted himself to the head of the bed and rested his cheek against the soft feathery pillow. "But for the record, your brother made me go help you buy that car."

"Excuse me?"

His eyes had adjusted to the darkness, and her soft features melted away his raw emotions. Everything about her made him feel like he'd lost control of his world. "Pat didn't think you could handle it. I tried to tell him you were fine, that you'd done all the necessary research, but he wouldn't let it go."

"I'm not sure how to respond to that."

"Just wanted you to know I'm not the only control nut."

"You mean to tell me that you let me ream you out that day, in front of half that dealership? And it wasn't even your idea?"

He chuckled. "Following you there wasn't my idea. But I did do my share of spying."

"What kind of spying?" A wave of emotions washed over her face. Too many for him to try to figure out.

"I sort of peeked at all your printouts, then pumped you for information. You were only twenty-one. It wasn't that I didn't think you could do it; I was just checking up on you."

"Prom night?" she questioned, turning toward him. A hint of fascination glimmered behind her cool blue eyes. "Your idea or my brother's?"

"Both," he admitted. "I only wanted to hang out and wait for you to get home. Your brother made me follow you."

"How does my pansy-ass brother make you do anything?" Her eyes were wide. She truly looked baffled.

"I suppose he played upon my sense of honor and duty. Not to mention he reminded me of our prom night."

She rolled her eyes. "The two of you made parts of my life miserable."

"Only because we care." He swallowed. Caring about her wasn't an issue. Feelings of love in the forever kind of way were beginning to grate on his nerves. He didn't want it, and he'd fight it. Even if he knew she was the kind of woman he could love. The kind of woman who'd be able to hold her own with him.

"I'm sorry if I made you feel unappreciated today. It's just that sometimes you're so overbearing, you make me feel inadequate."

He glided his hand across her firm belly. Unable to resist the fresh scent of roses on a warm spring day, he snuggled closer. "I don't mean to, honestly. I think you're an amazing woman."

"Thanks." Her gentle fingers roamed his forearm. "And I want to keep those appointments tomorrow. That really was very thoughtful of you."

He lowered his head and lifted a playful brow. "Not trying to be overbearing, but just because we're not in Lake George doesn't mean you can let your guard down."

"I know." The covers shifted and exposed more of her bare skin. She cupped his face. Her eyes filled with determination. "I'd like to make love now."

His breath hitched. Not the response he'd expected. He'd been more prepared for another argument. When his mouth opened, only a faint groan escaped.

"But," she said.

"But what?" His body had responded to her proposal.

"This is goodbye."

"What?" He blinked. It wasn't like he'd never see her again.

"I mean this will be the last time."

"Why? I won't be completely packed up and gone until next week. We like each other and the sex is good." Did he just say that? What a fucking moron.

"I don't want you thinking that you can come back for a visit and I will let you in my bed. My life doesn't work that way."

"I wouldn't expect that." He scowled, even though

part of him would enjoy that. His heart pounded unevenly at the insane thoughts that bounced about in his head. "I just thought it wouldn't end until I left." He held his breath. There was no future, no hope. He'd be miserable if he let her completely into his heart. It wasn't love he needed. He needed the thrill and excitement of police work. Not his present desk job.

"I don't regret being with you. I think it has been good for both of us. You've gotten a chance to see I'm all grown up, capable of taking care of myself. I think you needed that."

"I suppose." He rubbed his jaw, trying to organize his thoughts and push down any unreasonable ones. Remaining indifferent would be the only way he'd survive leaving her.

"And I've seen a different side of you. I used to worry that you were lonely. I thought you needed a woman to love you, to make you whole. Now I see that people don't have to have the happily ever after to be happy."

"No, they don't." Especially him. "But that doesn't mean I don't care about you or want to be with you." He adjusted himself on his elbow. "Just because my relationships aren't forever doesn't mean I don't care about the women I've been with. It ends because it's the right time."

"This is the right time." Something flirtatious illuminated her eyes. Something told him to push the issue.

"I don't think this is the right time or place to end this. We say goodbye at home, next week."

"As long as you understand it ends there. Affair over."

"Works for me."

Her hand slipped under his shirt and down the back of his pants, squeezing his ass and heaving him toward her. "Then get naked, or I'll have to call the cops."

"You're a crazy woman, you know that?" He grabbed her and pressed his already rigid body on top of hers.

"No crazier than you." Her legs shifted, allowing his body to settle in all the right spots.

"Promise me I won't hurt you." He fanned his thumbs over the lines her frown created on her forehead.

"You say you're immune to emotional relationships and..." She bit down on her lower lip. "And please don't get mad."

"Why would I get mad?" The muscles in his back relaxed at her tender touch.

"Because you're not the right kind of man for me, so you can't possibly hurt me, because I don't want that with you. Right now, I just want to be thoroughly satisfied." Her beaming smile sent his usually logical brain into a fury of panicked emotions.

"Mutual gratification," he whispered, pressing his lips against her soft earlobe. Getting lost in her body would help defuse the bomb of emotions about to explode inside his mind and heart.

He never expected to fall in love with her. Careful to hide his feelings, he ripped at her clothes with feverish intent. He needed to settle himself inside her, hopefully lose himself in the act of sex and forget about the pain lovemaking would cause his heart.

In the darkness of the night, her sensual eyes locked with his in a long tender moment of understanding. She had to feel it, too. The connection he had to her, as if she were made just for him, and he for her.

Slipping the condom in place, he pushed back all the craziness jumping inside his mind and then in one powerful thrust buried himself deep inside her. The more he tried to make the moment about the physical act, the more her body responded to his, like she belonged to him. Before he knew what happened, she'd taken complete control, and he feared he'd be in love with her forever.

There would be no going back and no denying his love for the one woman who had always been right in front of him, who he could never have. Not even now.

"Beautiful, Ryan," he whispered, feeling her release clutch at him as she moaned his name softly. "My beautiful Ryan." He let his own climax spill out. He buried his face in the crook of her neck, not allowing himself to feel anything but the numbness he'd need to get over her.

His job would demand it.

His heart would require it.

The following morning, Ryan forced her body to relax while the green mask on her face tightened and the cool compress on her eyes hopefully reduced the puffiness caused by a good cry. The moment Jared had closed the hotel door, she hadn't been able to hold the tears at bay any longer.

Normally she prided herself on making good decisions, considering all the obstacles that had been put in her path, but she'd really screwed up this time.

"Relax, honey," the beautician said. "Your hands are so tense." She rubbed the top of Ryan's hands with gentle circular strokes.

"I'm trying." Ryan took in a deep cleansing breath. "And I'm really enjoying this."

The beautician gently shook Ryan's hands. "I'm going to wrap your hands in a warm mud pack for a few minutes while we remove the face mask."

"Oh, that's nice." Ryan moaned while her hands and wrists were dipped in thick, hot liquid. "I could get used to this."

"You've never done this before, have you?"

Once the compress had been removed, Ryan blinked her eyes, adjusting to the dim lights. "I treat myself to manicures and pedicures every so often, but that's it."

"That's a start."

"What's your name?" Ryan asked, realizing how much she missed Penny.

"Cindy. Mind if I ask you a question?" Cindy continued to remove the mask with a warm washcloth.

"Ask away."

"My son's name is Ryan. How'd a beautiful young woman like yourself end up with that name?" Cindy gave Ryan's face one more washing. "Don't get me wrong, I love the name."

"But it's very much a man's name." Ryan adjusted herself in the bedlike chair so she could see Cindy better. "It's my mother's maiden name. She'd been so sure that I was going to be a boy. After a very long labor, she had to have an emergency C-section. When she came to, she filled out all the paperwork for the birth certificate before anyone could inform her she'd had a girl. She just never changed it."

Cindy sat across from her with a genuine smile. "That's a great story. What's your middle name if you don't mind me asking?"

Ryan laughed out loud. "Shamus."

"Oh, my." Cindy's large brown eyes widened.

"It's not so bad. Most people don't know my middle name, and I usually lie and tell them it's Suzanne or something."

"It's a beautiful Irish name."

"Yeah, for a boy."

Cindy's smile faded as she studied Ryan. "Why are you so sad? A sexy young woman such as yourself should have the world in her hands, not the weight of it in her eyes."

"It's not that I'm sad so much, but my life is changing," Ryan admitted, then let herself get a good whiff of the aromatherapy candles. She couldn't place the scents, but they were soothing. She could feel the swelling around her eyes reducing already. "My best friend is moving away."

"Does that friend happen to be the man in your life?" Cindy removed the wrapping from one of Ryan's hands, cleaned it off, then slathered it with cool vanilla lotion.

"I wouldn't call him the man in my life, but someone who's helped me a lot. Sometimes I think I owe him my life." She blinked, realizing her biggest mistake. Jared didn't see her as anything other than the one who survived. His lovemaking was out of a strange sense of duty. Jared always gave Ryan what he thought she wanted.

She'd made it clear she wanted him. Even if for only one or two nights.

"Then it's best you let him go. Owing someone doesn't make for a good relationship."

"He's not mine to let go," Ryan said softly.

"You seem like an intelligent woman, and you're drop-dead gorgeous. You'll find the right man." Cindy wiggled Ryan's hand and ran her index finger up her palm. "See this line? It's your love line."

"You read palms?"

"I read a book on it once. I really don't know too much."

"Well, tell me what you do know." Ryan shifted in her chair. She didn't believe in stuff like this, but at the moment, she didn't care. "What does it mean?"

"You have a strong heart. And the man who loves you will need an equally strong heart."

Ryan tried not to frown. She didn't think Jared's heart could be fixed.

"This man is not who you'd expect. You've avoided his type and only recently opened your heart to him." Cindy glanced up. "But you have to let him find his own way."

Feeling a little taken in, since Ryan had basically given Cindy enough information to form this kind of opinion, she tried to pull her hand away.

"Love is a funny thing. Even when it's meant to be, it doesn't always work that way."

"What does that mean?" Ryan asked, not hiding her annoyance.

"This line shows that you have a lot of love in your heart and it's destined to find love in return. It's not just about your soulmate, but friendships too. See all the branches? Lots of love. And it's longer than most because I suspect that you've already endured a great deal in your life." Cindy rinsed off Ryan's other hand, then quickly rubbed some lotion on it before studying the lines.

"You love because you don't know any other way.

Whether or not this man can hold on will be up to him, but you won't go without. Love is something you need to share. It's a part of who you are."

"Are you trying to tell me that no matter what, I'll fall in love, get married, and have kids?"

"No." Cindy wrapped Ryan's hands in a warm cloth again. "What I'm trying to tell you is regardless of what happens, your heart will mend and find love again. It's in your nature."

"I'm a sap," Ryan muttered.

"Join the club." Cindy lifted Ryan's foot and slipped it into a tub of warm water. "My heart has been stomped on more times than I care to admit." She held up her palm, showing the same long line. "I've been in love so many times, it hurts."

"Always the wrong guy?"

Cindy shook her head. "My first husband was killed in a car crash two weeks after we married. He never even knew I was pregnant."

"I'm so sorry."

"I'm not. I mean I'm sorry he died, but I have a beautiful son. I named him after his father." Cindy smiled; her eyes glistened with joy.

"Ryan?"

Cindy chuckled. "My second husband was killed by friendly fire in Iraq. We had two kids together. Lenny and Robby."

"Is there a man in your life now?" Ryan wanted to kick herself for asking.

"There is." Cindy lifted Ryan's foot and wrapped it in a hot wax coating, then shifted the tub. "Other foot."

Ryan did as requested and waited patiently. She wouldn't pry, not now.

After Cindy had both of Ryan's feet wrapped, she slid the cloth off Ryan's hand and began to buff her nails. "This one's a fireman. I think I like the strong silent type who barks a lot."

Ryan tried not to laugh, but she understood Cindy better than she wanted to. "Does he think family life and a fireman's life can't mix?"

Cindy stopped buffing and lifted her gaze. "I know he loves me, and I'm not asking him to give up his career. But he thinks he'd have to."

"I bet he says stuff like his job demands more of him. He can't worry about his job and you at the same time."

"Sounds like you've been where I am." Cindy moved to the other hand. "You've got great nails."

"Thanks." Ryan wiggled her toes, enjoying the wild warm sensation created by whatever Cindy had put on them. "So why stay with him?"

"I've dumped him more times than I can count, but he keeps coming back."

"Then what's the problem?" Ryan asked.

"I want to get married; he doesn't. Last time I brought it up, he mumbled something about what his dying would do to my kids if we were married. And he thinks my kids have been through enough as it is."

"Is he involved with your kids now?"

"He helps coach Robby's basketball team."

"So what's the diff?" Ryan checked out the polishes that Cindy brought over. "The pinkish one, please."

"Perfect choice." Cindy removed the wrap from Ryan's feet, then glopped a minty gel on them.

Ryan didn't have a clue what this woman was doing and didn't care. She loved it and loved the company.

"I keep telling him my kids are already attached to him, but he doesn't think it's the same."

"If you don't mind my asking, how long have you been seeing each other?"

"Two years. On and off."

"Hey, Cindy," someone called from behind the closed door. "Got a delivery here for you."

"Excuse me." Cindy gave Ryan an apologetic glance, then went to the door. "What is it?"

"Flowers," the same voice replied.

Ryan shifted, glancing over her shoulder. "Those aren't just flowers." Ryan smiled, looking at the huge assortment of different-colored roses. "That's at least five dozen."

"This man is going to be the death of me." Cindy sighed, pulling out the card. "Read this, I just can't."

Ryan took the card out of the envelope and glanced over the words. "Cindy?"

"Is it bad?" Cindy placed the large arrangement by the desk at the door. "We had an awful fight. Last night I told him to jump off a bridge and never come back."

Ryan continued to stare at the words "I'm sorry. I love you and I'd like to talk about forever. I'll pick you up after work," and wasn't quite sure what to say.

"Oh, God. I knew it. Only he would send roses as a kiss-off."

Ryan shoved the card at Cindy. "I think you need to read this."

Cindy plopped down in her chair across from Ryan and took the card in her trembling hands. "Love hurts."

"Sometimes." Ryan smiled. "And sometimes it just plain surprises you."

"Oh, my God. Like I said, the death of me." She mopped the tears rolling down her cheeks. "Just because he sends flowers, I'm supposed to drop what I'm doing and be there for him. Heck, he didn't even ask."

"I think it's sweet."

"Yeah, sweet when my guy does it, but how about when your man does stuff like that? Not so sweet, huh?"

Ryan reached for her green tea and took a sip. "I can't believe I thought that was sweet." But she did. Still did, and what did that say about her?

"What am I going to do?" Cindy glanced at her watch. "He'll be here in two hours. Do I give in and give it another try? Or do I call it quits?" Cindy lifted Ryan's feet, cleaned them off, and then started buffing. "Same color on the toes?"

"Go for it."

"The color?"

"Yeah, sure. But if he's willing to give it a try, so should you. I mean, if he's willing to give the marriage part a go."

Cindy shook her head. "I shouldn't let him do this to me. And if he even suggests he'll quit his job, I'll nail him right where it counts. He'd hate doing something else."

"Sounds like you know him well." Ryan leaned back. She knew Jared. Not only would he hate being anything other than a cop, but he'd hate having to answer to someone. She couldn't help remembering the early stages of his and Lisa's relationship. All the demands Lisa had made on him, and how hard he'd tried not to be miserable. For the baby's sake.

Even though Ryan suspected his feelings for her went deeper than he could admit, it didn't matter. No matter how much you loved someone, if you couldn't be true to yourself, you'd be miserable. And if you're miserable, that's the end of a solid relationship.

"So, if I'm going for it, why don't you?"

"Because I refuse to move." She blinked, wondering where the hell that comment came from. It wasn't like he'd even asked or offered. He'd probably run like hell if she even suggested she'd move. "I love living near my brother. He and his wife just had a baby. His name is Nolan, and he's the most adorable little creature. Not to mention my job at the Lake Side Hotel."

"You work there?" Cindy's eyes went wide with

excitement. "If I do get married, my honeymoon will be at that hotel. When I was a kid, we vacationed in the islands and always drove by the big white mansion. I hear it's magnificent."

"It's pretty spectacular, but not as nice as this place," Ryan agreed and eased back into her chair.

"I seriously doubt that."

Ryan focused on her own goals in hopes of easing her breaking heart. There were so many things she wanted to do in life. Being with Jared had been one of them. But it was time to move on.

Time to move past yesterday and on with tomorrow.

Chapter Fifteen

Jared jogged from his car to the hotel lobby. The day had been more than he'd expected. The job more than he dared dream of. Everything about his new post intrigued him, especially not having to wear a uniform all the time. So why was he running to the woman he wanted to leave behind?

Stepping around the corner toward his suite, his pace slowed, but his heart raced. *Maybe she'd move.* Abruptly, he stopped. The person behind him almost knocked him over. "Sorry," he muttered, then started walking again. Why would he even think that? He glanced around the beautiful hotel, figuring they had event coordinators in a place like this.

"Oh, for the love of God." He tossed his hands wide and glanced toward the ceiling. How could one woman flip his world upside down and toss him to space?

He'd given up this job once because he couldn't

leave her. She'd been too young and vulnerable. She was still vulnerable.

But that would soon change. They were close to putting an end to this case once and for all. And Ryan could move forward with her life. She'd proved time and again that she'd end up on top. And she sure as heck didn't need him.

He shoved the plastic key into the door; a green light flashed, letting him in. Part of him knew he'd had no choice but to bring her along. It was for her safety. But deep down, even if she hadn't needed the protection his badge offered, he wanted her by his side. That thought alone scared the crap out of him.

And there she was sprawled out on the sofa, book at her chest, eyes closed. Contentment seemed to shine from her face. It was as if she was smiling to herself. And she should. She had the whole world at the tips of her fingers.

He slipped into the chair across from the couch, watching her chest move up and down in a slow, rhythmic dance. Her head tilted, then her eyes fluttered while her body stretched, sending the book to the floor.

She jumped to a sitting position the moment she saw him. "Damn it." With her hand plastered across her chest, she took in a long, slow breath. "How long have you been there?"

"Five minutes, tops."

"I didn't hear you come in." Her fingers threaded through her hair, then she tucked it behind her ears.

"Did you color your hair?" he heard himself ask.

"I did what they call lowlights. I'm surprised you noticed."

"Me, too," he said under his breath. "I think we had a break in the case."

"My case?"

He shifted in his seat. The finality of this part of his life hit him between the eyes like the last page of a novel where the author filled in all the blanks, giving you the happy ending you wanted. But he wasn't happy. "It seems that Rudy Martin has had some contact with George, and Rudy's car was seen in Lake George last night."

"You're still skeptical."

"It's my job to question. Look for the loopholes."

"Do you remember the day of George's sentencing?"

Jared stretched out his legs and kicked off his shoes. He'd never forget that day. "He threatened me." Jared knew the man had meant it. George had never liked Jared and made a concerted effort to make Jared's life miserable.

"Actually, he said he'd kill you, after he took care of me."

The hair on the back of Jared's neck stood at attention. A memory of Ryan's torn shirt, breast exposed, with George groping at her, flashed in his mind. "Rudy doesn't have any motive for carrying out George's plan.

They weren't all that close on the inside, but he makes the most sense."

Ryan rose, stretching like a feline, then slipped between him and the coffee table. "Are you thinking out loud?"

"Something like that." With a gaping jaw, he let his eyes roam her body. The perfection of her curves, the softness of her silky skin, and wild tigress that lived beneath the surface still amazed him. She was all woman, and then some.

"Drink?" She bent down to open the fridge and glanced over her shoulder, her rear end sticking out. "Jared?"

"What?"

"You're staring."

"You're wiggling it in front of me."

She shook her hips, laughed, then pulled out two sodas. "Keep thinking."

"I can't with this distraction." He reached out, letting his hand linger on her rounded backside.

The soda fizzed when she cracked open the top and handed it to him. "Come on. George is behind bars."

He lowered his brow. "Doesn't mean Rudy's not dangerous."

"Didn't say that." The pink flesh of her lips curved around the soda can as she took a sip. She licked her lips, then said, "Anyone who'd befriend George would worry me. However, I'm honestly interested in how you think."

"I'm a Neanderthal. I can't think, remember?"

Her smile illuminated the room. "I'm serious. This is interesting, the way you approach a case. I want to hear the rest, and not just because it involves me." She scurried back to the couch and got herself comfortable while he squirmed. "What you do, how you do it, intrigues me."

A sense of connectedness washed over him, humbling him. No one, other than his parents, had ever really been interested in what he did. How he thought. Oh, people wanted the stories. Everyone always asked him if he'd shot anyone. Or how many times a day did he have to draw his weapon? The world wanted to know the gruesome details of being a cop. But no really cared what he thought, or what his work meant to him.

No one had ever seemed genuinely interested in what he actually did on a day-to-day basis. Just the gory details that made his job appear like a Hollywood movie. Her simple interest in his day meant he had someone to share it with. A thought that both bothered and comforted him.

"Suspect number one would be George and Rudy. Right now, Nick is focusing his attention on them, but with that said, ruling out the other possible suspects is just as important. You can never be too careful." His pulse increased with every word. Never in a million years had he ever expected to feel the importance of sharing his world with someone else.

He sipped his soda, trying to swallow his thoughts. His father always told him that change could be hard, even when you wanted it.

"Who's second on your list?"

"Tom."

Shock registered in her eyes. "I would put him at the bottom."

"That's why he's number two. He's not obvious, which makes him obvious, if that makes any sense. He does have access to your office, so planting that rat is plausible. Besides, you did turn him down, and men can get real mean when their egos are bruised."

"He's harmless."

"Not necessarily. You'd be surprised what people can do when they feel scorned."

"So, that makes him more suspicious to you?" The inquisitive look she gave him warmed his heart. And made him nervous as hell.

"There are too many unknowns with him."

"What do you mean by 'unknowns'? I mean, you know he's got some kind of record. You know that he doesn't take no for an answer."

Jared coughed, covering up a laugh. "You don't really say *no* too well. And even if you did say it flat out, it was probably done in a very 'nice' manner. He might feel like you led him on, and you owed him. Might be as simple as he snapped or something more sinister, some deep-seated sexual issue, like being molested as a kid or something. We just don't know his history, and that makes him dangerous."

"Lots of things about him you don't know." She nodded, like she really understood. "He never talked about his family or anything. On our date I tried to get him to open up, but it seemed like he didn't want to share anything about himself, only wanted to know about me."

Jared could see the wheels turning inside her mind. He enjoyed sharing his thoughts with her, but it was an unfamiliar sensation. One he shouldn't get used to. For the year he'd lived with Lisa, she never once asked him about his job, just when he planned on quitting and going into politics like his father. "It's important to dig up as much as possible on Tom so we can understand his frame of mind. The more people you can rule out, the closer you get to the real culprit, before he strikes again."

"Who's next?" She shifted in her seat, excitement sparkling in her beautiful eyes.

"It's a tie between Lisa and Eddy."

"Can I give it a try?" She bit down on her lower lip. She had no idea how sexy she looked when she did that.

"Go ahead." He smiled, unable to keep her at bay or his enjoyment from just being with her. They were friends, so this was normal, right?

"First, Eddy likes women's underwear. Mine went

missing. I also made a minor snafu with his name while—"

"That's not a minor thing. Crimes of passion happen all the time." Not to mention how every time he thought of the weasel touching Ryan, it made his teeth grind. Freaking pervert. How she could ever have liked that idiot was beyond Jared. "Jealousy makes people do some crazy things." But Jared wasn't jealous. No reason to be. Just concerned. *Right.*

"Eddy could be mad because I thought he was weird, I mean the underwear thing. I might have made fun of him."

"That could cause him to snap, but he doesn't really fit the profile, because he's more concerned about seeing women in their underwear and not with the act of sex. Wanting to kill me because I touched you really doesn't fit his profile, but it sure as shit fits Tom's. You turned him down, but not me. He's probably pretty pissed about that."

"I suppose. If he knows I didn't turn you down, which we don't know for sure."

"True enough, but he owns a camera and seems to know how to use it."

"I won't argue that. I can see why you love your job. It's fun." She tucked her feet under her bottom and stretched out her arms.

He undid the top button of his shirt. It bothered him that this situation felt like it should be a part of his daily life. "Dealing with whack jobs, it's hard work. And if I screw it up, someone could die. Not something I want to happen, especially when my friends are involved."

A slow smile spread across her flawless face. "I think you're very good at what you do. Now, on with Lisa. I don't like her much."

"The feeling's mutual, babe."

She narrowed her eyes.

"It's just an expression." He tossed his hands wide and laughed. "Never going to change, babe. Now let's hear your theory on Lisa."

"Okay, babe." She winked, a twinkle of mischief in her eyes.

"Funny." He laughed.

"This is based on my observations and what you told me."

"That's good police work."

She smiled at his remark, then adjusted her hair. "For some reason she thought I was a threat to her, and she planned on getting rid of me. When that didn't work, she tried to force you into realizing you couldn't live without her, but then Johnny...Johnny died." A sudden rush of sadness filled her eyes. "I loved him, you know."

Jared nodded. "That was obvious. You were very good with him."

"I didn't think you ever noticed."

"I was jealous," he admitted. "I didn't know how to connect with him; you did. He smiled at you." For the first time in years, he saw Johnny alive, in her arms, being loved.

"Lisa didn't make it easy for you."

"Our marriage was a mistake; Johnny wasn't," Jared whispered.

Ryan nodded, then took a sip of her soda. "To Lisa, I stood in the way of her happiness. It was easy for her to place all the blame on me. And from what I can gather, she still holds a grudge."

"No lie, she's definitely up there with Tom." Tired of fighting his desire to be closer to Ryan, he moved to the sofa. He slipped his hand through her silky hair and across the back of her neck. "There's more about her life I can't share with you, but just know she's a scorned woman."

"She feels wronged by us." Ryan sighed, then shifted her weight, resting her head on Jared's shoulder. "George feels wronged by the world."

"Still like my job?" He wrapped his arms around her firm body and lifted her into his lap.

"Is it hard to be so cynical about people all the time?"

He opened his mouth to give his standard cop response, that in the right set of circumstances, any person could be capable of committing some of the most outrageous crimes. But when his eyes locked with hers, for the first time in his career, he questioned his own reasoning.

The woman looking back at him was as pure and

honest as the winter snow was white. For the first time, he questioned his goals and what he really wanted out of life. He wasn't supposed to be able to love.

"Sometimes," he said. "But the citizens of this fine state need me to be cynical."

"I guess someone's got to do it. I'm glad it's you." She cupped his face, fanning her thumbs across his cheeks. "When does your new job actually start?"

"They'd take me tomorrow."

"I don't want you to stay behind because of my case. While I know you're probably one of the best cops around, Nick seems pretty good."

"Nick's the best." He kept his look serious. "No offense, but no matter what, I plan on being here by the end of next week. I've even got a place to crash until I can find a house."

"I'm glad to hear it."

Against his better judgment, he slipped his hands under her shirt. Her hot skin scorched his fingers. "If your case isn't wrapped up by then, I'd like you to consider a few things."

"Got it covered."

"Really?" He lifted a brow. "How so?"

"I promised Marci I'd come stay with her for a few days. I know she's not a cop, or a man, but safety in numbers. Besides, this manager of Pat's is starting to work out, so the bar can practically run itself, freeing up some of Pat's time."

He opened his mouth, but she covered it with her hand.

"Then, Penny's lease is up, but she won't live with Chuck until they're married, which won't be for two months, so if it's okay with you, she's going to move into the carriage house with me."

"What if the house sells?" Annoyed by her handling the situation, he tried to poke holes in her well-laid plan.

"I'm sure the culprit will be caught by then, and hopefully I will have found a new apartment and can still live with Pen until the wedding. But worst case, I'll move in with Pat." Undeniable confidence sparkled in her eyes.

"I guess I can't argue with that." He rolled her from his lap, gently resting her back against the couch, then pressed his rigid body against hers. "I'm glad you have a plan."

"I'm glad you approve." She glanced across the room. "What time are we meeting your friends? And don't we have to check out?"

"I paid for a late checkout, so anytime in the next hour, and we're meeting them across the street." He felt guilty because of his strong, powerful desire for her. He wanted to believe it was wrong, but she felt so right in his arms.

Temporary, he reminded himself. So much in his life had changed. The way he dealt with his agonizing grief, his job, his home, but this thing with Ryan was temporary.

The strong connection he felt for her only intensified because of the threats. This bond they shared was nothing more than him jumping into his job with two feet, like he always did. He wouldn't allow it to be love.

Ryan wanted to slap herself across the face. Would she ever learn? The more she made love to Jared, the worse she felt.

"You done in there?" Jared banged on the bathroom door, impatience in his tone. "The car is in the front loop."

She checked herself over one last time, knowing she looked fine. If she was being honest, she looked damn great. Twisting the handle, she pushed back the door. "Are you ready yet?" She smiled. Somewhere along the line she missed the boat. She should've been an actress.

He just laughed, shaking his head, then grabbed their overnight bags.

"What's the girlfriend's name?" Ryan asked. Why she wanted to impress these people was beyond her. She'd probably never see them again.

"His name is Brad Gloshen, and her name is Wendy something."

"Have you met her?" She slipped into the car, then Jared pulled out of the parking area and across the street to the Hensman Pub, a local hot spot. Looking down the street as the car zoomed across, she had to admit the town was quaint, but it wasn't Lake George.

"I just met him last month. Didn't even know he had a girlfriend until I told him you were coming."

"Oh." She stepped out of the car and headed toward the restaurant.

Jared pushed open the door into the noisy restaurant and bar. "He's kind of my superior, so when he suggested we go out, I couldn't say no, now could I. There he is."

She squinted across the crowded room, eyeing a very handsome older gentleman. He had grayish hair, but it offset his gorgeous eyes. His body wasn't too shabby to look at either. "Are all troopers hot?" she said, half to herself.

"I wouldn't know," Jared said with a chuckle. "But his girlfriend is a looker."

Ryan shifted her gaze to the tall brunette standing next to Brad. She didn't look old, but Ryan guessed her to be at least thirty-five. "She's too old for you."

"Breasts too big, too," Jared whispered. "I like mine a bit smaller." He patted her butt.

"Like I said, a Neanderthal."

"Jared, so glad you could make it. I know it's a long ride home. This is Wendy Brooks." Brad guided them to a table in the other room where it was a little quieter.

"Wendy, nice to meet you. This is my friend Ryan O'Connor," Jared said.

Ryan nodded, shaking Wendy's hand, then Brad's, feeling a little annoyed at being introduced as a friend. But what did she expect? That's what she was, and introducing her as his friend that he just had sex with wouldn't be very appropriate.

Once seated, the small talk began, and Ryan found herself enjoying the company. Wendy was a successful lawyer and one of the most interesting women Ryan had ever met. Not to mention Brad was just adorable and very smitten with Wendy.

Ryan listened to Brad and Jared talk about the job, and she had to admit, it worried her. His new job sounded very dangerous.

Her stomach fluttered when the waitress put their dinner plates on the table. Usually she loved the smell of sizzling steaks and piping hot potatoes loaded with sour cream, but at this moment, her stomach churned. Must have been the green tea.

She swallowed and fiddled with her food, hoping it looked like she was eating. She smiled and nodded a lot and tried to add to the conversation. Finally, she just couldn't stand it anymore, and she pushed her plate away.

"You okay?" Jared asked, leaning closer to her. His hand rested on the back of her neck while his thumb stroked the skin at the base of her head.

"I think I'm just tired," she said, forcing a smile.

"You can climb in the back and sleep on the way home."

Brad waved the waitress over, asking for the check. "We should let you guys hit the road. I hope I'll have the pleasure of your company again, Ryan."

"I did enjoy myself, thank you," she said, slipping out of the booth. "Just need to hit the little girls' room."

"I'll join you," Wendy said.

Ryan pushed back the door. She felt a little better, but her stomach was still queasy. An overwhelming fear loomed in the back of her mind. She could be pregnant.

"Are you sure you're okay?" Wendy asked.

"I think I had too much green tea at the spa today." Ryan smiled politely, then splashed cool water on her face. "Not used to being waited on. Maybe all that aromatherapy has gone to my head."

"Hardworking girl, huh?" Wendy joined Ryan at the sink, rinsing her hands. "I spent the last ten years of my life making it big and let the rest of the world pass me by. Not this time. I'm landing that guy once and for all."

"You look good together." Ryan turned, leaning her hip on the sink.

"He wanted to marry me ten years ago. I turned him down, so he married someone else."

"Excuse me?" Ryan's eyes widened.

"He's divorced now, but I'm not letting him go, not

this time. He's being a little wishy-washy, afraid I'll change my mind, my career and all. But I want kids, and I'm not getting any younger. Neither is he."

"Good to know what you want," Ryan said, holding her stomach as it did another flip. *Just nerves,* she told herself.

"What do you want?"

"Honestly, I don't know."

"I think you do; you're just afraid to ask for it," Wendy said. "But sometimes we have to learn the hard way. Come on." She pushed back the bathroom door. "You've got a long drive and a lot of thinking to do."

Ryan swallowed. Thinking would get her into trouble. The only thing she needed was for the psycho to be caught and Jared to move.

Chapter Sixteen

Jared stepped out of the restaurant into the spring air. He missed the cool lake breeze, but he liked Rochester. Or at least he knew he'd like it. What wasn't to like? His job sounded exciting. The guys he'd be working with seemed like decent men. Okay, so he'd miss Harmon.

"She plan on moving with you?" Brad asked. A beaming smile spread across his face.

Jared's gut twisted as though he'd been sucker punched. "We're just friends."

"You certainly don't act like 'just' friends," Brad said, his smile not fading, and that just annoyed Jared.

"You could say we have a temporary thing going. We've got a long history, but her life is there, and mine is here. End of story. It's nothing, really." A noise from behind him caught his attention.

"Ready?" Ryan asked with a sarcastic grin.

He knew she'd heard him. But she had no right to be mad. It was the truth, and she knew it.

"Thanks for dinner. I really had a great time," Ryan said, giving Wendy a hug, then kissing Brad on the cheek. "If you're ever in Lake George, look me up. My brother's got a great restaurant, and I'd love to return the favor."

"You are so on, girlfriend." Wendy gave Jared the evil eye.

What the hell had he done? Heck, he'd never understand women. You give them what they want, and somehow you ended up the bad guy. "Take care. It was nice meeting you, Wendy." Jared opened the car door, letting Ryan get settled before jogging around the front of the car and slipping into the driver's seat. "See you next week." He waved, then slammed the door and drove off.

Once on the highway, he glanced over at Ryan. Her eyes were closed, and her head was propped against the window. She was probably faking sleep, but he didn't feel like talking.

He didn't want to feel anything. But try as he might, no matter how he looked at it, leaving her would be hard. But he had to do it. Not just because he'd never be able to give her what she deserved, but because this job meant the world to him. Meant more to him than she did, didn't it?

He pushed down on the gas pedal. If he got pulled over, so be it. She could be mad all she wanted. Might even make things easier if she was pissed off enough to leave him alone.

His cell phone rang. She jumped.

"Sorry, forgot to put it on vibrate," he muttered, glancing at the number.

"Harmon?"

"I hope you're on your way home," Harmon said.

"What's going on?" Jared glanced at Ryan. She sat up and looked at him with wide eyes.

"Nick picked up Rudy an hour ago," Harmon said.

"For what?" Jared glanced at the speedometer, then pressed the pedal so he'd reach ninety. "Alert everyone I'm flying down the thruway just past Utica, and I'm getting off at exit twenty-eight. Tell them to leave me alone."

"I can handle the troopers, but the locals on the back roads, you're on your own, man."

"I know, now tell me about Rudy."

"The guy was lurking around your house. Your friend Rory called it in, and we got him on trespassing. Nick was able to search his car, and guess what he found."

"Underwear," Jared said under his breath.

"Jared, you just drove past a cop," Ryan said, looking over her shoulder.

He glanced in the rearview mirror, and the trooper pulled out. "Crap. Frank, got a cop on my tail. Call it in." Jared moved over to the right lane but didn't slow down. "Ryan, grab my badge from my pocket." He shifted, giving her better access. "Take the phone for a minute."

The trooper pulled up next to him, and Jared waved, flashing his badge. The trooper held his radio in his hands, then nodded and flicked his lights on, giving Jared an escort. "Give me the phone back." He pushed down on the accelerator. "You got your seat belt on?"

"What's going on? You're scaring me."

He squeezed her leg. "Don't be scared. Nick picked up Rudy, and it looks like we got our man. I just need to get home, okay?"

"Home works for me," she said, keeping her eyes on the road.

"You feeling okay?"

"Speed makes me a little dizzy."

"Put your head between your legs if you have to." He grabbed the phone from her hands. "Frank, you still there?"

"Yes, sir."

"I need you to find Penny Swartz and have her meet us at my place." He glanced at Ryan. "I need to go to the station and figure out what's happening, and I don't think you should be alone, okay?" He pleaded with her.

She nodded, then looked back at the road.

"Anything else, boss?" Frank asked.

"Are you at the sheriff's office?"

"That I am, sir."

Jared smiled. “You stick to Nick like a fly on shit, okay? I want to know everything, you got it?”

“Oh, I got it, and I’ll enjoy it, sir.”

Jared laughed. “I’m sure you will.”

“Oh, and Jared?”

Since when did Frank call him by his first name? “Yeah?”

“Thanks.”

“For what?”

“The glowing recommendation to the scuba unit.”

Jared smiled. “I’m sure you’ll like it.”

“Prichard said you set some swimming record in college. Why haven’t you gone through the training?”

Why indeed? Jared glanced over at Ryan. Her hands gripped the armrests and her eyes locked on the darkness ahead. “See you shortly.” He closed his phone, unable to think about the scuba unit. While the post would be demanding and challenging, it could mean staying in Lake George, since he already did lake patrol. Not going to happen. He needed a change.

Once on the back roads, he slowed to a normal speed, having lost his escort. He’d picked up a lot of time, but his pulse still raced. The adrenaline pumped out of control. Not being there to see and question Rudy was driving him nuts.

Okay, so he was a control freak.

“Almost there, babe.”

She shook out her hands. “I don’t think you ever have to worry about me getting a ticket.”

"You know to just drop my name, right?"

She laughed. "I've never been pulled over and never plan on it."

"Well, if you do, just ask them if they know me; most likely you won't get a ticket."

"I'll remember that."

They remained quiet for the rest of the ride. He kept glancing at her, wondering what she was thinking, but he didn't dare ask. If what Harmon said was true, he'd be packing most of his clothes and heading out, saying goodbye.

His heart paused for a moment before pounding wildly against his chest. He told himself it was just the anticipation of catching the bad guy. It wasn't the pain his heart felt for having to let go of Ryan, but wanting to give her something he couldn't.

"We'll be fine, Jared," Ryan said, practically pushing him out the door. "Now go and take care of business."

"Lock the doors," he said, looking over her shoulder.

"Is he always this paranoid?" Penny asked.

"I'm not paranoid."

"Yeah, right. Okay, now scoot," Ryan said.

"You always this controlling?" He smiled.

"Yes," she said, fighting the urge to grab him and kiss him passionately. Sometimes his controlling ways really weren't so controlling. She had to admit he did care for her, on some level. And that felt good, even though she didn't want it to.

She clicked the lock on the door, then watched him jog down the path and hop in his pickup. He waved before backing up. She turned and dropped her gaze to the floor, unable to face Penny's scrutinizing glare.

"You're in love with the big goof." Penny's voice echoed in Ryan's ears.

"Am not." Ryan pushed past Penny, making her way into the family room.

"And I'm not pregnant. Mind if I raid the refrigerator?"

"Help yourself." Ryan paused, then turned. "Then again, it's not my refrigerator."

"Whatever." Penny waved her off, ducking her head into the icebox.

Ryan rubbed her eyes and plopped herself down on the couch. One minute she was listening to Jared reduce their affair to an understanding, the next she wanted to kiss him for being there for her. She didn't understand. If this was love, she wanted nothing to do with it. It reminded her too much of a roller coaster ride, which generally made her want to toss her cookies.

"Want some?" Penny sat down next to her with a huge bowl of chocolate chip ice cream. "I so wish I had morning sickness. I'm going to be fat by the time I get married." Penny shoved the ice cream in Ryan's face.

"No." Ryan shoved it aside, her stomach flipping again. "I had way too much to eat earlier. Jared treated me to a bunch of spa treatments, and they had all these decadent chocolates and stuff." Ryan had eaten a lot of stuff she'd been offered during her day at the spa, but she knew that hadn't caused her upset stomach.

Not knowing if this Rudy guy was behind the bizarre things that were happening to her had caused her stomach to churn. She found herself mentally counting the days of the month again. She let out a sigh of relief when she realized she wasn't late. Tomorrow. She'd get her period tomorrow and all would be well in the world.

Well, not really. "Can you take a few days off next week?"

Penny shrugged. "Probably. I'm thinking about going part time anyway."

"You've got to be kidding me." Ryan felt her eyes go wide.

"Trudy, another girl at work, just had a baby and she hates working full time. We're trying to see if we can work out a job share thing."

"Does Chuck want you to stay at home?" Ryan had a hard time believing career-minded Penny would consider giving up her marketing job. "Do you want to stay at home?"

"I'm not quitting my job, just shifting things a little. The worst is, I've got a lot of vacation time saved up, but he doesn't. We'll only be taking a long weekend for our honeymoon."

"That sucks," Ryan said.

Penny shoved a large hunk of ice cream in her mouth, then tried to talk, but gave up when she didn't make any sense. "As I was saying, he wants to save the time for when the baby's born and take a couple of weeks then. Or maybe take some time off when I go back to work."

Ryan shook her head. Never in a million years did she think she'd be seeing a grown-up Penny, making life-altering decisions. "Wow," she muttered.

"What?"

"I'm blown away."

"Why?"

"I don't know. When did we grow up?"

"Speak for yourself, honey." Penny stuck out her tongue, then licked her spoon before scooping another oversized bite. "Tell me, why am I asking for time off on such short notice?"

"Because Jared plans on packing up and hitting the road next Friday, and I don't want to be around when he does. I thought we'd go on that camping trip a few weeks early."

Penny looked to the ceiling, still licking her spoon. "I could take off Thursday and Friday, but if we do this, the trip ends Saturday so I can have the rest of the weekend with Chuck."

"Deal, but let's wait to finalize the plans until I know for sure the bad guy is behind bars."

"Probably a good idea. So, when do you plan on telling Mr. So-Interested-In-You that you love him?"

"On the twelfth of never."

Penny set aside the empty bowl, then placed a firm hand on Ryan's shoulder. "You have to tell him."

"Why? So he can feel guilty, then consider giving up the best thing that's ever happened to him, for me? Out of guilt? No way."

"I don't think you're giving the man enough credit. I saw how he looked at you tonight."

"You're killing me, Pen. First you tell me to go for it, then to drop it because you don't think I can handle it, and now you think I should tell him how I really feel?" Ryan blinked, forcing back the tears. Admitting to herself she loved him was hard enough, but to tell even Penny hurt like hell.

Penny scooted closer, putting a sisterly arm around her. "If you don't take that risk, you'll never know."

"If I tell him, he might turn down that job, and I can't do that to him again."

"Again? What does that mean?"

"He was offered that job six years ago but turned it down because of George's trial. Because he felt like he had to stay and take care of me. I was only seventeen when the trial started, and he felt obligated. I don't want to pressure him in any way, because then I'd always wonder." Tears rolled down her face. She brushed them away, but it didn't stop them from coming.

"Oh, Ry. I understand how you feel, really I do. But what's the worst thing that could happen if you told him?"

"He'd stay, and not because he loves me."

"He does care for you; anyone can see that."

"Would that be enough for you with Chuck?" Ryan tilted her head.

Penny's shocked face gave Ryan the answer she needed. It wouldn't be enough, and nothing Penny could say would sway her mind. She'd only tell Jared if he came to her, giving himself to her freely.

But she knew that would never happen. "This sucks." She threw her arms around Penny. "Love really sucks."

"I know, honey, I know," Penny whispered, stroking Ryan's hair and giving her the opportunity to let it all out.

Ryan didn't know how much time had passed, but when she didn't have a tear left, she pulled away and wiped the mascara from her cheeks. "You're going to make a great mom," Ryan said, meaning it.

"God, I hope so."

"How are the wedding plans?" Ryan asked, genuinely interested. She wanted to focus on something other than her own issues. She glanced at the clock. An hour had passed since Jared had left, and not knowing what was going on was driving her crazy.

"The church is booked; the only issue is the reception."

"What's the problem?"

"My mother. She and Chuck's mom don't see eye to eye on this point."

"What about you and Chuck?"

"He wants to please my mother and I want to please his."

Ryan laughed. "Sounds like fun."

"Oh, yeah. Loads. At this point I'll settle for anything. We're having a meeting of the minds tomorrow morning, and we're going to make the final decision since we have to put money down."

"Who do you think is going to win?"

"My mother, since she's footing the bill. But Chuck's not too happy about that either. He wants us to pay for it."

"Why look a gift horse in the mouth?" Ryan eased back on the couch, getting lost in Penny. She loved Pen like a sister, and her sheer happiness had started to rub off on Ryan.

"He won't insult my mother, but I think he likes being the man. By the way, I stopped by the hospital today to see Nolan. Oh, my God." Penny fanned her face. "That little boy is adorable. And your brother is just beaming. He even gave me a huge hug and kiss."

Ryan's entire being warmed at the mention of her nephew. "I can't wait to spend some real time with him. This whole thing has really put a damper on his arrival."

"I'm sure Marci and Pat will be calling on good old Auntie Ryan."

A click from the other room made Ryan jump. "Did you hear that?"

Penny nodded, looking over her shoulder.

"I'm home," Jared bellowed.

"Damn that man." Ryan leaped from the couch. "Come on. Let's go find out what happened."

Without checking to see if Penny followed her or not, Ryan bolted into the kitchen, meeting a long-faced Jared. "I'm not sure I like that look."

"Me neither," Penny said. "Did you get the bad guy?"

"We did," Jared said, raking a hand across his head.

"So why the long face?" Ryan asked. Her body trembled in fear, but not for her life this time. "George was behind this, right?" Ryan gripped the chair, locking gazes with Jared.

His face softened. "We can't get a confession out of either of them, but Rudy has been arrested. Nick needs you to come down to the station and identify your underwear."

"Oh, that should be a blast," Penny muttered. "You want me to go with you?"

"You should go home," Ryan said, turning to Penny.

"You call me if you need me, day or night, got it?"

Penny looped her arms around her and squeezed tight. "I love you," she whispered.

"I love you, too."

"Hey, since this nightmare is coming to an end, any reason she can't go shopping with me tomorrow afternoon?" Penny looked at Jared.

"I don't see why not." He shrugged.

"Great. Oh, you do want to be my maid of honor, right?"

"As long as I don't have to wear pink taffeta."

"Oh, good God, no." Penny laughed. "Call me in the morning, okay?"

"You got it."

"I'll walk you to your car." Jared pulled back the door.

"Thanks."

Ryan stood on the back porch and watched Jared open Penny's car door, helping her slide behind the steering wheel. He was quite the gentleman. To everyone. Ryan realized all his actions were the same. He treated the world with the same respect he'd treated her. Nothing special, it was just the way he was. God, she hoped he'd get called to Rochester in the next twenty-four hours. Her acting abilities wouldn't last much longer.

Jared stood in the still of night and watched Penny's car disappear in the darkness. He couldn't understand why he was still tormented. As long as Ryan identified her underwear, the district attorney assured him they had enough evidence to bring full charges against Rudy.

George was a different story, unless Rudy blew him in. But George was already behind bars and wouldn't be getting out anytime soon.

Jared turned and faced the main house. The large home glowed against the clear lake. Everything about the solid structure sparkled. It needed a family to fill its quiet walls. He could picture a swing set with a sandbox and a couple of kids running around in the yard. He could see Ryan with a few kids, managing a career and home life, and doing a damn good job.

But he couldn't picture himself in that family, no matter how hard he tried. Loving her had become the easy part. Telling her, well, that was impossible, because he still couldn't give her what she desired most in life—stability.

Leaving would be best for both of them.

He took a few steps toward the house, where she stood on the porch, arms around her middle. The possibility of a baby still loomed in his brain. To his knowledge, she hadn't gotten her period.

When he reached the porch, he wanted to tell her so many things, but just couldn't bring himself to. None of it mattered anyway. "They can hold Rudy tonight, so we don't need to go to the station until morning."

"What if it's not my underwear?"

"Then he walks," Jared answered matter-of-factly. No need to beat around the bush; she'd been through too much for him to sugarcoat this.

"What if I can't identify them?"

Her soft skin calmed his nerves when he took her by the elbow and led her back into the house. "I'm sure that won't be a problem."

"What about at trial? I mean, lots of women shop at Victoria's Secret." Her voice trembled.

Closing the door and securing the lock, he pulled her into his arms. "One step at a time, okay? The D.A. thinks we have a good case, and he wouldn't go to trial if he thought he might lose."

"Is this really over? Can I really let my guard down?"

He cupped her chin. "You should always be aware of your surroundings, but yes, this is over."

"Thank God." She pushed herself from his clutches, then rolled her neck.

He scowled. "I still want you to stay clear of Tom."

"I have to work with him."

"Don't care."

"Oh, trust me. I think this experience has taught me a thing or two about being a bitch."

He wanted to laugh. Ryan could never really be a bitch. She was too nice. One of the many things about her he admired and adored. She had an uncanny ability to see the good in most people.

"Jared?" She touched his hand. "What's going on?"

"I'm just tired." He threaded his fingers through hers. "Closing a case is always anticlimactic. The experts say it has something to do with the rush of adrenaline, then the letdown when it's all over or some such nonsense." What a line of bull that was. And he wasn't tired. He was restless. "Should we take a pregnancy test or something?"

"We?" She laughed. "Don't think your urine would tell us anything."

"You know what I mean."

She patted her hand on his chest. "I'm not pregnant."

"How can you be so sure?" He narrowed his eyes, checking out every feature of her face. As a cop, he was trained to detect liars.

"Let's just say we won't be mixing friendship with sex for the next few days." She didn't blink, not once. Nor did she look nervous. Besides, she had no reason to lie to him. They'd always been upfront with each other.

"You can still sleep in my bed, if you want."

She shook her head. "Thanks, but I think the right time is right now. Besides, the real-estate agent left a message on your machine saying she has an offer. One you should take. It sounded like they were close to the asking price."

His pulse raced out of control and his chest actually

hurt, like a heart attack might. "That's good, but what about you?"

"It can't be that hard to find an apartment this time of year. I've already circled a few in the paper over in Bolton."

"You don't miss a beat, do you?" He fought his desire to tell her how he really felt, because he wasn't so sure.

"Nope." She smiled proudly. "I can't afford to."

He opened his mouth to ask her what she'd do if he stayed, but then he remembered her look of disappointment when she'd found out he'd turned down the job once before. He didn't want to disappoint her or have her hate him. Those two things he couldn't bear. "I want you to know how much you mean to me. How much this time with you has helped me deal with... Johnny. I think I can finally move past his death, thanks to you."

She smiled, her eyes twinkling in delight. "That means a lot to me. It broke my heart to see you in such pain."

"It still hurts, but I know it's not my fault."

"Good."

He stood there and stared at her, not knowing what to do. His heart wanted to take her into his arms and hold on tight, never letting go. His brain told him to run like hell and never look back. "Is the message from the real-estate agent still on the machine? If someone is willing to pay list, I'd be a fool not to take it."

She turned, fiddling with some papers on the counter. "I took all the information down." When she turned to face him, she smiled, but her eyes looked sad. "It's a good offer. She said she'd fax it to you in the morning." She held the paper in her trembling hands. "Leaving this house, the carriage house, will be hard." She wiped a tear that had dropped to her cheek.

Was there something more in her eyes? He searched but couldn't tell. His heart told him she wanted him to stay and give them a try, but he couldn't commit to that feeling. What if he was wrong? What if he put his heart out there and she didn't want him? "Ryan," he whispered.

"I'm tired. I'll go to the station in the morning. Good night, Jared." She eased into his arms to kiss his cheek, then slipped out and disappeared up the stairs, taking his heart with her.

But he wouldn't follow it. He couldn't. He didn't know how to love her.

Chapter Seventeen

Jared watched the sun begin its descent behind the tall mountains as he loaded the last of his suitcases into the back of his pickup, then looked around the place he'd called home for as long as he could remember.

"Is that it?" Pat asked.

"For now. I'll fly back in a few weeks to get the BMW. And until I sell the house, I won't move the furniture."

"What about that offer?"

"Still negotiating." Jared rubbed the back of his neck. He should've taken the offer up front, but he decided to hold out for a few more thousand. Now the real-estate agent said the couple was looking at another house on Assembly Point. "You know how it is."

"I know you're stubborn as a mule."

"One of my more redeeming qualities." The empty carriage house caught his attention. Ryan had moved in with her brother until her new apartment became available in just two weeks. Jared couldn't help but feel like he'd taken her home from her. And now she was off with Penny, camping. He scowled. She couldn't have waited a few days to say goodbye to him? She'd been able to ID most of her underwear. The district attorney had gone after Rudy with both barrels loaded. And since then, she'd been avoiding Jared.

Or at least that's how he saw it.

"Tell Ryan to take her time getting her stuff from the garage. I can help her when I come back. I'll probably take a long weekend."

"Having a tough time letting go?" Pat asked, giving him a brotherly pat on the back.

"I suppose. I've never lived anywhere else, besides college. It is a little weird."

"I meant Ryan."

Her name made his heart ping. He missed her, and he didn't want to. He could smell her peach shampoo and feel her skin against his.

"I'm not sure how to say this," Pat continued, "but you've changed, and I think my sister has something to do with it."

"She's a good woman, and I care about her. She's helped me through some tough times, and I'll always be grateful."

"I think she feels the same way about you."

Jared chuckled. He'd never really thought about how much Ryan had been there for him. He'd always been worried about being there for her, protecting her from the world. But she'd proved she could take care of herself, and then some. "I just wish she'd waited to say goodbye."

"It's not like you'll never see her again. You just said you'd be back in a few weeks." Pat slapped him on the back. "And don't forget about the christening a few weeks after that. And I'm sure you'll be back for Penny's wedding."

"I think I'm in it." He chuckled, wondering how he'd been suckered into that one. "Well, I'd better hit the road."

He pulled open the door, then looked Pat square in the eye. "Thanks for everything, man."

"Anytime." Pat craned his neck. "Are you sure this is what you want?"

"Yep." Jared didn't hesitate in his response, but he'd been hesitating in his heart. "I know I've been a little on the sentimental side these last few days." He rubbed the back of his neck. "Change is always harder than we think."

"I suppose." Pat took a step back from the truck. "Take care."

"Watch your back," Jared said, then slipped behind the wheel. He didn't look back when he pulled away, but he knew things would never be the same again. He managed to keep his emotions in check until he pulled onto the Northway. He swiped at his eyes, infuriated with himself. He glanced at himself in the rearview mirror. A horn honked behind him. He swerved, pulling into the right lane, noticing he'd been going slower than the flow of traffic. Then he pulled onto the shoulder and rolled to a stop.

Gripping the steering wheel so tight his knuckles turned white, he blinked a few times, then pulled back out into traffic. For the next few miles, he blasted the radio and tried to get into the music, singing along. He forced his mind onto his new job and off Ryan.

He yanked his cell phone from his hip and pressed star three, staring at her cell number. "And what the hell would you say to her?" He tossed his phone to the passenger seat. Like he'd tell a woman he loved her over the phone. "Shit." He gunned the truck, trying to ignore the U-turn coming up, but to no avail.

Once again, he rolled his truck to a stop between the north and south lanes of the highway. He hadn't driven more than forty miles from Lake George. "This is nuts." He backed out and continued to head south. He just needed some space. He figured the more miles he put between them, the better he'd feel.

But as he approached the thruway, he didn't feel any better. Pulling into a deserted parking lot, he reached for his cell and stared at it. "I love her," he said, feeling like a fool for talking to himself, but a weight had suddenly been lifted. Just saying it out loud gave him some freedom. The question then became: was admitting it enough? Could he continue to drive away knowing the woman he loved would move on with her life, never knowing how he felt?

And what about his job? Wasn't that what he'd been working toward for the last few years? The scuba unit had been his second choice. He stared at the cars rolling by toward their own destinations when it hit him. His restlessness had never been about his job, but what was right in front of him.

Ramming the gearshift out of park, he peeled out of the parking lot and headed toward home. It wasn't about being needed by the good people of the State of New York, but being needed by one person. And him needing her.

And now he was going to get her. A sudden panic shot through his system. What if she didn't want him? He flipped open his phone, hitting Pat's number.

"Hello?" Pat answered.

"Where is she?" he practically yelled.

"Jared?"

"Where's your sister?" he asked again. This time a little more calmly.

"Camping, why? Something wrong? George break out of prison or something?"

"Nothing like that, although you won't like what I've got in mind."

"What the hell are you talking about?" Pat asked.

"Just tell me where she is. I'll explain later."

"I don't know. She went camping with Penny somewhere in the narrows."

"A lot of help you are. If you find out, call my cell. I should be back in town in a little less than an hour."

"You're coming back?" Pat's voice rose up an octave. "Should I be worried about her safety?"

"Ummm, that all depends on what you think about me sweeping her off her feet."

"What?"

Jared held the phone from his ear while Pat swore up and down. "You done yet?"

"Go to Rochester," Pat said.

"No can do. Not unless Ryan breaks my heart." Jared sucked in a breath. That could be a reality, something he might have to deal with.

"You come anywhere near her, I'll...I'll...oh hell, good luck. You're going to need it when it comes to my sister."

"Yeah, I know." Jared clicked his phone shut, then called Frank, bypassing Chuck. He knew he shouldn't use his police resources to find her, but his heart was on the line.

"If you want to go back, we can," Ryan suggested. "I know it's a little chilly, and I'm sure Jared's long gone by now."

"Nah, I'm fine." Penny wrapped a blanket around

her body, then settled back in her chair. "So, what are you not telling me?"

"What are you talking about?" Lying to Jared was one thing. But lying to Penny would be damn near impossible.

"I've sat with you for hours while you cried your eyes out over that man. But I know you, and there is more to this story. So spill it."

"I might be pregnant," Ryan said, a little shocked she didn't even try to lie.

Penny fell off her folding chair.

"Crap. Penny! Are you okay?" Ryan leaped over to help her up.

"Not okay. In shock. Did you say pregnant? As in having a baby? Jared's baby?" She held on to Ryan's shoulders.

Ryan nodded.

"Holy shit, Ryan. Are you sure?"

"No, I'm not sure, but I'm about a week late."

Penny settled herself back in the chair. "You have to tell Jared. He has the right to know."

"After I find out for sure. I figured on telling him after he'd gotten settled in Rochester."

"That's so not fair." Penny glared at her. "How can you do that to him?"

"I don't want him staying here again because of me." Ryan shoved a stick in the fire, sending the flames high in the air. The smoke almost choked her.

"That's his baby. He has the right to make that decision."

Ryan turned. "I don't know if there is a baby yet. I've been late before. Besides, if there is a baby, I will tell him."

"If you don't, I will."

"You wouldn't dare."

"Don't tempt me, Ryan. You're playing with fire." Penny stood, then moved toward the tent. "I love you with all my heart, but think about what you're doing. Not only are you playing with Jared's emotions, but your child's. That's just not fair. And I can say that from experience. Imagine where I'd be if I hadn't told Chuck."

"That's different. Chuck loves you, and he asked you to marry him before he knew."

"You don't know how Jared feels, because you never gave him the chance to tell you. Nope, you hid from him instead. Telling him he didn't mean enough to you to see him off." Penny shook her head, then slipped into the tent.

"He had ample time to tell me how he felt," Ryan muttered, but she knew that wasn't the case. How had her life gotten so screwed up? She rubbed her temples. "Does Chuck have Tylenol on his boat?"

"There's some in the cuddy in the first aid kit," Penny yelled. "Hey, Ryan."

"Yeah?"

"You know how much I care about you, right?"

"I know, Penny." She sighed and headed for the boat. Her head pounded.

A twig snapped behind her. "Penny?" She spun around, but no one was there. "Damn nerves." She continued toward the boat but couldn't shake the feeling someone was watching her.

Jared screeched to a halt in his driveway next to Frank's patrol car. "What did you find out?"

"They're on Turtle Island, site five." Frank took off his hat and rubbed his head. "Randy did some more digging around regarding Tom."

"What are you talking about?"

"He mentioned the other day that Tom fit the profile of another case he'd been working on."

"What the hell are you babbling about?" This was the last thing Jared wanted on his mind. Hell, he didn't want anything taking up space in his brain, just Ryan in his bed. Then it hit him. "Wait a minute. Tom is involved in something the FBI is looking into? And you're just telling me this now?"

"Really, they're different cases, but when Randy faxed me this—" Frank held out a piece of paper. "I thought you might want to know, but you called me, barked out an order, and I followed it, figuring I'd see you when you got here."

Confused, Jared took the sheet of paper, glancing

at the picture. "Who is this?" He scanned the sheet for a name. "William Crommly? This guy looks like Tom."

"We think it is Tom. I mean, he stole Tom's identity."

"Then he didn't get arrested for flashing?" Jared glanced over the sheet again, staring at the words *rape* and *murder*. "Wait. These two are one and the same?"

"Not sure yet. But this guy is wanted in two states in connection with at least two rapes and one murder. All obsession-stalker cases. Nick already has all the details. I made sure of it."

"Where's Nick?" Jared blinked, crumpling the paper in his fist.

"Getting a search warrant."

"Screw the damned search warrant—find the bastard. I'm going to get Ryan."

"I'll go with you," Frank said as a car rounded the corner.

"No, you'll work with Nick and catch the asshole." Jared waved to Chuck as he parked his car. "Let's get a move on."

"No way, Jared," Chuck said. "The last thing I need is another lecture from my fiancée on the importance of girls' night and such."

"I screwed up—"

"Not my problem."

"Not with that, but this." He shoved the paper in Chuck's hand. "Ryan's still in danger, and I need Frank here to find Tom and nail his ass. You and I are going to get the girls."

Chuck glanced at the paper, then back at Jared. "Okay," he said. "Turtle Island. But I don't know the site."

"Five," Jared said, jogging toward the docks. "Stay in touch, Frank." He waved but didn't look back. Frank knew what to do. Now to get Ryan and find a safe place for her to hide out until he got the situation under control.

It took Jared all of five minutes to start his boat and head out into the deadly calm lake.

"Do you really think they're in danger?" Chuck asked.

"Honestly, I don't have all the facts." Jared glanced around the open waters. "When I called you, I planned to talk to Ryan about…things. I didn't want to have two boats to deal with and well…"

"You're rambling," Chuck said, annoyance in his voice.

"Frank was supposed to call me with the site information. Instead, he showed up at the house with that piece of paper. That's all I know."

"Surprised you're not out there in the hunt." Chuck didn't try to hide a small smile. "Isn't that what you live for?"

"My job is to protect and serve. Right now, I'm doing the protecting aspect." He turned his head, lifting a brow. "Let's not forget your fiancée is with Ryan."

"I haven't forgotten, but that's not the point."

"That's exactly the point." Jared pulled the throttle back a tad as he entered the narrows and looked around for anything out of the ordinary. Jared rested his hand on the butt of his weapon.

"Guns make me nervous," Chuck said.

"Yeah, well, when it's not my gun, they make me nervous too."

"That doesn't make me feel better. All those cop buddies of yours know where we are, right?"

Jared slowed the boat to a crawl as he navigated his way through the islands. "I won't let anything happen to them." Jared scanned the area as he approached Turtle Island. "I'm kind of in love with her, ya know."

"Really, you don't say." Chuck laughed, shaking his head. "Glad to see you finally figured it out."

"Let's hope I'm not too late." Jared pointed. "That your boat?"

"Yep. I don't see the girls."

Jared glanced at his watch. "It's early for them to be asleep, but they could be inside the tent."

"Penny loves to sit outside on a chilly night." Chuck squinted, peering over the bow of the boat.

"What would Penny do with the keys to your boat?"

"Knowing her, she'd leave them in the boat." Chuck glanced over to Jared. "This doesn't seem right, does it?"

Jared ignored the panic setting in, using every trick in the book to clear his mind and think only about his job. "Once the boat is docked, give me a minute to check things out. I'll wave you up when I know it's safe."

Chuck jumped out on the dock, securing the boat, all the while looking up at the site.

Jared held his finger to his lips, then pulled his weapon out. He set his feet on solid ground.

He scanned the site. The fire in the pit had reduced to hot coals. Voices echoed from other sites. "Ryan? Penny?" he whispered. If they were sleeping, he didn't really want to scare the crap out of them. He paused about ten paces from the tent. The hair on the back of his neck prickled. "Ryan," he said a little louder.

Something stirred inside the tent. "Ryan, it's Jared, is everything okay—" A twig snapped behind him. He glanced over his shoulder. Chuck stood on the dock, then took a sudden step. Jared held up his hand, hoping Chuck understood he needed him to stay... "Shit."

"Drop it, asshole." Tom pushed something cold against Jared's temple. Jared tossed his weapon to the ground. "You don't want to do this, Tom. Or is it William?"

"Actually, if you must know, the name's Fred, but I've had so many, I've lost track." He pressed the barrel of the gun harder. "However. I likeTom. Now, Ryan, get your ass out here. I want you to watch this.

And you down at the dock—get up here, unless you want me to kill your girl, too. And toss the keys in the lake."

Jared nodded to Chuck. "Do what he says."

Chuck reached into the boat, dangled something, then tossed it to the lake with a splash.

"Move it, asshole. You don't want a bullet hole in your head, do you?" Tom asked.

Chuck practically ran up the path. "Where are they?" he questioned, his lips set in a determined line.

Jared had to give the guy kudos for being so ballsy.

"Come on, girls. Out you go," Tom said.

Two shaky shadows moved behind the thin layer of nylon before the zipper echoed across the night. A few seconds later, Ryan stepped from the tent, her face bruised.

Jared swallowed his breath.

"Ahh, there you are. Come over here." Tom's voice echoed insanity.

"Stay where you are," Jared said, surveying the situation. Those bruises hadn't just appeared on her face without help, and Jared planned on making sure Tom paid for them. Big-time.

"He'll kill you, Jared." Her voice trembled.

"I might not. Not if you cooperate," Tom said.

Jared watched Ryan take a tentative step from the platform. Her body visibly shook with fear. He figured he had about three seconds before losing any chance of taking control of the situation.

"You fucked with the wrong man," Jared whispered, then sent his elbow crashing into Tom's gut.

Something hard and cold smacked Jared in the back of the neck at the same time a loud pop rang out. Jared hit the ground. Closing his eyes, he focused on the sounds around him; a scream from Ryan and loud gasp from Penny, along with a few unflattering curses by Chuck echoed in his ears. None of which helped the pounding pain in his head. Thank God the bullet missed.

"Stupid man," Tom said.

"You killed him?" Ryan whispered.

Feeling footsteps approach him, Jared held his breath and kept very still. A bullet in the back wasn't part of the plan.

"You belong to me, remember that," Tom said.

The footsteps moved away. Slowly, Jared let out his breath until he could no longer feel the earth shake.

Tom's voice echoed, but Jared couldn't hear the words as the engine to the boat sputtered to life. Then two gunshots rang out. Jumping to his feet, he ignored the blinding pain in his head and wiped the dirt from his face.

"Jared?" Penny squealed. "You're okay?"

"He shot the engine out," Chuck said, pulling Penny into his arms. "What are you going to do?"

"Steal a boat." Jared picked up his weapon, then headed toward the next campsite, focusing on the sound of his boat. "Call 9-1-1 and tell them what's going on," he yelled over his shoulder, then whipped out his badge. "Sorry, folks, police business. I need to borrow your boat." He jumped in, ignoring the stunned faces, grateful the keys were in the small cruiser, and headed out onto the dark lake. The bastard wouldn't get away with it. He'd make sure of it.

Chapter Eighteen

Unable to take a deep breath, Ryan could feel the panic set in. She blinked, trying to get her bearings. They were headed north, toward a group of islands called the Mother Bunch. Easy to dodge behind and around, but once past the islands, it was open water.

Swallowing, she prayed Jared wasn't dead. Seeing him lying on the ground, his body not moving, she felt like her whole world had crashed around her.

It took every ounce of courage she had to keep herself from passing out. She glanced around the boat. There had to be a way out of this mess. She couldn't die without finding out why Jared had come back. Not without telling him how she felt.

The fire extinguisher rattled next to her leg. She wondered if it was loose. She looked up at Tom who seemed to be lost in driving. He kept glancing over his shoulder and all around. Another boat hummed in the distance.

If Jared had been shot, he was going to need her. *Here goes nothing.* She grabbed the fire extinguisher and yanked. Thank God it broke free. She swung the metal canister up at Tom as hard as she could.

Smack!

His head jerked to the side and his eyes went wide. He stumbled but caught the steering wheel. "You bitch." He held his head with his free hand as he tried to pull himself up, but he stumbled to the floor.

She wasn't going to let him get the upper hand. "You messed with the wrong woman." She rose, lifting the extinguisher high over her head, then slammed it into Tom's head.

This time his body sprawled out on the bottom of the boat. His head rolled to the side, and his eyes fluttered closed. Her hands trembled. She dropped the canister to the side. Then, without thought, Ryan grabbed the wheel and turned the boat around. She headed straight for the oncoming boat. If Tom wasn't dead, he wouldn't stay unconscious forever. She had to get back to Jared.

She slowed the boat down, waving both hands over her head. Hopefully, whoever it was had a working cell phone and could call for help.

The boats collided with a bounce. She blinked and focused on the driver. "Oh, my God! Jared!"

"Ryan," he said calmly. "Grab the wheel and maneuver the boat again."

"You're not hurt?" Frantically, she turned the boat to the left, then back to the right, trying desperately to get to Jared. "He didn't shoot you?"

"Missed, but I got a nasty bump." He held the boats together with one hand, reaching for her with the other. "Come here, please."

"I was so scared," she whispered, leaping into his arms. "When he showed up…I couldn't believe it. At first I thought, the nerve of the guy, I mean I told him to buzz off earlier."

Jared cupped her face. "Are you okay?" His finger traced a path over her swollen cheek. "He hit you." Jared's eyes narrowed, then he peered over her shoulder. "Bastard," he muttered. "Wait right here." He vaulted from one boat to the other.

A loud moan echoed in the still of the dark night.

"Oh, shut up," Jared said. "One of your rights. Along with the right to an attorney, but you already understand those rights, don't you?" Jared pulled Tom to the driver's seat, yanking his hands behind his back and tying them with the stern line.

"I'll get you for this," Tom sneered.

"Not where you're going."

Sirens rang out in the distance.

"Here comes the cavalry." Jared looked over his shoulder and pointed, then looked to Ryan and frowned. "Let's get you to the hospital."

"I'm fine, really." She rubbed her tender cheek. "He only hit me once, and I'm more worried about that lump on the back of your neck. It's huge."

"It's nothing, but we'll go together, okay?" He heaved her to his chest and held her tight but said nothing.

She clutched at him like he was the air she needed to live, but before she could muster up the courage to tell him how she felt, cops surrounded them.

A few hours later, she found herself in the back of Frank's personal car, getting a ride home. Jared sat next to her, holding her hand and staring out into the dark night. He seemed distant and unreachable.

Why would she think he'd be anything else?

He'd only come back because he'd found out about Tom.

"Thanks, Frank," Jared said.

Ryan blinked, then realized they'd pulled into Jared's driveway. He held his hand out to her. She glanced at her watch; it was well past two in the morning. "Pat's probably worried sick. We should just go there."

"I spoke to him before we left the hospital. He'll be here in the morning. Besides, we need to talk." He tugged at her hand.

Swallowing, she glanced at Frank. "Thanks," she

mumbled, feeling the exhaustion hit her bones as she scooted from the car.

"See ya around." Frank waved, then backed out, his taillights disappearing down the road.

"Finally," Jared muttered. He yanked her to his body, pressing her against the cold metal of his pickup.

She opened her mouth, but couldn't say anything because his tongue dove in. Grabbing his shoulders, she intended to shove him away, but just rested her hands there instead, lost in the moment. But the better the kiss got, the more she knew it had to stop. She gave him a good shove.

"What?" He scowled. "I've been waiting hours to do that."

"Thought you said we need to talk."

"Oh, that." He took a step back. "I suppose we need to do that, too."

"I appreciate you coming back here to help when you heard about—"

He chuckled, pressing his fingers against her lips. "I turned around long before I knew what was going on with Tom."

"You did?" Her heart raced in a panicked frenzy. "Why?"

"To do this." He walked over to the For Sale sign, kicked it a few times, then lifted it from the ground.

"You sold the house?" she asked, anger surging through her body.

"Usually when that happens, a Sold sign goes up for a while. I'm taking it off the market."

"What?" She put her hands on her hips and shook her head. Nothing made sense. "I'm tired. I need some sleep."

"Might happen, eventually." He tossed the sign behind the garage, then sauntered over toward her with the weirdest smile on his face.

"I must have fallen asleep, because this doesn't make any sense."

He laughed and pressed his hand on the small of her back. "Come on, I think I have some explaining to do."

"Can the explaining happen when I'm awake?" she mumbled, unable to believe any of this was real. "Are we still at the hospital and I've just fallen asleep on that ugly blue couch or something?"

He pushed open the kitchen door and nudged her forward. The bright lights forced her to blink a few times before she adjusted to the brightness.

"Let's go into the family room. Would you like a drink?"

She shook her head, letting her body relax into his strong arm. "I hope you won't get in trouble with your new boss."

Jared laughed.

"I don't think that's funny. I know what that job means to you."

"You mean more," he whispered, pressing his soft lips against her neck.

Dropping her head to the side, she closed her eyes, getting lost in the sensation.

"Sit down," he said softly, easing her back onto the couch. "Open your eyes."

"I don't want to wake up. Jared just told me I meant more to him than his job." She curled herself in a ball, fiddling with what she assumed was a pillow and let herself drift off into a land where Jared loved her.

It was nice to dream.

Jared listened to the soft, even breathing of the woman he knew he couldn't live without, waiting for her to wake up. He shifted, hoping to upset her sleep, but she just kept snuggling in, using his lap for a pillow.

"Great," he mumbled, letting out a long breath and threading his fingers through her hair. He couldn't sleep if he tried. How the hell could she? He tossed his head back and stared at the ceiling. Hours had passed since Frank had dropped them off. Jared couldn't wait any longer. "Ryan," he said.

"What?" She jumped, smacking the back of her head against his face.

"Damn it." He covered his nose as water welled in his eyes. "Sleeping with you is going to break my nose yet."

"Huh?" She sat up, recoiling to the other side of the sofa. "What happened? What's going on?"

"I was trying to have a serious conversation with you, but you fell asleep on me."

"Oh." She adjusted her hair, tucking her feet under her butt. "I do remember you telling me you wanted to talk. Then I had the most bizarre dream."

He rubbed his nose, satisfied it wasn't really hurt, then scooted closer to her. "Tell me about your dream."

"No way."

"Was I in it?"

"I'll take the Fifth." She reached out and ran her finger down his nose. "I'm sorry about that."

"Seems to be a habit with us."

"Did you take the house off the market?"

He nodded, inching closer. "I'm not taking that job."

Her lips pursed together.

"I took a different one, right here. And it's not because of you, well, not entirely."

She rubbed her temples. "That job was everything to you."

"Not when some lunatic was waving a gun at the woman I love." His heart skipped a beat and his hand trembled when he touched the bruise on her face. "I do love you, Ryan."

She met his gaze dead-on. "That's not love. That's guilt."

"Oh, no, you don't." He cupped her face. "I won't let you tell me how I feel or don't feel."

She laced her fingers around his wrists. "You care about me, always have. But you don't just all of a sudden fall in love with someone in a situation like that." She pushed him away.

"Damn it, Ryan." He stood up and started to pace. This wasn't going quite like he had planned. Then again, he didn't know what he was doing. "You're right." He stopped and stared at her. "But that's not when I fell in love with you. Hell, I have no idea when it happened, and I sure as hell didn't want it to happen. I pulled over on that damned highway half a dozen times before I decided I had to tell you I loved you. Now, either you love me or you don't. So just tell me one way or the other." He let out a puff of air and planted his hands on his hips and waited.

She just sat there an with an open mouth and wide eyes.

The longer she sat there, the faster his pulse raced. "Well," he said. "I can't stand here much longer. Do you love me, yes or no?"

She blinked a few times. "You came back because you love me? Not because you knew that Tom wasn't who he said he was?" She stood, facing him dead-on.

"Yes," he said. "I wanted you to know, and I hoped you'd let me spend the rest of my life proving it to you."

"Are you suggesting we get married?" Her brows shot up.

"Well, yeah. I'd like that." This really wasn't going as planned.

She turned from him and did her own pacing on the other side of the coffee table. "What about my job? I mean, I won't quit."

"Wouldn't ask you to," he said with a scowl.

"What about kids? That would be a deal breaker." She locked gazes with him.

"I didn't realize we were making a deal." He swallowed the large lump in his throat.

She narrowed her eyes. "This isn't a joke, Jared. I'm not putting myself out there for you to tell me I can't have what I want."

"I want to give you everything," he admitted. "I want it all, and I want it with you." He shoved his hands in his pockets and stared into a pair of scrutinizing blue eyes. He couldn't blame her for being suspicious. He'd given her every reason to believe that love, marriage, and kids weren't for him. Hell, a few weeks ago he thought the same thing. "I love you. I don't know how else to say it."

"That works." She put her foot on the coffee table, then hurled herself at him.

"Humph. Good Lord, woman, are you trying to kill me?" He stumbled backward, landing on the couch with her on top of him.

"Just wanted to let you know I love you, too." She smiled, tears rolling down her cheeks.

"Don't cry." He kissed the salty tears. "I don't like it when I make you cry."

"Trust me, these are happy tears."

He pushed the coffee table back with his foot, and rolled, settling himself in her arms where he belonged.

She ran her hands across the top of his head, then down his back. "Tell me again," she whispered.

"I love you." He pressed his lips against hers. "I think I always have; I've just been too stubborn to admit it." His pulse hammered in his ears so fast he didn't think he'd be able to breathe. But the softness of her body pressed firmly against his gave him everything he needed. "Condoms are upstairs," he said with a ragged breath. "Unless you want to work on that aspect of our lives right now. Not sure I want to wait." He couldn't believe how much his life had changed. "I want to have children with you." He stroked his thumb across her bruised cheek, then kissed it with tender care. "Whenever you're ready. Don't want to rush you or anything."

Her head hit the floor with a clunk, then her arms dropped to the sides while she shut her eyes tight.

"Ryan, you okay?"

She shook her head, covering her face, mumbling a bunch of words he couldn't understand.

"Ryan, you're kind of wigging me out here."

"Sorry," she mumbled from behind her hands.

He shifted to his knees, pulling her to a sitting position, and leaned against the couch. "Come on, what's wrong?" He pulled at her hands. When she finally looked at him, she had chomped down on her lower lip and had a guilty look on her face. "You lied to me."

"Not really."

"Are you pregnant?" He swallowed, not able to tell if he was angry or happy. Or both.

"I don't know."

"You didn't get your period, did you?" He rubbed his hands across his unshaven face.

"I sort of lied to you about that."

"And if you're pregnant, were you planning on telling me, ever?" He hated hearing his angry tone, but he couldn't help it. She'd lied to him about something really important. Not a good way to start out.

She jumped to her knees. "I wouldn't have kept that from you, but understand I didn't want you giving up everything just because I might be having a baby. You did that once and look how bad that turned out."

"I didn't love Lisa. I love you. Big difference." He shook his head. "And wouldn't that be my choice to make?" He looped his arm around her. Staying mad at this woman would be impossible.

"And you could've come back, if you wanted to. I would never keep your child from you. I just didn't want you to give up something for me again."

"Leaving you would've been giving up something, something wonderful. You're the best thing that's ever happened to me. I don't want to know what it would be like not to have you in my life."

"That's sweet." She slumped her head into the crook of his neck, relaxing. "When I got around to taking the test, I planned on calling you."

"You'd tell me that over the phone?" He snapped up his head.

"No, I would've told you I wanted to see you when you came back to get your other car. You're not moving, are you?" She wrapped her arm around his middle.

"Nope, and neither are you. Well, actually you are. Please don't tell me you won't make me wait and you'll live with me before we get married."

"Oh, good grief, no." She laughed. "Poor Pen. She didn't want to wait, but her father wouldn't have married them if she did. He didn't take the pregnancy too well."

"I guess I wouldn't have a pregnancy test lying around the house, would I?"

"I've got one in my bag. I was going to take it with Penny in the morning."

"It's the morning, so take it now, with me." He leaped from the floor, pulling her with him. "Where is it?"

"Wherever my overnight bag ended up. Do we have to do this now? I can think of something much better we can do."

"The bag's in the kitchen. I'll meet you upstairs." He pulled her into his arms. "We'll get to everything, I promise. But let's find out if you're pregnant first. I need to know." He paused and looked at her soft-blue eyes. "I want to know."

Ryan locked herself in the master bathroom and read the directions three times before putting her sample where it belonged. She left the test strip on the sink, then pushed back the door.

"Well?"

"We have to wait five minutes." She flung herself on her back on the bed and stared at the ceiling.

"You've been in there for fifteen." Jared rubbed the back of his neck as he sat next to her.

"I read the directions a half dozen times. I don't want to screw this up."

"Like I screwed up my proposal?"

She slipped her hand under his shirt, rubbing his back, feeling truly at home for the first time in her life. "I didn't know you asked."

He glanced over his shoulder. "I mentioned it."

"But you didn't ask." She smiled at his wide eyes. "And I certainly didn't answer." She sat and scooted to the edge of the bed.

"You want me to do the one knee thing, huh?" He slipped off the bed and reached into his pocket.

Her breath hitched as she clutched her emerald

necklace. She'd only been teasing him. She thought it was a given at this point, but she'd let him ask again.

He looked up at her from bended knee, holding up a sparkling diamond.

"Oh, my, God! Where the hell did that come from?" She reached for it, but he pulled it back. "Jared?"

"I stopped at the jeweler's on the way home."

She stared at him, her pulse beating fast and furious. "You're kidding, right?"

"Nope." He swiped at his eyes. "I think this is about as spontaneous as I can get."

She gasped when he slid the ring on her finger. "It's beautiful."

"You're beautiful." He kissed her hand. "Regardless of what that test says, I want to marry you. Will you marry me, Ryan?"

"Yes," she whispered, pressing her lips against his as he eased her back on the soft mattress.

He lifted his head and stared into her eyes. She felt his love right through to her core. How could she have missed it before?

"You've always been right in front of me," he whispered.

"And that's where I plan on staying," she said, drawing his lips to hers, leaving the outside world. This moment would be forever ingrained in her mind as the happiest moment in her life. She'd once said she wanted it all, and now she had it.

And she'd never let it go.

Epilogue

Jared rolled his ring around on his finger, then glanced at the blue sky. No matter how long he'd been wearing the ring, he'd never gotten used to it. But he couldn't bring himself to take it off. It reminded him of what he had almost lost.

"Da, Da!" Caitlyn squealed, stumbling down the pathway, arms flapping at her sides like a drunken sailor.

"I thought it was cute when she started walking. Not so much now that she's running." Ryan let out a sigh as she chased behind the little girl.

"Come to Daddy." Jared knelt, holding out his arms. Caitlyn flung herself at him. He lifted her to the sky and twirled her around while she belly laughed like there was no tomorrow. "Say 'Mama.'"

Caitlyn shook her head. "Da, Da." She cupped his face, then planted a wet kiss against his lips.

"Mommy." He pointed to Ryan, who smiled.

"She does this because you think it's cute." Ryan laughed.

"Onny." Caitlyn pointed to the car.

"Did she say Johnny?" Jared stared at Ryan.

"Been working on that one all day." Ryan pulled back the car door. "Show Daddy what you've got for Johnny."

Caitlyn rummaged in the oversized pocket of her dress. "Ca."

"Car?" Jared questioned.

Caitlyn nodded her head up and down in a wild motion.

"If you can say car and Johnny, you can say Mommy."

"No." Caitlyn pursed her lips.

"Come on. Let's go visit your brother," Ryan said, slipping into the car.

Jared buckled Caitlyn in her seat, then scowled at her. "Say 'Mommy,' please. It would make Daddy happy."

Caitlyn pursed her lips, then tilted her head, looking up as if she was deep in thought.

"That's the daddy look."

"I do that?" He glanced to Ryan, who just laughed.

"Mommy!" Caitlyn laughed, covering her face with both hands. "Onn! Ove Onny!"

"That's 'love Johnny.'" Ryan smiled proudly.

Jared never thought he'd be reduced to tears by two

words a little girl could barely manage, but as he slipped behind the steering wheel, he had to wipe away the tears stinging his cheeks.

"I love you," he whispered, reaching for Ryan's hand.

She laced her fingers through his. "I love you." She glanced over her shoulder. "So, you want more?" Ryan asked.

"More what?" He lifted his chin. "You're not?"

"I think we need to stop at the drugstore on the way home and buy one of those tests," Ryan said, her eyes dancing with joy. "But I'm pretty sure."

"Really?"

"Baby!" Caitlyn bounced her arms and legs up and down. "Mommy! Baby!"

"I guess you and Mommy have been working hard today, huh."

"She loves to play games." Ryan shrugged.

"And my life just keeps getting better and better." Jared cupped the back of Ryan's head, heaving her toward him for a quick, but passionate kiss.

"Right back at ya, babe," Ryan said, laughing.

Jared just shook his head, knowing life was as it should be, always having everything he needed, right in front of him.

Thank you for taking the time to read IN TWO WEEKS. I hope you enjoyed! Next up in the NY STATE

TROOPER SERIES is Frank's story. Check out ***Dark Water*** at jentalty.com.

Don't forget to check out the *First Responder Series,* in which Jared often makes an appearance as well as the *Legacy Series* and the *Love in the Adirondack Series*.

Also by Jen Talty

Brand new series: SAFE HARBOR!

MINE TO KEEP

MINE TO SAVE

MINE TO PROTECT

Check out LOVE IN THE ADIRONDACKS!

SHATTERED DREAMS

AN INCONVENIENT FLAME

THE WEDDING DRIVER

NY STATE TROOPER SERIES (also set in the Adirondacks!)

In Two Weeks

Dark Water

Deadly Secrets

Murder in Paradise Bay

To Protect His own

Deadly Seduction

When A Stranger Calls

His Deadly Past

The Corkscrew Killer

Brand New Novella for the First Responders series

A spin-off from the NY State Troopers series

PLAYING WITH FIRE

PRIVATE CONVERSATION

THE RIGHT GROOM

AFTER THE FIRE

CAUGHT IN THE FLAMES

CHASING THE FIRE

Legacy Series

Dark Legacy

Legacy of Lies

Secret Legacy

Colorado Brotherhood Protectors

Fighting For Esme

Defending Raven

Fay's Six

Yellowstone Brotherhood Protectors

Guarding Payton

Candlewood Falls

RIVERS EDGE

THE BURIED SECRET

ITS IN HIS KISS

LIPS OF AN ANGEL

It's all in the Whiskey

JOHNNIE WALKER

GEORGIA MOON

JACK DANIELS

JIM BEAM

WHISKEY SOUR

WHISKEY COBBLER

WHISKEY SMASH

IRISH WHISKEY

The Monroes

COLOR ME YOURS

COLOR ME SMART

COLOR ME FREE

COLOR ME LUCKY

COLOR ME ICE

COLOR ME HOME

Search and Rescue

PROTECTING AINSLEY

PROTECTING CLOVER

PROTECTING OLYMPIA

PROTECTING FREEDOM

PROTECTING PRINCESS

PROTECTING MARLOWE

DELTA FORCE-NEXT GENERATION

SHIELDING JOLENE

SHIELDING AALYIAH

SHIELDING LAINE

The Men of Thief Lake

REKINDLED

DESTINY'S DREAM

Federal Investigators

JANE DOE'S RETURN

THE BUTTERFLY MURDERS

THE AEGIS NETWORK

The Sarich Brother

THE LIGHTHOUSE

HER LAST HOPE

THE LAST FLIGHT

THE RETURN HOME

THE MATRIARCH

More Aegis Network

MAX & MILIAN

A CHRISTMAS MIRACLE

SPINNING WHEELS

HOLIDAY'S VACATION

Special Forces Operation Alpha

BURNING DESIRE

BURNING KISS

BURNING SKIES

BURNING LIES

BURNING HEART

BURNING BED

REMEMBER ME ALWAYS

The Brotherhood Protectors

Out of the Wild

ROUGH JUSTICE

ROUGH AROUND THE EDGES

ROUGH RIDE

ROUGH EDGE

ROUGH BEAUTY

The Brotherhood Protectors

The Saving Series

SAVING LOVE

SAVING MAGNOLIA

SAVING LEATHER

Hot Hunks

Cove's Blind Date Blows Up

My Everyday Hero – Ledger

Tempting Tavor

Malachi's Mystic Assignment

Needing Neor

Holiday Romances

A CHRISTMAS GETAWAY

ALASKAN CHRISTMAS

WHISPERS

CHRISTMAS IN THE SAND

Heroes & Heroines on the Field

TAKING A RISK

TEE TIME

A New Dawn

THE BLIND DATE

SPRING FLING

SUMMERS GONE

WINTER WEDDING

THE AWAKENING

The Collective Order

THE LOST SISTER

THE LOST SOLDIER

THE LOST SOUL

THE LOST CONNECTION

THE NEW ORDER

About the Author

Jen Talty is the *USA Today* Bestselling Author of Contemporary Romance, Romantic Suspense, and Paranormal Romance. In the fall of 2020, her short story was selected and featured in a 1001 Dark Nights Anthology.

Regardless of the genre, her goal is to take you on a ride that will leave you floating under the sun with warmth in your heart. She writes stories about broken heroes and heroines who aren't necessarily looking for romance, but in the end, they find the kind of love books are written about :).

She first started writing while carting her kids to one hockey rink after the other, averaging 170 games per year between 3 kids in 2 countries and 5 states. Her first book, IN TWO WEEKS was originally published in 2007. In 2010 she helped form a publishing company (Cool Gus Publishing) with *NY Times* Bestselling Author Bob Mayer where she ran the technical side of the business through 2016.

Jen is currently enjoying the next phase of her life...the empty nester! She and her husband reside in Jupiter, Florida.

Grab a glass of vino, kick back, relax, and let the romance roll in...

Sign up for my Newsletter (https://dl.bookfunnel.com/82gm8b9k4y) where I often give away free books before publication.

Join my private Facebook group (https://www.facebook.com/groups/191706547909047/) where I post exclusive excerpts and discuss all things murder and love!

Never miss a new release. Follow me on Amazon:amazon.com/author/jentalty

And on Bookbub: bookbub.com/authors/jen-talty